EMPIRE OF RUINS

Also by Arthur Slade

The Hunchback Assignments
The Dark Deeps

EMPIRE OF RUINS
THE HUNCHBACK ASSIGNMENTS

ARTHUR SLADE

Angus&Robertson
An imprint of HarperCollins*Publishers*

Angus&Robertson
An imprint of HarperCollins*Publishers*, Australia

First published in Canada in 2011
by HarperCollins*Publishers* Ltd
First published in Australia in 2011
by HarperCollins*Publishers* Australia Pty Limited
ABN 36 009 913 517
harpercollins.com.au

HarperCollins*Publishers*
25 Ryde Road, Pymble, Sydney NSW 2073, Australia
31 View Road, Glenfield, Auckland 0627, New Zealand
A 53, Sector 57, Noida, UP, India
77–85 Fulham Palace Road, London W6 8JB, United Kingdom
2 Bloor Street East, 20th floor, Toronto, Ontario M4W 1A8, Canada
10 East 53rd Street, New York NY 10022, USA

National Library of Australia Cataloguing-in-Publication data:

Slade, Arthur G. (Arthur Gregory)
    Empire of ruins / Arthur G. Slade.
    ISBN: 978 0 7322 9046 7 (pbk.)
    Slade, Arthur G. (Arthur Gregory) Hunchback assignments ; bk. 3.
    For secondary school age.
    Disfigured persons — Juvenile fiction.
    Supernatural — Juvenile fiction.
    Spy stories.
813.54

Cover illustration © Christopher Steininger 2010
Cover design by Priscilla Nielsen
Typeset in Sabon 11/16pt
Printed and bound in Australia by Griffin Press
60gsm Hi Bulk Book Cream used by HarperCollins*Publishers* is a natural, recyclable
product made from wood grown in sustainable forests. The manufacturing processes
conform to the environmental regulations in the country of origin, Finland.

5 4 3 2 1   11 12 13 14

For Tori and Tanaya,
with all my love

A Savage Pursuit

In a Queensland rain forest, over ten thousand miles from London, Modo leaned his humped back against a strangler fig tree. He bound his handkerchief tightly around the stump of the little finger on his left hand. The sabre cut had been clean and he was surprised there hadn't been much blood. The pain threatened to cloud his every thought. But he'd been trained to ignore pain and so, with several deep breaths, he cleared his mind. He had other tasks to perform.

The first was to test for broken bones. There were scratches and bruises, of course—one would expect that after falling from such a great height—but he systematically checked his bones and found all of them intact. The goggles had prevented his misshapen eyes from being poked out and his thin wooden African mask had saved the rest of his face from any deep gouges. His hands had been burned to blisters from lifting the boiler, but they would heal.

He did find a large thorn in his shoulder and grimaced as he pulled it out and tossed it aside. He'd been convinced as he plummeted earthward that death was waiting for him on the rain-forest floor. But Fate had been kind. He couldn't even attribute his survival to his acrobatic skills, because he had been screaming and flapping his arms all the way down like a frightened gosling.

The sky, the sun and the airship battle above were blocked by the canopy of branches, vines and leaves. Even the rumbling of steam-powered engines had disappeared. He panicked a little when he thought of his companions. Was his fellow agent Octavia still alive? His master Mr Socrates? Were they even now dodging the gunfire of the enemy? He pictured Octavia wounded, and nearly burst out with a sob of fear.

Snap to! he told himself. *Keep the mind steady. Be in the present.* These were the words Tharpa, his weapons master, had drilled into him. *Think about what needs to be done, not what you cannot change.* Those words belonged to Mr Socrates.

Modo took stock of his surroundings—shrubs, woody vines, knee-high palm trees, larger palms, massive roots for massive trees—all completely unfamiliar. The forest was quiet, as though holding its breath. He imagined that his screaming, crashing arrival had surprised the wildlife. Here and there was a peep of a bird, or the hissing of a snake, as the jungle came back to life.

He turned to the task of listing his useful possessions. He searched his pockets and belt pouch and came up with a knife, a packet of matches, a pocket watch and a compass. He took the goggles off and saw that one glass lens had been shattered. His khaki clothing was adequate now, though he had no idea how cold it would become at night. He guessed it would be warmer than sleeping in the drafty balloon car. At least the compass would allow him to discern his direction. In a front pocket he discovered a graham wafer. He munched a quarter of it.

Modo knew very little about Australia—only that there were many poisonous creatures that could bite you and then you'd die within the hour. "Just avoid them," he whispered. "You can get through this, old pal."

The insect and animal noises were growing louder. Bolder. Some of the hisses seemed to be coming closer. He felt as though a thousand eyes watched his every move.

At least they won't recoil in horror from my face, he thought. Animals and insects couldn't perceive ugliness. And still, he couldn't take off the mask. He required its protection.

As the minutes passed he became more aware of his many aches and of the grumbling in his stomach. He'd need to eat more than a cracker in the next few hours. He could break off a stick and tie his knife to it using strips of clothing to make a crude spear. He wouldn't want to take on a wild boar, but a rabbit would do just fine. Or a kangaroo.

That gave him pause. He wouldn't eat a kangaroo, would he? It would feel wrong to kill anything that stood on two legs and could stare you in the eyes. He didn't even know if there were any kangaroos in this part of the country.

Then he noticed that the forest was quiet again. After years of training he instinctively held his breath, let his heart slow so that he became only ears and eyes.

An owl hooted. An odd sound in the daylight. The noise had come from many yards behind him. A screech rattled the branches fifty yards to his right. Could it be a monkey? Oh, he should have studied what animals lived here! Surely Darwin or some other naturalist had written about the flora and fauna. Another hoot. There was a quality to the tone of it that made the hairs on the back of his neck stand on end. At first, he thought it was just a natural reaction: fear making his heart speed up. Then another hoot, even closer.

They were humans masquerading as animals! He was certain of it! They were sending messages—probably surrounding him.

As he pulled his knife from the sheath he heard a *hiss* race past him, and a small *thud*. He turned to see a quivering spear sticking out of the fig tree. He jumped forward as three more spears missed him by inches. His attackers were on his left, judging by the angle, so he ran, pell-mell, to his right, breaking through overhanging branches.

Savages! Mr Socrates had spoken of such tribes on the journey. On Caribbean islands, in Africa, and here in Australia. According to the penny dreadfuls they killed for pleasure and ate the flesh of fellow humans. *Cannibals!*

It was important not to panic; it would only lead to poor decisions. He tried to hear over his own crashing and panting. No footsteps behind him. Another hoot ahead of him made his heart go cold.

He shifted to his left only to see rattling branches and hear shouts. They were herding him! He dodged right, but saw a blurred white-painted face, nostrils wide as he sucked in breath. The man leapt, spear in hand. Modo grabbed him by his necklace of what looked like shrunken heads, and used his own momentum to throw him down. The man's spear struck Modo's mask and was deflected away.

Out of the corner of his eye Modo saw the tribesmen running to either side of him, shadowy limbs and floating faces, bodies hidden by the foliage. There was only one direction for him to go. If he turned, he'd be shot full of spears in an eye-blink. They were forcing him to move forward, but to where? It was clear they were directly behind him.

Modo leapt over a fallen tree, nearly tripping on the rotted trunk. He heard a waterfall. Maybe he'd be able to dive into a pool and escape! He dashed over a flat, open area, then realised, a moment too late, that he had made a horrible mistake. The leafy ground had looked solid enough, but cracked asunder and he plunged into a pit, shouting in fear. There was just enough light as he fell to see the bottom lined with sharpened stakes.

CHAPTER 1

The God Face

Nine months earlier Alexander King, adventurer and explorer, was clinging to sheer rock on the lowest peak of Mount Kilimanjaro when his partner casually mentioned the God Face. They were still a day's climb from the summit. Above them were the other two snow-covered peaks, below them the surrounding African forests. The men had no intention of being the first to reach the top; this expedition was only a lark, as King had explained, something to pass the time.

It was turning into much more.

"What is this God Face?" King asked.

"It iz a skull or a mask or someting like dat," his climbing partner said.

King had known fellow explorer Josef Stimmler for eight years, had climbed with him on three different mountain ranges on three different continents. It had taken a long time and a lot of shared wine to gain the German man's confidence and friendship.

"Da God Face holds magic. It does make your enemies, how do you English say it, mad as hatters."

King didn't correct him. He was actually a Canadian. His father had been British, though, and long ago King had perfected his British accent. He found that people respected him more once he dropped his colonial accent. The thought of a new treasure made King salivate. The world was running out of treasures and he was running out of money.

"What's the artifact made of?" he asked.

"Oh, dat is interesting. Da usual exaggerations. Gold, diamonds, platinum. I'm certain da British Museum vould pay dearly for it, even if it was made of dried dung. Ha, now dat vould be laughingstock."

"Yes, it would." King found a good foothold and climbed a little higher, then hammered his hook into the rock, careful to ensure it was tight and would hold their combined weight. When he was finished, he looked down at his partner.

"Who told you about it?"

"About vat?"

Beads of sweat trailed down Stimmler's forehead and face, catching in his jowls. He was far too pudgy for mountain climbing, King thought. There was nothing worse than seeing an adventurer becoming a bumbling middle-aged man.

"The God Mask."

"Oh, da God Face. It vas da old man."

"Which old man?" King asked carefully.

Stimmler lifted a sausage-shaped finger to point south west towards Lake Tanganyika. "*Da* old man of Africa. Dare ees only one."

King nodded. He knew exactly who Stimmler was referring to. "Thank you, Stimmler," he said, solemnly. "You have been a great partner over the years. I'm certain your discovery of the Ibys River will be remembered by future generations." Then King pulled the Buck knife from his belt and quickly sliced through the rope below him. Stimmler didn't even have time to scream, a look of stunned shock on his face as he tumbled to his most certain death.

It was all somewhat comical to King. He put his knife away and tied his spare rope to the remaining section of the climbing rope with a tight knot. Then he headed back down the mountain. The descent was much faster, now that he didn't have his partner.

After returning to Moshi to resupply, King hired two guides and began the trek into Ruandi. He didn't know this part of Africa well, but he'd read the newspaper accounts of the old man he was about to visit. He was the most famous explorer of them all, the articles had said. King snorted. What had the old man really done? Discovered a river or two and not much more. He'd never found the source of the Nile.

In the fortnight it took to complete the journey, King lost one of his guides to malaria and a mule to snakebite. The remaining guide led him and the remaining mule to a small village and soon King was sitting in front of a fire, waiting for the water to boil for tea.

His companion was a tall, pale old man with youthful eyes. He'd been living among the tribes of Africa for many years now. Just the thought of it made King shiver. Why spend your life with these backward savages? The tribesmen had all retired to their huts, which suited King fine.

"The God Face?" the old man asked, a Scottish lilt still present in his gravelly, tired voice. "It's in Australia, that's what Bailey told me. He heard from the natives there that deep in the rain forest is hidden a great temple bulging with riches. Exaggerations, exaggerations! That's what we thrive on, my friend."

"Of course we do. Why did your friend not seek out the source of these rumours?"

"Bailey is a botanist. If the rumours had involved an undiscovered plant he would have carved his way there with a machete. Gold? God-Faced skulls? They mean nothing to him."

King sipped his wine. "But every once in a while there's truth at the core of these rumours."

"Yes, yes. And this is a good legend. I was impressed by the detail the local tribe provided. They tell of the sky falling and great spirits rising, and of how the God Face would drive anyone who viewed it raving mad."

"But when was this 'treasure' last seen?" King asked.

"Oh, these tribes often speak in riddles that befuddle our civilised minds. Was it last year or a thousand years before? The description of the temple does suggest an ancient, long-forgotten civilisation. Which is odd, since we both know there were no civilisations in Australia before we arrived."

"Which tribe was it again?"

"The Rain People, that's what Bailey called them. What they called themselves I cannot say."

King filled another goblet with red wine from France. He'd brought it in his own pack, a bottle that was twenty years old now. A perfect vintage. A wine, he thought, that a man would be happy to drink on the last day of his life.

"Who else have you told?" he asked.

The old man laughed. "No one, Mr King, no one. You, that Stimmler fellow and no one else. It's not worth more than a moment's thought. The vagaries of these stories." He lifted a palsied, blue-veined hand. "The vagaries of our occupation."

"That's what we thrive on," King said softly. "Now where would one find this vagarious place?"

The old man chuckled. "It's in the Queensland rain forest. Bailey drew a map for me. I've been using it as a bookmark for years now."

King poured a second glass and with a flick of his hand a powder fell into the wine.

"Well, it's good to finally meet you," he said, and handed the glass to the old explorer. "Cheers, Dr Livingstone, I raise my cup to all your accomplishments."

The powder was strong. King had traded a pygmy shaman two gold buttons for it. He watched as Livingstone sipped his wine. He slowly closed his eyes and his head nodded as though he were answering a question. He murmured something that could have been "the waters" or "the vines" or "Queen Victoria," then he excused himself and retired to his tent.

By early morning the old explorer was dead, and King was gone, but not before having retrieved the map from Dr Livingstone's copy of the Bible.

As King had tramped eastward through the steaming jungle he'd read the map by moonlight. It became tattooed on his thoughts. He pushed his guide and the mule harder every day. He had to be the first to discover the God Face. He'd be on the cover of the *Illustrated London News* within six months. Every sacrifice would be worth it.

It took King another week to reach the island of Nosy Boraha, just off the northeast coast of Madagascar. He rented a room at a storm-battered hotel built on stilts. The island had been home to pirates for years, and though their ships had long ago been sent to the bottom of the ocean by French and English warships, their kin and offspring still lived there. These men and women could navigate the waters without a compass; could fight like hardened marines. And loved to gamble.

It was this last vice that was most important to King. He'd long ago decided the only people he could trust were those who were *un*trustworthy. No sense trying to put together an expedition from London, or any other civilised city. He didn't have the money or prestigious connections for that. But soon he'd win enough to assemble his own team of guides and workers.

He spent his time at the card and wheel tables, ignoring the beer and whiskey they served. Someone with his mind could easily outsmart these half-breed pirate offspring and castoffs. And he did win, at first. He gathered up fistfuls of cash and howled at the dimwits. But then began a downward spiral of lost bets. He turned to the whiskey and what followed slowly became a blur. He may have climbed onto a table and hollered, "I'm Alexander King the greatest explorer alive!" He may even have shouted out something about the God Face and made the laughing hyenas tremble before him.

Then one night he awoke to hear a whirring of wings and a scratching at his door. There had been no footsteps, even though he had requested a room with the longest rickety staircase in order to hear anyone approaching. A screeching noise, half-animal, half-banshee, followed and he knew Death was on the other side of that door. He drew his revolver and pointed it, hands shaking. He stayed in that position, rarely blinking, until the sun came through his tattered curtains.

Sober now, he saw the paper that someone had slid under the door. Still holding his revolver, he went and picked it up.

The letter had no address, only his name. And in the upper left hand corner was a triangle symbol over a clock. Three neat holes, as though pierced by talons, perforated the corner. He opened the envelope. Inside was eight thousand American dollars and a note that read: *For your expedition. We ask only to be kept informed of your findings. We will contact you when you have accomplished your task.*

He poured himself a whiskey as he stared at the money, swigged it. Then, with a smile, he smashed the shot glass on the floor.

* * *

Within a week he was on a steamship to Penang, then New Guinea, and finally to the tiny port of St James, Australia. It took another week to organise carts and hire a red-eyed guide named Ned Land. As he downed beers, the man swore that he knew the rain forest "like the back of me hand." That night he disappeared with the map and several hundred dollars.

It surprised King how little the theft bothered him. The map was burning in his mind, lighting up his thoughts. He would be the first white man to gaze upon the God Face. His photo would be in every newspaper in the world.

This time, he hired only Indian and Chinese porters and guides from the poorest part of the port. They spoke little English; his Hindi and Mandarin would suffice. A guide would no longer be necessary. After all, he was destined to find the temple.

He led his expedition westward on foot, ponies and a mule carrying their gear. The cart wheels broke after the second day, the ponies died on the third. The glowing map led him deeper into the dark rain forest. The sky never stopped crying, the Indians complained. The insects never stopped biting, the Chinese moaned. Soon larger creatures were biting; as they crossed a river clearly indicated on the map, he lost a man to a crocodile. Even when a fever overtook him, King drove them on.

After that they wandered for days and King began to fear he wouldn't find the temple Livingstone had spoken about. Was he remembering the map accurately? But yes, it shone like a constellation in his mind.

Then, one day as he climbed a rock face he discovered two falcon-headed statues, their features mostly crumbled with age, marking the entrance to a cave. Around the open door were hieroglyphs. He stared at them, stunned. Egyptian hieroglyphics? Here in Australia? Now *this* was a discovery the world would remember! Paperboys across the colonies and America would soon be shouting, *"King discovers ancient Egyptian temple!"*

His crew wouldn't follow him inside, so he wiped sweat from his forehead, loaded his pistol, and entered the cavern alone. There he discovered more Egyptian symbols and wondered how they'd come to be in this place. Who had carved this temple out of a mountain?

After two hours King stumbled out, drool dripping from his lips. He awkwardly kicked aside the dice his men were playing with and fell to the ground, moaning and jittering.

The guides looked at him and then at each other. Should they just leave him to die? He'd been a cruel boss, after all.

"Let's tell the port people a snake bit him," an Indian suggested.

"No," said a Chinese man in broken English, "a spider."

One suggested they just leave him in the river for the crocodiles. But the largest of them looked at King, whose eyes now stared directly at the sun as though searching for some secret in that burning orb.

"There may be reward," the man grunted. "He easier to travel with now."

Still they couldn't agree, so they threw their dice—and rolled the number seven. A lucky number.

They strapped King to the lone mule and began the journey back to the coast.

CHAPTER 2

The Unexpected Guest

Modo sat at the window of a London mansion known as Safe House, a teacup in his right hand. Behind him were his training tools—straw-stuffed dummies, kenjutsu swords, wooden dumbbells. Through the window in front of him he could see Kew Gardens—April showers had turned London's largest garden lush green and brought the flowers to life. In the distance they were a blur of colour.

Modo had spent a quiet winter in Safe House. His most recent mission as an agent of the Permanent Association had involved the pursuit of a submarine from New York to Iceland and he had returned to England with more bruises than he could count and a chest infection that had taken two months to cure. It was a small price to pay. They had dealt a blow to the Clockwork Guild by sinking their giant warship. He felt some satisfaction, but as the days passed he wondered when their secret organisation would surface again. At this very moment Miss Hakkandottir was likely tapping her metal fingers somewhere. The image gave him the shivers.

Over the months his fatigue had ebbed away and he was training again, honing both his martial arts skills and his "adaptive transformation" ability—the shifting of his shape. But training every day was growing maddeningly boring; he'd been languishing in this mansion for so long now that he worried Mr Socrates had forgotten him. There had been a few brief visits from his master; the last was two weeks ago.

"I will go batty!" he whispered. He set his teacup down and pushed aside the latest edition of the *Illustrated London News* and his cloth workout mask. He hadn't been given permission to leave the mansion, and it was beginning to feel like a jail sentence. No, he decided, what was really riling him was that it reminded him of his childhood in Ravenscroft. Thirteen years in a country house without being able to take so much as one step out the door! It had all been part of Mr Socrates' plan to raise him as an agent, and it had worked, but Modo had no wish to be trapped like that again. He itched to be climbing and swinging his way across London, as he'd been free to do only a few months ago.

"Enough sitting around!" He marched to the centre of the room and began snap-kicking and palm-smashing the stuffed dummy hanging from the ceiling. Each move had been taught to him by Tharpa, his weapons trainer. It was a combination of kalarippayattu, an Indian fighting art, and wushu, a Chinese martial system. Occasionally he caught his reflection in the mirrors on the training room walls and grimaced at his ugliness. He punched and kicked even harder.

When he had exhausted himself, he bowed to the dummy and sat down to do his breathing exercises, hoping to clear his mind of anger and frustration. Instead, Octavia's face appeared. He hadn't seen his friend and fellow agent since their return from Iceland. Nearly four months had passed! Did she even know he was here? Did she miss him? He missed her, even the way she raised her eyebrows when she was annoyed. Or toying with him.

The doorbell rang. A minute later there was a knock at the door to his room. He walked to the table, picked up his mask and slipped it on. Then he said, "Enter."

A Chinese servant in a silk suit came in. He answered only to the name Footman, and as hard as he tried Modo could never get him to give his real name, let alone have a conversation with him.

Footman bowed slightly and said, "A requesting visitor seeks your presence."

Who could be visiting? Mr Socrates and Tharpa always arrived unannounced. It could only be Octavia!

Modo nodded. "Thank you. Please bring the visitor to the tea room in five minutes."

Footman bowed again and walked quietly out of the room. He moved confidently, which suggested that he too had been steeped in the martial arts. This wasn't a surprise; Mr Socrates would only have the best-trained servants. Modo dreamed of testing the man's skills. It would be good training for a change to fight a living, breathing opponent.

For Octavia he would transform into the Knight. She

already knew that character and seemed to like him. So he removed his mask and, with much determination, set about changing his features. As the pain seared through his bones and flesh, as his nose grew straighter, his cheekbones more chiselled, he wondered how many times he'd used this ability since his birth. Did chameleons feel pain when they changed their colour? The months of rest made it somewhat easier—shifting his shoulders, making the hump squash flat into his back, growing a dark swath of hair. He was wearing his sweaty training clothes, but that wouldn't be too improper. She'd see that he hadn't been twiddling his thumbs!

He went to the tea room and had a full minute to dab away his sweat and comb his new hair.

Footman opened the door to the room and gestured to the guest. *This is it!* Modo thought, his heart skipping a beat. He could have slowed it down using his breathing techniques, but his heart *should* beat faster! It was Octavia, after all.

A woman in a large, fashionable bonnet, her face hidden by a veil, traipsed into the room. Footman closed the door behind her. Modo was distracted by the flowers—real flowers—poking out of her hat. She was taller than Octavia. He had been so certain that it would be his friend, had secretly hoped they would greet each other with a hug. Instead, a stranger.

"Are you da vun vat is called Modo?" she asked.

Her tone was smooth and controlled; he couldn't place her accent. German? Scandinavian? He froze. Was it Hakkandottir? Her hands were tucked into a sable muff, so he couldn't tell if one was made of metal. But she looked about the same size as Miss Hakkandottir and carried herself with the same confidence. How had she found him here?

There were no weapons in the room, just a butter knife on the tea table a few feet away. But if he broke the decanter …

"I am who I am," he said. A lame reply, but his voice sounded steady.

"You look taller."

"Do I know you?" he asked.

She took a step closer, her hands moving inside the muff. A concealed weapon?

"I have known you as long as you have known me."

His muscles tensed. No, stay loose, he reminded himself. You'll react faster!

"Is this a riddle?" he asked her.

She pulled her hand from the muff—a glint of metal! He jumped to the tea table, grabbed the butter knife in one hand and smashed the decanter with the other, then pointed the jagged end at her.

The woman let out a shriek and dropped her weapon. It rolled across the hardwood floor between them and came to a stop at his feet.

Modo stared at the object—not a weapon, but a toy train—and then looked up at the woman. She lifted her veil, and he gasped.

"Mrs Finchley!" He hadn't set eyes on his governess for nearly a year. He glanced at the smashed decanter and the knife in his hands, then dropped them both on the table, feeling utterly foolish.

"I hoped to greet you with some drama," she explained, "but my acting was far too convincing. I sometimes forget how good I am." She laughed.

It was such a familiar, comforting laugh. How Modo had longed to hear it.

"I'm sorry! I'm sorry." He sidestepped the shattered glass and ran to her, stopping a few feet away. How he wanted to embrace her! What was a gentleman to do? But she did not reach out to him.

How old she looks, he thought. Then she smiled and she was just as he'd remembered her.

"Is that you, Modo? You look taller."

"I am taller," he said. "At least an inch." He'd grown in the last year, though height was hard to measure in someone who often changed his shape.

"I don't doubt it." Mrs Finchley stroked his face with a gloved hand.

During the battles of the last year, Modo had often longed for her healing touch. Any scratch or bruise he'd had as a child had been attended by her.

"The Knight face, isn't it?" she said. "We invented that one, you and I. From a drawing that I made."

"Yes, yes, it's your creation as much as mine."

"You are the artist and the canvas," she said, removing her hand.

He grabbed the toy train. "I remember this." It looked tiny in his huge palm.

"I—I thought you might. I kept it after you were taken—or rather, after you moved to London for further training. I've carried it with me ever since. I'm too sentimental for my own good."

He rubbed the wheels. He'd nearly worn them to nubs, pushing it around on the hardwood floor of Ravenscroft. It was the only toy he'd had, and was hidden whenever Mr Socrates visited. His master had wanted only science and history books and weapons for Modo.

"Yes, I remember 'Choochy' well. Our little secret, wasn't it. Oh, I do really miss those days."

"As do I, Modo," she said warmly, patting his head.

To hear her say this warmed his heart.

"And you are well, my pupil?"

"I am, Mrs Finchley. I've accomplished several missions since our time together. You've been healthy and well employed, too, I presume."

"Yes," she said, though a familiar tired sigh accompanied her answer.

"What are you employed at?" he asked.

"Oh, this and that. Work for Mr Socrates. Nothing important, really."

"What sort of work?"

"Housekeeping. And other details."

It occurred to Modo that she might be training someone else, practising accents and teaching acting to another agent. Maybe even mothering him, as she had Modo. Did that boy have a normal face?

Modo crossed his arms. "I see."

"I must admit you got my heart racing with that display of glass smashing and acrobatics. My fault, though. I should have remembered that this is not Ravenscroft and your life is under threat every day."

"Well," he said, waving a hand, "maybe only every second day. Truth is, I have been waiting here for far too long and I feel I'll soon die of boredom."

"Boredom won't kill you, Modo, but you can always kill boredom with a good book."

"I've read all the books here."

"Good. Good. Perhaps I've come to alleviate your boredom."

"You have? Will we finally be leaving this house?"

"That's the thing—I don't know exactly why I'm here. I received a rather mysterious missive from Mr Socrates. I was given this address and was told to arrive at exactly 11 a.m."

"So you don't even know why Mr Socrates sent you?"

"As you know, Modo, he has his reasons for everything. All missions are well thought-out, but we aren't privy to the reasoning behind his perfect machinations."

Modo didn't sense any sarcasm or bitterness in her voice. She seemed sincere. But, he reminded himself, she was a brilliant actress who had once played on some of London's great stages.

"Mr Socrates asked me to give you this." She handed him an envelope.

Modo opened it and pulled out a note in Mr Socrates' perfect handwriting.

Please ask Mrs Finchley to help fit you with the costume of a physician. In the next 45 minutes the two of you will work on a persona and develop a new facial physiognomy. At precisely 12 p.m. a carriage will arrive to take you to Bethlem Hospital. Once there, you will interview Prisoner 376 in the prison section.

Mr Socrates

"He wants me to dress up as a doctor and go to Bethlem Hospital."

"To 'Bedlam'?" she said. "Why on earth would he send you to an asylum?"

Modo shrugged. He knew that *Bedlam*, a word used to describe confusion and uproar, was the nickname of Bethlem Royal Hospital, and that out on the streets of London Town a "Bess o' Bedlam" was a lunatic female vagrant. He'd seen his share of them. The ones who were inside Bedlam must be even worse. Well, at least he would be getting out of the house and back to work.

"I'm to interview a prisoner there who goes by the name 376. Odd name, isn't it."

She laughed. "Well, it sounds like a curious mission, but at least a safe one."

"Safe? There are numerous mental degenerates there."

"I know," she said softly, "I've visited Bedlam more than once myself."

Modo was about to ask who she had visited when a thought struck him: Had she been an inmate? He thought of her son dying at a young age, of her sometimes frightened look. *No, no. It couldn't be.*

"I can only say that the unfortunates there are treated more kindly now than they used to be," she said. "In the not-so-distant past they were chained to the walls, their various madnesses on display for curious tourists."

"That sounds horrible." Modo pictured himself in his own infancy as a member of a travelling freak show. Of course, he had no memories of that year of his life, but Mr Socrates had described it to him often enough that he had no trouble imagining it. Had they chained him up?

Footman knocked and entered with a steamer trunk. He set it on the floor, then bowed before exiting.

On the trunk's side was the name *Huntsman & Sons,* the tailors Modo knew were a favourite of Mr Socrates. Inside, Modo discover a neatly pressed frock coat, a top hat, and a doctor's bag, complete with several instruments and a magnifying glass.

"Mr Socrates always has things planned down to the T," Mrs Finchley said. "Don't delay, Modo. Get dressed and we shall begin. I'll need a pencil and paper. I'll draw you a new face."

She put her hand on his shoulder. "We both know Mr Socrates didn't reunite us for our own happiness. He sent me here for a reason." She gave his shoulder a good squeeze. "Whatever the reason, I'm glad of it. I have missed you."

CHAPTER 3

Into Bedlam

The horses snorted as the Hansom cab came to a stop at the Lambeth Street entrance to Bethlem hospital. Modo stepped out onto the cobblestones, walking stick in hand. He paid the driver, then strode confidently to the closed iron gate. His frock coat was of the finest quality, his top hat fit perfectly—he'd adjusted the size of his head to the hat—and the walking stick was adorned with a gold-plated lion's head. He exuded confidence; the fashionable cut of his suit helped straighten his spine. And he held his doctor's bag with authority, just as Mrs Finchley had instructed.

The hospital was larger than Modo had imagined it would be, the dome cutting into the sky. The Roman columns contributed to the building's majesty. He assumed many of the patients inside were cracked and that was why the authorities kept the gates locked.

He approached the gate and could see the true length and breadth of the hospital. Were there really so many men and women in the city and surrounding countryside afflicted with insanity that they filled this huge hospital?

He rapped on the gate with his walking stick, and a guard in a black uniform stepped out of a booth, carrying a ledger in one hand. Modo could see a holstered pistol just inside the guard's jacket and he wondered if the pistol was to keep people out, or the inmates in.

"Morning, sir," the guard said.

He looked to be no more than twenty years old. That gave Modo some comfort; the young man might be easier to manipulate. He took a deep breath and put on his most authentic voice. "I am Dr Jonathan Reeve. I have an appointment to see Prisoner 376."

The guard examined his ledger. "I don't seem to have your name on the list, sir."

Modo tapped on the gate hard enough that the guard edged back. "Now hear this! I won't suffer any more bureaucratic buffoonery. Do you want me to report you to your employers? It was very difficult to arrange this appointment. I'm a busy man! Are you telling me the office didn't send word of my visit? Look again! I'm Dr Jonathan Reeve of the Humanities Institute."

The guard studied the list again, his hand shaking. "You aren't listed, sir," he said quietly. "There must have been a mix-up." He pulled out a key and unlocked the gate, swinging it wide enough for Modo to walk through. "I'm sure the proper papers will arrive with the afternoon post, Dr Reeve. I'm so terribly sorry for the mistake, sir. "

"Tut-tut, my man! Speak no more of it."

With that, Modo brushed past the guard and marched down the main walk that split the brilliant green lawn, carrying his walking stick under his arm.

Men played croquet in groups while women with fancy hats looked on. He wondered what form of insanity had struck them.

He climbed the stairs between the Roman columns, passed through the front doors and glanced down a long hallway. Milling about were several men in various types of dress, from bathrobes to proper suits. He'd expected clamour and frenzy, but it all looked rather civilised. Well, except the bathrobes.

Then one of the gentlemen turned to face him. The hair on half his head had been shaved off completely and one cheek was red with blood. Modo sucked in a sharp breath before he realised the "blood" was, in fact, a bright rouge.

A broad-shouldered matron in a grey dress approached him. Modo guessed her to be about fifty years old. She wore a tight cravat around her neck, her jowls dangling over it. Her hands were large and callused, indicating to Modo that she wasn't afraid of hard work. A key ring hung from her belt.

"May I help you?" she asked curtly.

"I'm here to see a prisoner."

"We have no prisoners, sir," she replied. "The prison wings were demolished years ago."

At this reply, Modo was taken aback for a minute, then he collected himself. "Ah, well, that's rather peculiar since I'm here to see Prisoner 376."

She frowned. "And you are?"

"Dr Jonathan Reeve," he said, sounding slightly haughty. "I'm from the Institute."

She nodded. "I see, Dr Reeve. Perhaps I spoke too quickly. We weren't expecting any more inspectors. Please come along."

She led him down the hallway and through several corridors, her keys jangling as she walked. Every few feet a door opened to a room, and Modo couldn't resist looking in. In one, a man was painting bright orange cats on the wall. In another, a short bald man was playing a violin, while two nurses clapped along to encourage him. The tune stuck in Modo's ears; he had heard very little music while growing up in Ravenscroft, other than Mrs Finchley's singing, so music always sounded as if it were coming from another world.

"Where are you taking me?" he asked.

"This is your first visit to Bethlem hospital?"

"Yes. Though not my first visit to these types of asylums, of course."

"Well, it's not entirely true that we are rid of the prison section. We did keep a few—how shall I put it—private cells."

"Private? For the rich?"

"For those our government deems to be of interest."

They turned a corner to find a soldier standing by a thick metal door. A scar cut across his left cheek and he showed no sign of having smiled in his lifetime. He had corporal chevrons on his right arm.

"Greetings, Mrs Hardy. Greetings, sir."

"I'm Dr Jonathan Reeve," Modo said. "I've come to see Prisoner 376."

"No disrespect, doctor, but if I haven't been forewarned about your visit, I cannot let you inside. Do you have the required documentation?"

"Documentation?" Modo asked. Why hadn't Mr Socrates given him more specific information? Now he would have to find some other way to see the prisoner. Could he break in? Knock the soldier out? But what to do with the matron? She was standing with her arms crossed as if she had already started to doubt he really was a doctor. "I do have papers."

Modo searched through his doctor's bag. During his spare time at Safe House he had gone through boxes of military records. Mr Socrates had given them to him so he'd understand more thoroughly how the army was organised, and who the important people were in the chain of command. He thought of the Secretary of State for War, but any half-literate bumpkin would know it was George Robinson, Earl de Grey. Modo tried to bring all the names to mind. Generals, major generals, colonels. Who would this soldier report to directly?

"Sir, do you have papers?"

Modo breathed in, then sighed. "They are misplaced." As he was about to give the guard a quick palm strike to the jaw, he glanced at the badge on his chest. He was with the Queen's Own! Aha!

"Captain Brooks would not be pleased to know there'd been a delay in my visit. This is a most urgent interview."

The man's eyes widened. "The captain sent you?"

Modo was relieved he'd memorised the names of

officers in several different regiments. "Of course! It's not as though I could steal the prisoner from under your nose. So I guess you have a choice: turn me away and face your captain's wrath or let me pass. Which will it be?"

"You may go in, sir." He opened the door to a dark hallway.

"Thank you, corporal," Modo said. He stepped through the door with all the authority he could muster.

"To the left," the matron instructed, moving past Modo and leading him down a narrow corridor. Every ten feet or so were hung dim gas lamps. They were obviously pinching pennies in this unit.

"Would you like the patient manacled?" she asked.

"I don't believe in manacles."

She shrugged her immense shoulders. "It's your choice, of course." She stopped at a large oak door and squinted through a spy hole. "He seems to be sleeping. I recommend you keep your distance from him, sir. There's a bell inside to the left of the door. Ring it when you want to leave. If he becomes violent, do ring it vigorously. Corporal Salton will get to you as quickly as possible."

Modo wished he knew how strong the prisoner was.

"I understand," he said, as she unlocked the door with one of her many keys.

It squeaked as she pulled it open and Modo couldn't stop his muscles from tensing. The matron gestured for him to go in, so he did. A man was lying on a bare cot, his head and body wrapped tightly in a white sheet so that he looked like an Egyptian mummy. One arm was left uncovered.

"His name is Alexander King," she said. "He will occasionally answer to it."

She closed the door with a solid *thunk*.

Modo glanced around the room, noting the details. A gas light hung from the high ceiling, well out of reach. A barred, oval window was situated at the top of the north wall. Below it, drawn in dark red, were neat rows of hieroglyphics. In the patient's own blood?

"Good afternoon," Modo said.

The man didn't stir.

"Mr King. Are you awake?"

Again, no reaction. Modo wasn't certain the man was breathing. But a second later the patient's chest rose slightly.

"Mr King. I am Dr Reeve and I'm here to ask you several questions. I would appreciate your answers." Modo had no clue what those questions would be. He didn't know the man's state of mind, nor any details about him. Mr Socrates was testing him, no doubt. Obviously King was a criminal of some persuasion; an insane criminal, no less. But what had he done? Perhaps he could start with that.

"Could you tell me your occupation?"

He made no sound. The sheets had been so tightly wound around his face that Modo wondered that he could breathe at all.

"Mr King, I would appreciate your cooperation. What is your occupation?"

King's right arm, a palsied limb, rose and his fingers touched his own sheet-covered face. His forearm, Modo noted, was still slightly tanned, but his upper arm was pale as alabaster.

"Ah, Mr King, you are awake."

The man was small and wiry and looked to have been athletic before his incarceration. Modo walked over to the end of the bed. He could likely restrain King easily enough, but he had read about the surprising strength of those who were maniacally deranged. Better to keep his distance.

"Mr King, can you hear my questions? Please nod if you do."

King continued to stroke his face through the sheet, as though exploring it for the first time. The action reminded Modo of his own habit of feeling his face, in the vain hope that this time it wouldn't be so ugly. Modo couldn't make out any of King's features through the sheet, other than his nose.

"Why do you touch your face?" Modo asked.

The hands froze. King suddenly sat up, giving Modo a start. From behind the sheet, he said, "I have no face." He had a vague colonial accent.

"But you can hear me?"

"I have no ears."

What was he playing at? Modo could see the outlines of the man's ears through the cloth.

"Well, where did they go?" Modo said, humouring him.

"No eyes," King continued. "No nose. No mouth. No tongue. No brain. No thoughts. No me."

"Then who am I speaking to?"

"The mountain keen, the forest green, the God Face burns inside."

"Pardon me?"

"The west at your spine, the face divine. Through the doorway go, beneath the Horus stone. The face it waits, it waits, it waits!" He was scratching at his own face through the sheets so hard that Modo worried he'd gouge out his eyes.

"Mr King, please control yourself!"

Then King began to slap and punch his own head, and Modo, fearing he would grievously injure himself, grabbed the man's arms. It took all his strength to hold the prisoner. The man struggled so fiercely that the sheet began to unravel.

He'd been shaved bald. His face was painted red, but there were gouges all along his cheeks. His luminous eyes shone with cold anger.

"Never touch a god."

He shoved Modo so hard that he flew back against the wall. King grabbed the sheet and frantically wrapped it around himself, then lay there, shaking and trembling, on the bed. After several moments, he became still. He was clearly unable to entertain any rational thought.

Modo pressed his back against the wall and rang the bell. Within seconds the matron opened the door, and Modo joined her in the hall, the door clunking shut behind him.

"He is a hard case," he said.

The matron nodded. "One of the hardest."

CHAPTER 4

The Funeral

Octavia groaned as yet another diplomat stood up to praise the life of Dr David Livingstone. If she had known that Mr Socrates was sending her to such a long and numbingly humdrum funeral, she would have stayed in her room at the Ivory reading *A Tale of Two Cities*, a book full of guillotines and such that kept her entertained. Instead, she was sitting ramrod straight on a pew in Westminster Abbey, which was packed to the rafters with mourners. She guessed that nearly every bloated aristocrat of English society was sharing the air with her, and half of them seemed to have a Scottish accent.

The achievements of Dr Livingstone were certainly impressive; each speaker described the explorer's many incredible discoveries in Africa. She would have been amazed to meet the man while he was living and breathing, but now that he was dead he was rather a bore.

She passed the time by glancing around the crowd through her veil, a handy tool for such covert surveillance.

She wondered if Modo was here. He could be any one of the gentlemen in the pews or extra wooden chairs; he could be watching her at this very moment, which gave her a slight tingle, but also angered her. It meant he always had the upper hand, could sneak up on her, even spy on her. By some magic he was able to change the appearance of his face. Which was his *real* face; who was he?

Still, she missed him. Mr Socrates' policy of not allowing his agents to have contact between missions was so annoying. Next time they worked together she would find a way for them to meet again behind their master's back.

Octavia huffed out her exasperation and continued to observe the crowd. She was unimpressed by the other women's dresses, all black as crows. She herself had on a black crepe dress with a plain collar and her hair was tucked under a widow's cap. Her hat, though, featured a purple band around the crown, making it stand out. If anyone asked, she would say it was Uncle Livingstone's favourite colour, and sniff and sob towards the casket.

Through it all she feigned sadness. The funeral eventually ended and a gentleman threw a palm branch into the grave as a final act of respect. She heard a portly man in the pew ahead of her whisper, "For a Scotsman he was a fine Englishman."

The mourners shuffled out of the church, off to tea parties or to watch cricket matches, Octavia imagined. She salivated. Tea and a sandwich would be wonderful right now, but she had work to do. Her stomach would have to wait.

She found a dark corner near a pillar and pretended to be silently mourning. She ran through her orders again, not that there was much to them. The letter that had explained this assignment had said only to attend the funeral and wear a purple ribbon on her black hat. She would be approached by an operative, who would exchange information with her and in return receive the cash that accompanied the letter. Just another errand. She ran many of them for Mr Socrates.

She couldn't help but gaze in awe at the beauty of Westminster Abbey; the stained glass windows, the buttresses rising into the air as though holding up the heavens. She had no idea how men dreamed up such majestic buildings. Kings and queens had been crowned here. Even fat ol' Henry the Eighth.

A clicking could be heard near the balcony and she glanced towards it, but could see no one. Probably some priestly type locking up the wine, she decided. She wandered through the nave of the church and was drawn to a small marble statue of a man lounging on a couch, leaning on a stack of books. Above him was a marble globe. According to Mr Socrates, that was the shape of the earth. She was dubious. If the earth was round instead of flat, why didn't people fall off? She read what she could of the epitaph. By Jove, it was the grave of Isaac Newton. Admirable resting place for a man who was famous for an apple smacking his head. Here was more proof that all great men die eventually. Though only the greatest were buried in Westminster Abbey.

There were still several men in robes attending to
their duties, and a few other mourners or visitors in the
church, but no one was at Dr Livingstone's grave. Why
not pay him final respects? she thought. She approached
and read the words on the marble slab:

> *For 30 years his life was spent*
> *In an unwearied effort*
> *To evangelise the native races,*
> *To explore the undiscovered secrets ...*

She stopped. Some of the words were harder and she
had to work at remembering what they meant. Octavia
hadn't learned to read until she was employed by Mr
Socrates. So Livingstone had been a priestly type, too. Or at
least fancied himself so. She wondered what all the African
tribes thought of these English explorers. Why didn't the
savages just boil them all up and eat them for dinner?
Maybe English fat didn't taste good. She giggled to herself.

Beside her, a man cleared his throat. She hadn't
noticed him come up. He was also reading the gravestone.
She gave him a once-over: he was in his thirties, wearing
a rather ragged-looking sack coat. He hadn't shaved in
several days.

"A right brave man," he said, rubbing his forehead
with a handkerchief. There was a singsong nature to his
accent but she couldn't place it.

"Yes, he was brave," she agreed.

"I admire your purple swatch. It's as bright as a fig
marigold."

He was Australian! She was certain of it. She'd heard a few sailors with that accent swearing at the pub. She lifted her veil and smiled. "You are very kind to say so."

"Ah, kind I am. In fact, you have dropped something, mademoiselle," he said. He bent down and from his mud-splashed boot pulled out an envelope. He handed it to her and she tucked it into her purse.

"Again, how kind of you."

"I also dropped something," he said. "Could you return it to me?"

"I don't believe you dropped anything." She surveyed the floor at his feet.

"If you look carefully, mademoiselle, you'll see that I did indeed drop something, and you must give it to me. I insist."

There was a trace of anger in his voice. Octavia nearly slapped herself in the forehead. The money! Of course! She opened her purse again and handed him an envelope containing a thousand pounds. Mr Socrates must have wanted the contents badly to pay that many quid for it.

The envelope disappeared into the man's jacket pocket. "As much as I would like to discuss the weather with you, mademoiselle, or even see more of your pretty smile, I must be on my way. As of now, I'm on the wallaby track."

She smiled at the expression, even though she had no idea what he meant. "Good luck with it," she said.

He was rather handsome. He winked at her and flashed a mischievous grin, making her blush.

His grin became a grimace. A shadow descended between them, then shot back into the air, and a red slash gleamed on the man's neck. Blood began to leak down his dirt-grey cravat. He moved his lips silently for a second, then let out an *ugggh* and fell to the floor.

Octavia staggered back just as another shadow swooped near her face. She couldn't believe what she was seeing: a falcon with glowing eyes, and wings that flashed with metal. A second falcon dove at her and she ducked. The bird ripped the hat and veil from her head, then both birds shot up into the great heights of the nave.

Octavia kneeled and touched the man's neck. No pulse. The wound wasn't much more than a scratch, so there was only one explanation: poison! She glanced up and saw the birds still hovering far above her, their eyes bright against the darkened ceiling. She yanked open his jacket and retrieved the envelope of cash. The money was no use to a dead man.

The mechanical falcons were circling, their wings hissing and clicking as they drew closer and closer, waiting for the perfect moment to strike. She glanced around for help, but the few remaining mourners were fleeing in fear. Even the clergymen had backed away.

She spotted a man in a grey greatcoat standing in the balcony above her, watching the attack. His face was hidden in the shadows, but she could see a third falcon on his wrist. His other hand was raised as though he were signalling someone, and a moment later she realised he must be controlling the birds. He flicked his fingers and a falcon dove at her.

Octavia tore a wooden cross from the wall and struck the bird in the air. It spiralled into a row of chairs, splintering them, then hit the floor with a metallic crash. The creature let out a screech unlike any bird she'd heard before.

"Who are you?" she screamed at the man.

He waved his hand and another falcon attacked her. She swung again and the cross snapped in two as it deflected the bird.

The man released the third falcon.

Octavia decided it was high time to scarper to freedom, but her long dress would slow her down. She reached for the hem and easily tore a swath off, revealing her legs. Her seamstress had, at Octavia's request, designed all her dresses this way. It made running so much easier.

She drew her stiletto and ran full speed towards the closest exit, glancing back to see the falcons whirring and screeching behind her, beaks open and talons extended. Each time they struck she'd first hear the ticking of their clockwork and swishing of their wings, giving her time to duck or slash with her stiletto. She managed to poke one right below the eye and drive it back.

She shoved open the west door and ran outside, then threw herself against it, slamming the door closed. She heard the birds pecking and cawing and ramming their metal bodies so hard at the door that she feared the thick wood might actually break. There were shouts behind her and she turned to see constables and even a few Royal Guards rushing towards the door.

"You'll need guns," she shouted, as several of the young men froze at the sight of her stockinged legs. "Oh for heaven's sakes," she implored. "Draw your guns!"

Far above her the stained glass shattered and showered all around her. A falcon, glittering in the sunlight, screeched madly. A moment later two more smashed through the windows.

"Good Lord," one of the Royal Guards shouted. The men were stunned.

"Shoot them! Shoot them!" Octavia shouted. Then she ran for the street, bumping past the constables and shoving a clergyman out of the way. "So sorry, Father," she muttered.

Finally, shots rang out, but one of the damnable birds was still following her and it plunged so close its wings brushed her head. She expected a talon to rake her skin, but there was only a tickle down her neck, then it shot back into the air.

On the street, she waved down a cab, and as she climbed in, shouted at the cabbie to "Drive! Drive like a madman! I'll pay you thirty pounds!"

Without pausing, he snapped the reins and the cab raced ahead.

Through the window, she watched the sky. After twenty minutes she began to feel safe again. She pulled the envelope out of her bag. She hadn't been told to look at what was inside; then again, she hadn't specifically been instructed not to. And she'd just risked her life for this bit of paper. She opened the envelope with her thumb.

Inside she found an old, tea-stained map of a coastline and forest. She held up the flimsy paper to the light. She'd risked her life for a map that doubled as a napkin! Mr Socrates would have a lot of explaining to do.

CHAPTER 5

The Key Master

On the alcove of Westminster Abbey, Gerhard Visser spun his noisemaker. Its clicking echoed throughout the church. The clockwork falcons sped back through the broken windows and returned to him, the first landing on his extended arm, talons digging into the leather protection there. The other two falcons touched down at his feet. The church visitors had fled and the clergymen were cowering in the sanctuary. He crouched to be out of sight of anyone on the ground floor. Visser grinned. Soldiers or constables bumbled along far too slowly. He'd be long gone before they made it up to where he'd been perched.

The falcon on his arm stared at him, his thin metallic skull a parody of that of the original creature. The birds never blinked and, so long as they were wound properly, they didn't tire. With a clicking of gears the falcon turned its head and opened its beak as though it wanted food. Visser chuckled at the witless display. The birds no longer needed food, but Dr Hyde hadn't been able to stop them from mimicking their natural behaviour.

Visser inserted a key into the falcon's skull and it closed its eyes. The second falcon hopped up to his arm and he repeated this procedure, but the third moved to avoid him and only after he gave it a *tut-tut* did it stay still long enough for him to use his key. It glared until its dark eyes closed. He had no idea what went on in the little mind inside the metal brainpan. He carefully placed the falcons in a portmanteau and closed the case. The birds had followed his gestures perfectly. He had trained them for hours and hours under the watchful eye of Dr Hyde.

He glanced down at the dead Australian. The poison had been a particularly good batch. Dead in less than five seconds. Visser had, over his lifetime, perfected the art of ending other people's lives. For a fee, of course. Ropes, knives, guns, bare hands—he had used many methods. But he found these clockwork falcons to be particularly effective. It made for a great show, too.

Over the last two months, Visser had pursued Ned Land from Sydney, Australia, to London, England. Though Visser was an expert tracker, he had consistently been one ship, one port or one pub behind the man for far too long. Only this very morning had he discovered Land's hidey-hole at the Black Sheep Inn and followed him to the funeral. A nice idea to carry out the exchange at such a public event, but it hadn't saved the man's life.

Visser hadn't expected a female agent. The woman was brave enough, he had to give her that. To actually question him while the birds were swooping around her and then to knock one out of the air … Most victims just fled in fear and were cut down as they ran.

So, she had the map. Now he would have to retrieve it. That was the thing about being an agent: sometimes plans had to be altered on the fly. He'd fully intended to kill her and be done with it, but once the soldiers and constables arrived, there was no point. She'd be dead and someone else would have the map. Instead, at the last moment he'd signalled one of the falcons to drop a special instrument on her.

This might be good, he decided. She would perhaps lead him to a bigger catch. At least that's what he would tell his masters at the Clockwork Guild. He would send them a telegraph within the hour.

Visser felt satisfaction slowly building. This was how he liked things to work. Each gear clicking into place like the perfect timepiece.

Taking a compass from his pocket, Visser was particularly pleased to discover that it was not pointing north. Instead it was pointing towards the door that the woman had exited. As he watched, the needle slowly moved. He guessed she would be in a cab by now.

It was time to follow her. He dishevelled his blond hair, picked up the portmanteau, and fled down the stairs and out of the church, shouting, "The birds! The birds are in the balcony!" He ran right past the soldiers who were still waiting for orders from their officers.

CHAPTER 6

A Trusted Associate

Modo sighed as the gate to Bedlam closed behind him. The fact that it was still light out was surprising—it felt as though several hours had passed inside the hospital. And he hadn't learned anything from the meeting with Alexander King.

The man's madness was disturbing; Modo had never before been nose to nose with someone who had lost his faculties. Perhaps most disturbing of all was the man's face. The self-inflicted scratches. The blood. Could it be he hated his appearance? Modo himself, in moments of frustration, had wanted to tear his own face off. Would it one day drive him as insane as that poor fellow?

Concentrate, he told himself. *Why were you sent here?* He sifted through every detail of their conversation and couldn't find a single clue as to why he'd been given this mission.

Smartly dressed ladies and gentlemen, out for a walk, watched him leave Bedlam and then observed the walls of the madhouse with curiosity and perhaps a little fear. No doubt they wondered what was inside. *Madmen,* he wanted to shout at them, *madmen and violinists and painters! That's what I saw!*

You're a doctor, he reminded himself, *and you are an agent. Control yourself.*

He hadn't been told where to go after the interview, so he decided to return to Safe House. He was about to raise his hand for a cab when he noticed a black carriage at the edge of Lambeth Road. The wide-shouldered driver in a greatcoat sat staring ahead with his back straight, suggesting a military background. The carriage door swung open. Modo knew who would be inside even before Mr Socrates leaned out and motioned him over.

Modo strode up to the rig, removed his hat and climbed into the carriage, closing the door behind him. He sat down on the red velvet bench across from his master. Mr Socrates was wearing a black dress coat with a fur collar, opened to reveal his blue jacket, white vest and the gold chain of his watch. His top hat sat beside him like a companion. Modo would have considered Mr Socrates an old man, with his white, closely cropped hair and wrinkled face, but his eyes held a wellspring of energy and strength that would have intimidated anyone half his age.

He tapped his walking stick on the ceiling of the carriage and they began to roll down the street. He appraised Modo for several moments and nodded to himself as though a question had been answered, then leaned forward on his stick.

"So, what did you discover about the illustrious Alexander King?"

"He is quite mad."

"One would expect so, since he is housed in Bedlam. Did you ascertain anything specific from meeting him? Details about his past perhaps? His occupation?"

Modo leaned forward on his walking stick, until he realised he was unintentionally mimicking Mr Socrates. "Uh, well, he had rough hands, so that suggests that he had done some labour. His diction wasn't of the lower classes, though. He was partially tanned, so he spent a good deal of his time outside. I would guess that he is a naturalist or an engineer."

Mr Socrates nodded. "Good observations, though the last is incorrect. King is an explorer. A second-class one, to be sure. But we keep tabs on all the explorers, even the unsuccessful ones."

"His accent was Canadian," Modo added.

"Yes, he's from Vancouver."

Ah, another morsel from my master, Modo thought dryly. "You seem to know quite a bit about him. Why didn't you give me this information before the interview?"

"I wanted an unprejudiced view, so to speak. I have now told you most everything I know about our mutual friend. The only other fact is that he was recently brought back to London from Australia by our government."

"Why?"

"He's suspected in a death or two."

"Whose deaths?"

"A fellow adventurer from Germany. And the death of Dr Livingstone."

"But Livingstone died of natural causes!"

"According to the papers, yes. And that's the story they will always give to the public. But the evening he died, he wrote in his diary—a diary that's been kept a secret—that he was about to dine with Mr King. The same Mr King who was reported to have been climbing with Josef Stimmler a few weeks earlier on Mount Kilimanjaro. Stimmler fell to his death that day. Odd to have two explorers die within such a short period of time and in the company of the same person. I wouldn't call this coincidence."

"So why did he murder them?"

"That's what I was hoping you'd shed some light on. Alas, you haven't been successful in gathering any pertinent information."

"I did my best, sir," Modo snapped, surprised at the ire in his voice. Well, what did Mr Socrates expect? He'd locked Modo away in that mansion for months, then thrown him into an assignment expecting him to be at the top of his game. "And besides, I haven't told you everything yet, sir."

"When you finish your huffing and puffing, do please tell me."

"There are hieroglyphics on the cell wall, written in his own blood, I believe."

Mr Socrates nodded as though he heard these sorts of details every day. "Anything else?"

"He recited a nonsense rhyme." Modo paused to recount the rhyme word for word. "*The mountain keen, the forest green, the God Face burns inside. The west at your spine, the face divine. Through the doorway go, beneath the Horus stone. The face it waits, it waits, it waits.'"*

"Well, he won't give Coleridge a run for his money," Mr Socrates said, and chuckled.

Modo smiled broadly. He loved Coleridge's poetry and was pleased to think his master read him too. Mr Socrates might even be old enough to have known Coleridge himself.

Mr Socrates rubbed his chin. "His poetic rantings do sound rather mad. Most likely pointless drivel. But could it perhaps be a riddle?"

So I was sent to discover pointless drivel, Modo thought. "I do wonder, sir, why I had to sneak in. Why didn't you just pull a few strings and make an appointment yourself?"

"Sometimes it's best not to tip your hand, Modo. Even to members of one's own government. A formal request would have resulted in questions and I would have had to provide answers, which likely would have involved reams of paperwork. An undocumented visit solves all of that."

The carriage rattled along. Modo wanted to ask him several questions, including why he had not been given any assignments for over two months, but he took a deep breath. It was not his place to question. He was here to follow orders.

They crossed the familiar iron and granite Westminster Bridge, clogged with traffic. The sight of the Houses of Parliament made him feel a little nauseated. Would he ever be able to view them again without remembering the monstrous creation the Clockwork Guild had built to attack the government? If not for Octavia he would have drowned in the Thames. Twice now she had saved his life, and she would hold that fact over his head until the day he died. Unless, of course, he could find a way to save her life in return.

As the carriage plowed through the traffic, Modo turned his attention to Westminster Abbey, next to the Houses of Parliament. Together they were a majestic sight. The seat of civilisation, of the very Empire. Mr Socrates was looking at the abbey too.

"They buried Livingstone today," he offered. "I'll miss the old man."

"You knew Dr Livingstone?" Modo asked.

"Yes, he had a great mind, though he was a little too much of a missionary for my taste. I supported his appointment as a consul for the east coast of Africa by the Royal Geographical Society. He was a good friend."

"Why didn't you attend the funeral?" The question had slipped out. "I'm sorry, sir, was that too personal?"

"I'm not one for long goodbyes, Modo. When I depart this world, just set me on a burning boat and push me out to sea. The Norsemen knew how to do funerals."

Modo pictured Mr Socrates in an icy grave and a sharp pain touched his heart. For some moments he considered what would become of him if his master died.

"And did you have a productive visit with Mrs Finchley?" Mr Socrates asked after they had rumbled a few more blocks.

"I did, sir."

"It wasn't a lot of time, but I hope she was able to sharpen your acting chops."

"She did, sir. Thank you for letting me see her again." He stared at the top of his cane. Thirteen years spent raising Modo and then Mrs Finchley had been ripped out of his life by Mr Socrates. Admittedly, it had toughened him, but the fact that he hadn't been allowed to see Mrs Finchley in such a long time made him burn with outrage.

Mr Socrates drummed his fingers on top of his hat. "Don't thank me for that. I don't appreciate sentimentality in my agents. If I had known you were becoming so attached I wouldn't have allowed you to work with her again."

"Yes, Mr Socrates," Modo said. It took all his acting skills to hide his resentment.

When the carriage pulled up to the front of Victor House, they climbed out and Mr Socrates set a quick pace through the iron gates and across the yard. Modo, a half-step behind, tapped the shield on the statue of Mars that guarded the property. He believed it would bring him good luck, plus he felt daring in showing superstition in Mr Socrates' presence.

The door to the house opened and Tharpa nodded to them. He was dressed in tan trousers and a tan kurti that hung to partway down his thigh, and a white turban. Modo nearly rubbed his hands with glee. He finally had the chance to pull one over on his martial arts trainer; Tharpa had never seen Modo in his latest face.

"Good afternoon, Mr Socrates," Tharpa said, pausing to look directly at Modo, "and good afternoon to you, young Sahib."

"How did you know it was me?" Modo squeaked.

"You have a certain smell," Tharpa answered, no sign of guile in his eyes. "Plus I knew you would be travelling with Mr Socrates."

Of course! Modo cursed his fractured thinking.

"Always examine the most obvious answer first, Modo," Mr Socrates said with the same tone he used to impart any lesson. "Any news, Tharpa?"

"Yes. News in the form of Miss Milkweed. She is waiting in the study." He stepped aside so they could enter, then closed the heavy door behind them.

Octavia! Modo was glad for his extra acting lessons. He pretended he hadn't noticed her name and tried to ignore his rapid heartbeat. As he followed Mr Socrates into the study, he checked his buttons and made certain his cravat was straight. He adjusted the chain of his watch so that it hung from his pocket in a perfect U.

"Ah, Miss Milkweed, I see you've made yourself at home," Mr Socrates said.

Octavia was wearing a black dress and seated in a red velvet chair, a book in her hand. It looked as though the bottom portion of her dress had been torn. Her stockinged legs were visible from shins to ankles and her feet were buried in a dark fur rug. Her leather shoes rested next to the chair. A teacup sat on the small table beside her. It had been four months since Modo laid eyes on her. He had to stop staring at her legs!

"Yes. It's good to see you, sir," Octavia said. "Will you introduce me to your companion?"

Modo laughed to himself.

"Of course," Mr Socrates answered. "This is Dr Jonathan Reeve. He's in the employ of our Association."

"At your service," Modo said, and bowed with exaggerated courtesy.

"Oh, a doctor," she exclaimed, brushing a loose curl from her eyes. "It's an absolute pleasure to meet you."

The way she spoke took Modo aback. Was she flirting with him? Did she flirt like this with all men? How many doctors did she know, anyway?

"I'm pleased to be at your service," Modo said.

"You're repeating yourself," she said smartly, and gave him a wink.

A wink! Modo nearly snapped his walking stick in two. She *was* flirting!

"Come, sit at the table, Octavia," Mr Socrates said. "We have much to discuss. And do cover up your legs and put your shoes on; you may not be a real lady, but that's no excuse for such vulgarity."

"Ah, but me feet ache so, Mr Socrates. Perhaps the doctor could soothe them with some rubbing lotion."

Modo swallowed as he pulled out a chair at the table. He didn't dare look at her. Then it dawned on him why Mr Socrates hadn't revealed Modo's true identity. This was another test of his acting abilities! Well, Modo would show him. And her, for that matter.

Octavia, after making a production of putting on her shoes, wrapping a blanket around her legs and muttering under her breath, brought her cup of tea to the table. "Is the good doctor to be part of our meeting?" she asked, sitting down with them.

"You may speak freely in front of Dr Reeve," Mr Socrates said. "He's a trusted associate and an integral part of our Association."

Modo wondered about that. Was Mr Socrates actually complimenting him now? The Permanent Association was a secret organisation that included some of the most powerful people in all of Britannia. Or was the compliment just part of the ruse?

"I would appreciate your report, Miss Milkweed," Mr Socrates said.

"First off," she said, "in the future, could you indicate in your instructions that my life may be at risk?"

"But that should be presumed. Now stop delaying and tell us what you found."

"Well, Dr Livingstone is still dead." Octavia scratched the back of her neck.

"One would expect such, since he has been dead for nearly a year, not to mention the fact that he was missing his heart."

"He was?" Modo said, imagining the gruesome dissection.

"Ah, didn't you read that in the papers, Dr Reeve? When he died in Africa the tribe he'd been staying with at first refused to give up his body. After some persuasion, his two servants carried it in a coffin for nine months, to a port. The authorities there opened the coffin to discover that his heart had been cut out by his tribe. A note had been tucked under his arm. It said, 'You can have his body, but his heart belongs in Africa.' Apparently, they buried his heart under a mvula tree."

"How savage!" Modo said.

Mr Socrates shrugged. "I prefer to think of it as noble. Livingstone himself would have approved, I am sure. Besides, we civilised people have even more savage rituals. Have you ever seen a man hanged? It's only education and upbringing that differentiates them from us. And a bit of English blood." He laughed. "Enough of that. What did you discover, Octavia?"

"Well," she said, "I waited until the mourners were gone, and then a man with an Australian accent approached me. He gave me a document." She slid the envelope across to Mr Socrates. "Oh, and then he died." She threw an envelope stuffed with cash on the table. "So I retrieved his payment."

Mr Socrates pocketed the envelope. "Good work. Please explain his manner of death."

"Three mechanical birds attacked him."

"Mechanical birds?" Modo exclaimed. "But that sounds like the Clockwork Guild!"

"Ah, you know of the Guild," she said. "You really must be a trusted member of the Association. These birds seemed to have poison on their beaks, or their talons perhaps, for the Australian died immediately after having been scratched by one, even though his wounds weren't deep." She scratched her neck again.

"It takes some skill to procure and administer contact poison," Mr Socrates observed. "Please continue."

"Well, a man was observing the attack from the balcony. He was waving his arms, signalling to control the birds. I won't bore you with details about how I escaped and left my mechanical feathered friends behind. I changed cabs twice to be certain no one followed me."

"Good work!" Modo said, completely out of character.

Octavia gave him an odd look. "There's something familiar about you, Dr Reeve. Is there any chance we've met before?"

"Uh, I don't believe so."

"But we have. I'm growing more certain of it. I've heard your voice before. And there's something about your eyes."

"I have never met you, Miss Milkweed," he said, trying to deepen his voice.

Mr Socrates waved his hand. "The charade is over, Modo. Obviously your acting needs more work. My boy, you must be a consummate actor, especially around people who know you."

"Modo?" Octavia glared at him. "So this is another of your faces? And it was all a lark on Miss Milkweed, was it?"

"Not a lark," Modo said, stunned. This was not at all how he'd pictured their reunion.

"What was it then, clever-pants?" she replied.

"It wasn't anything. It wasn't!"

"Enough!" Mr Socrates pronounced. "It was only a minor test for both of you."

"Well, I ..." Octavia lifted her hand, and Modo wondered if she were going to throw something at him, but instead she scratched at her neck again. "This horrid itch," she said, then, wide-eyed, she pulled something out of her hair. Opening her fist, she looked at her palm and let out a little shriek as she dropped an object on the table.

A metal spider, an inch wide, lay there on its back, its silver legs kicking at the air. It ticked like a watch. "What the deuce is that!" she exclaimed.

Mr Socrates picked up a butter knife from the table and poked at the thing. It closed its legs tightly around the knife and began to climb. "Hmm. A curious device. Incredibly fine clockwork." He slowly turned the knife, then dropped one of his cufflinks onto the table. He bumped the spider close to it and the cufflink moved slightly. "It's magnetic. Powerfully so, for something that size. Any idea how you came to get it?"

"I haven't the faintest idea," she replied.

Tharpa found a tin in a desk drawer, and Mr Socrates placed the spider inside and closed the lid.

"I'll have it examined. And, Octavia, we'll have to have a *real* doctor examine your neck. Thank you, Tharpa." He handed the tin to Tharpa, who then left the room.

"The spider is troublesome. One can only guess at its purpose. Fortunately it wasn't covered with contact poison or you'd be dead right now."

"Well, that's a comfort," Octavia said. She crossed her arms.

"It might be a different kind of poison," Modo suggested "something with a delayed action."

"You sound as though you wish it were so," Octavia said.

"No. I just … you should see a doctor."

Mr Socrates shrugged. "Once we're done this meeting, she'll be attended to. But here's what's important now."

He opened the envelope and unfolded the map, holding it so only he could see. Modo stared at the back of it to avoid looking at Octavia, who he knew was still glaring at him. He could see a dim outline but couldn't tell what area of the world the map represented.

"Well, that settles it," Mr Socrates said finally. "Prepare yourselves for another mission. We are going to Australia."

CHAPTER 7

A Hidey-Hole Discovered

Gerhard Visser pounded his fist on the side of the cab. When it didn't stop he smacked the roof several times and shouted, "Halt! Halt!" Now he understood why English gentlemen were always carrying walking sticks. The cab stopped. "Hold your position!" he shouted, and the cabbie muttered, "Your orders is my command, guv'ner."

Visser let the compass needle come to a rest. He'd circled this large, walled house and each time, the needle had pointed towards it, which meant the spider was inside—and the woman as well, of course. He glanced at the statue of a Roman god standing imperiously at the gate.

So this is one of their hidey-holes, he thought. It was a word he'd picked up from his time in pubs in Sydney, trying to find Ned Land. The Australians often talked about scaring wombats out of their hidey-holes.

Visser had no idea what a wombat was, but he knew a good find when he saw one. He didn't have the map. But he had located the home of one of their enemies. That would mean something, wouldn't it? And he'd have ample amounts of information to give his masters. He'd send a telegram.

He made a mental note of the address, pounded on the roof again and shouted out the name of his hotel. He sat back and grinned ear to ear. His masters would be extremely pleased.

CHAPTER 8

An Uneasy Journey

For the next seven days Modo waited in Safe House, training by himself, dining by himself and wondering if he had been forgotten. For all he knew Mr Socrates had decided to go to Australia without him and he'd rot here. There'd been no further communication from him, nor had Modo seen Tharpa, Mrs Finchley or Octavia. Footman attended to Modo's needs, but the man rarely spoke.

Modo read as much as he could about Australia, but only three books in the mansion even mentioned the country and the only newspaper reference was an illustration of the Taradale Viaduct on the Melbourne-to-Sandhurst line. Apparently, gold had been found there back in the 1850s. If Modo had had permission to leave Safe House he could have changed into a gentlemanly shape and gone to Mudie's on Oxford Street, his favourite library.

Then one morning Footman came into the tea room with a package wrapped in brown paper. Modo thanked him and unwrapped it to discover a thin wooden mask. It looked like something an African would have created, with large round eye-holes and a slit for a mouth. Inside the mask was a folded note in Mr Socrates' perfect handwriting:

> *A gift for you, Modo. This African mask was the best I could find on such short notice. Artisans here know nothing of the Maori style, which would have been my preference. Please join us dressed impeccably and transformed into the good Dr Reeve. That persona has not been overused, though you shall be assigned a new name. We will travel first class. Immediately proceed to Victoria Dock to board the RMS Rome. Your clothing, weapons and other necessary equipment are already packed.*
>
> *Mr Socrates*

Modo held the note gently. His standing orders were to burn all correspondence, but instead he tucked the note into his pocket. Mr Socrates had given him a gift. He couldn't bring himself to destroy this proof of his master's kindness.

He tried on the mask, tightening the leather straps. It fit perfectly. Mr Socrates must have used the wax moulding of Modo's face. The doctors of the Permanent Association had made it when they were studying his adaptive transformation abilities.

He set about changing his features, returning happily to the face of Dr Jonathan Reeve—the Doctor face, as he'd come to think of it. He liked the straight jawline, the air of sophistication. Then he dressed in the same fine clothes he'd worn to Bedlam, but he chose a bowler hat this time. It seemed more appropriate for the voyage. Surely, the wind on a ship would toss a top hat out to sea. He threw on a greatcoat and, clutching the mask in one hand, ran downstairs.

Outside the front gates he climbed into the waiting carriage. "Victoria Dock, please," he said to the driver.

They rode east through the streets towards the docks, Modo all the while wondering what the ocean voyage would be like. The idea of getting back on a ship didn't make him particularly happy; in his last mission, he'd had too many terrifying encounters with the ocean. Ah, don't let that spoil your mood, he told himself. He was out of the mansion and actually going somewhere!

After an interminably long time, the carriage stopped and Modo jumped out. Victoria Dock was the greatest of the Royal Docks, the largest port in London, maybe the world. This was where many of the goods from across the Empire were brought into England. He stared at the mass of workers and travellers, like ants next to the enormous steamships. A man with a wagonload of bananas rolled by. A train had pulled to a stop behind him, unloading even more people. There was a crowd of people and a host of portmanteaus, large and small, carpetbags, brown-paper parcels, even canaries in birdcages!

Modo made his way down the dock to the RMS *Rome*. There, standing next to several large crates, were Mr Socrates, Tharpa and, he was happy to see, Octavia.

Even more surprising was the woman in the red dress and long coat: Mrs Finchley! He ran up to them.

"Well, Modo," Mr Socrates said, "late is better than never."

"It's good to see you too, sir," he said somewhat flippantly. "And you as well, Mrs Finchley."

"Yes, Modo," she answered, "always a pleasure." She sounded a little distant, aloof even. Ah, thought Modo, she didn't want to show too much affection in front of Mr Socrates.

"I assume you are pleased to see me, too," Octavia said with a haughty smile.

"Of course, of course." He clutched the mask close to his heart.

"Interesting mask," she said.

"Oh, this?" Modo knocked at the wood. "Mr Socrates gave it to me."

"Yes," his master said, "you cannot hold that shape forever, you'll need it to cover your face so as not to alarm the other passengers. We'll explain it as an affectation. These are also for you." Mr Socrates handed several official papers and a ticket to Modo. "You're to play my son."

"And what would your name be, Father?"

"Robert Reid, son," Mr Socrates replied, smiling. "And your name is Anthony Reid."

"I'll be the best son you ever had," Modo said, meaning it to be a joke, but it came out sounding too serious.

Something like sadness crossed Mr Socrates' face, then was gone. "You'll be extremely busy with studies and training. Mrs Finchley is joining us to help you with your acting. It's almost a two-month trip, so I expect you to be a brilliant actor by the end of it. Mrs Finchley will also chaperone Octavia. She can't be seen travelling alone with three men." At this Octavia rolled her eyes at Modo and he struggled to hide a grin. "This will give Mrs Finchley opportunity to refine Octavia's upper-class accent. And etiquette. *Especially* her etiquette." He stood impervious to her glare. "She will be my niece," he added. "Miss Charity Chandra."

Eight men in dark greatcoats passed them on two wagons. *Ah, our luggage,* Modo realised when he saw all the trunks they carried. Five large, twelve-foot-long crates were on one wagon. Being a mail steamer, the *Rome* was designed to carry a goodly amount of freight. Modo was curious: what could be inside such huge crates? But Mr Socrates didn't offer an explanation, and Modo didn't ask.

A bell on the ship began ringing, warning the passengers that it was time to board. As they climbed the gangplank to the first-class cabins, Modo studied the ship. It was fully four hundred feet long, with four masts and two smoke funnels. A grand enough beast, Modo thought, but he remembered the monstrosity that was the *Wyvern*. That Clockwork Guild battleship would have dwarfed this royal steamer. But this would be a fine ride all the same! The idea that he could travel, in this modern age, all the way from London to Sydney in less than two months was mind-boggling. Going first class was the icing on the cake.

A porter led them to their cabins. Modo would be sharing one with Tharpa, right next door to Mr Socrates' cabin. Octavia and Mrs Finchley's cabin was on the other side of their master's.

Modo was impressed by the size of the cabin, the rich red carpets and curtains, and the view the porthole allowed, looking out over the docks and other steamships waiting in their berths. Below the porthole was a teak table with a chess set, the pawns and knights and such already in place.

Modo picked up the king. "I shall defeat thee mightily," he said, and Tharpa laughed.

Both beds were luxurious, though Tharpa took the smaller one.

"There will be just enough room to spar," Tharpa said. "We shall do so every morning."

"I look forward to it," Modo said jovially.

They sat and waited for their luggage, but Modo quickly grew bored. "I'm going to scout out the ship," he said.

"Yes, go, young Sahib. Scout to the contentment of your heart."

Modo strode along the top deck, passing a good number of lifeboats, which made him feel a little more secure. He crossed under the bridge and spotted the captain, a white-bearded man watching a seaman unfurl the Union Jack from the crow's nest. The captain looked as though he'd been at sea for the last hundred years, and that was fine with Modo.

He made his way among the passengers, avoiding the bustles of the ladies and sidestepping gentlemen with their walking sticks. As he reached the forecastle of the ship, the horn sounded and the RMS *Rome* began to move out of the docks, pulled by a smaller steam-powered tugboat, through the locks to the Thames.

"Are you feeling seasick, cousin?"

Modo turned to the voice. Octavia gave him a wink.

"No," Modo answered, pleased that she may have been looking for him. "I seem to have conquered my seasickness."

"Funny, when we were married you were a husband with a rather delicate constitution."

Modo often relived that trip across the Atlantic and his "job" of acting the part of her husband. He'd spent most of his time in the cabin feeling nauseated. Since that mission he'd sometimes found himself wishing Mr Socrates would arrange for them to be married again.

"Perhaps it was married life that made me ill," he said, smiling his cheekiest smile.

"And maybe your French mistress cured it." She seemed to have lost her lightheartedness.

"What do you mean by that?" he asked, though he knew full well.

"Oh, nothing," she said. "I'm only blowing hot air. I'm feeling a little flushed—I shall return to my cabin, cousin."

Modo watched her sashay away until he could no longer pick her out in the crowd of passengers on the deck. French mistress my eye, he thought. In the days after he had fought alongside Colette Brunet, a French agent, Octavia had often given him the cold shoulder. Perhaps that was why she had chosen not to see him over these last few months.

Modo would never understand Octavia. One moment they were best of friends, the next she was angry at him for some perceived slight. And yet, when they were apart, he couldn't stop thinking about her.

Given how things between them had started off, it seemed it was going to be a very long trip.

CHAPTER 9

One Last Passenger

Visser followed his targets up the gangplank of the RMS *Rome*, carrying his portmanteaus in either hand. He'd dyed his blond hair black and dressed himself in a derby hat and jacket, adding gold-rimmed glasses to give him a bookish, artistic appearance. All this was to prevent the young female agent from recognising him as being from Westminster Abbey. In his pocket were papers that said his name was Albert Carpenter, an American citizen. He always enjoyed mimicking an American accent.

It had been a simple enough task to hire several urchins to watch the house of his enemy and, once alerted, to follow them to the port and purchase tickets to Sydney, Australia. He even had time to send a telegram to his masters providing details regarding the group. He was the last to board the ship.

He recognised Mr Socrates from sketches in the Guild files. He was a brilliant and accomplished man. His Indian servant, Tharpa, was the deadlier of the two. It would be wise to kill him from a distance. Perhaps to be safe, both of them would best be dealt with from a distance.

Not that he'd been instructed to kill them. His orders were to follow Mr Socrates and report on his progress. He didn't know the names or backgrounds of the other three people with Mr Socrates, but he would uncover their secrets soon enough. He'd already seen what the young woman was capable of with his clockwork falcons. He'd also be wary of the other two, who were most likely agents. The older woman might even have a trick or two up her sleeve.

As he walked across the deck he heard the occasional click from within the portmanteau and wondered if he hadn't wound down the falcons properly. Though he'd had several lessons about their intricate levers and gears, there were still a few things about the birds that perplexed him. They were more than just machines, that much he knew.

He noted the cabins his targets had been given, then followed the steward to his own.

CHAPTER 10

A Game of Cricket

Because Modo couldn't maintain his appearance for longer than five hours, he was forced to spend much of his time in his cabin. Each morning, after a breakfast of bread rolls and eggs in the dining room, Modo would return to his room and let his Doctor face slide into the face he had been born with. Then he'd spar with Tharpa, earning new bruises every day.

In the afternoons Mrs Finchley would arrive to give him his acting lessons. Modo was reminded of his days in Ravenscroft and his heart ached for that simpler time when it was just him, Mrs Finchley, Tharpa and occasionally Mr Socrates.

"'Is this a dagger which I see before me, the handle toward my hand?'" Modo recited. "'Come, let me clutch thee!'"

Mrs Finchley clapped her hands. "You have outgrown me!"

Modo enjoyed the part of Macbeth, one of his favourite characters. "But I haven't outgrown *you!*" he answered.

She patted his shoulder. "I mean in your talent. I hope you never outgrow spending time with me. I'm so proud, though. There are times when you are completely involved, when you become the character you are playing. That's at the heart of great acting. You have tremendous ability for someone so young—but you need to forget something."

"Forget what?"

"Yourself! The best actors must believe in their hearts that they are who they pretend to be."

There must be something to that, Modo decided. But he never felt as though he could forget who he was, so he could never completely throw himself into a part. How could he forget his life, his face?

He set down the imaginary dagger.

"How is Octavia progressing in her studies?" he asked. He hadn't had more than a few private conversations with her since they'd boarded the ship. She would join them for meals, but was busy with her own training.

"She's progressing nicely. A smart, raw talent, that one," Mrs Finchley said.

"As talented as *moi?*" he asked, feigning light heartedness. Mrs Finchley had sounded so proud of her and his fists had involuntarily tightened.

"Ah, each of you has your own unique talents. Now, let's work on your accent and bearing."

After the fourth straight day of training, he knocked Tharpa onto his back twice. Each time, Tharpa stood, brushed himself off and gave Modo a grin. "Good! Good!"

When Modo wasn't training, he wandered the *Rome*, looking out at the Atlantic, stopping at the saloon for lemonade or lime juice. He was relieved the steamship hugged the European coast. He shivered when he pictured falling into that water again, as he had only a few short months ago. He'd come so close to freezing to death; his body remembered it well. And every time he looked down into the deeps he thought of Captain Monturiol and Cerdà and swallowed a lump of sadness. The Atlantic was their grave, a sunken submarine ship their coffin.

He distracted himself from his memories by following one of Mr Socrates' orders: to learn as much about the other passengers as possible. There were 125 saloon passengers in all. It had been a simple matter of asking for a tour of the clerk's office, then sneaking a look at the list while the clerk was called out to answer some lieutenant's question about pay stubs. The names were common enough: *Mr and Mrs Henderson, Mr and Mrs Hare, Messrs. M. Collier and C.P. Davis, Mr Carpenter, Miss Hoddle, Miss Fulton. Mr and Mrs O. Sheppard and two children. Mr Robert Reid and Son, Anthony Reid and servant. Charity Chandra and Mrs Finchley.*

He read the last few lines again. There it was in writing. Anyone who read it would believe he was Mr Socrates' son and that Octavia was named Charity. He assumed Mrs Finchley hadn't changed her name because she wasn't an agent. And, it was curious that Tharpa wasn't listed by name as a passenger. If the ship went down and all souls lost, would he even be counted?

Modo memorised the list. He would make it a game

to put a name to each of the faces. He would do the same with all of the ship's cabin boys, stewards, seamen and officers too. Mr Socrates didn't expect there to be any sort of trouble on the ship, but it was wise to know with whom they were spending so much time.

There were other distractions, of course. Being in first class meant painting lessons, which he skipped, card games, singalongs, croquet on the deck, and even cricket in one of the open holds. He'd never played cricket, but he'd read the rule book over a year ago. A passing knowledge of cricket would be important to survival in the British Empire, he'd decided.

He'd expected to be spending more time with Mr Socrates, but his "father" was either in his cabin doing research or with the officers of the ship. Mr Socrates did dine with Modo and Tharpa at breakfast, but the discussion was mostly about the weather.

"Will we be playing any cricket, Father?" Modo asked on the sixth morning of their voyage. There was something about calling him "Father" that was pleasurable. Mrs Finchley had said he should throw himself into his part and so he would!

Mr Socrates laughed. "My cricket days are done."

"Would you play, Tharpa?" Modo asked.

"The rules of propriety don't allow me to play," Tharpa said.

"What do you mean?"

"Don't be soft-headed, son," Mr Socrates said. "Tharpa is a servant. He cannot play cricket with the first-class passengers. Besides which, his place is at my side."

"I bet you could knock the ball right across the Atlantic," Modo said. "You'd hit it so hard their first-class lily-white pants would fall right off."

Tharpa laughed. "You are kind, though incorrect. It is their socks I would knock off."

Modo signed up for the next game that afternoon and spent a few hours in the open hold playing against a collection of officers, doctors, a hotel owner, an engineer and even a priest, memorising their names as he did so. It was a sunny day, and down in the hold he began to sweat.

When it was his turn at bat, Modo stood behind his wooden wicket and stared at the bowler, Mr Haroldson, a clerk from London. He knew the point of the game was to prevent the ball from striking his wicket and to hit it far enough to give him time to change places with the second batter fifteen feet away. He glanced at the upper deck and was surprised to see Mr Socrates looking down at him. Alongside him were Captain Adamson and a few other elderly gentlemen.

Modo gripped the white willow cricket bat too tightly and his first swings were utter misses, allowing the ball to strike his wicket and knock down two of its "stumps." He was already nearly out and he hadn't even hit the ball! He released his breath and relaxed his shoulders, just as Tharpa had told him to do a thousand times. With his next swing he struck the ball hard, ringing it off the metal wall and hitting Lieutenant Sanders in the stomach, knocking him to the ground.

"My son doesn't know his own strength," he heard Mr Socrates say.

Modo rushed over and apologised to the lieutenant, but even as he did so he couldn't help but feel a little pride. He could play cricket! He was just like a regular Englishman, after all. Who needed a fancy education at Oxford? Ravenscroft had been good enough.

The lieutenant waved him away. "It's a minor wound, take your place."

As Modo walked to his wicket he glanced back up at the spectators. Mr Socrates had turned away and was discussing something with the captain. Wasn't he going to watch the rest of the game? There were only five other spectators. Modo was pleased that he could immediately recall the names and occupations of four of them. The fifth was a dark-haired man with glasses who seemed to be travelling alone. Modo had yet to match a name with his face. However, as he picked up the cricket bat it came to him with a laugh. The only name he hadn't matched was Mr Carpenter. Now that he knew his name, he'd have to discover his occupation.

Modo was delighted. A run scored in cricket and now he had matched every passenger's name to a face. He glanced back at Mr Carpenter, who was still watching him. Modo nodded at him and prepared to swing, whispering at the bowler, "You can't have my wicket!"

CHAPTER 11

Stop. Expendable. Stop.

When the *Rome* resupplied at Gibraltar, passengers were given a few hours to visit the shops. Visser took a cab from the docks and down the central streets. His cabbie, like most other residents of the port city, had a British accent; essentially this little jut of rock in the Mediterranean at the bottom of Spain was British soil. It irked him to know that they had already left their footprints on so many parts of the world. Their incursions and domination of the Boers in South Africa was particularly galling. His people. He'd learned to hate the English at the knee of his father, a Dutch farmer, who eked out his living in the Orange Free State.

He stopped at the Piazza, stepped out onto the paved square and went into the Club House Hotel, a three-storey building. After waiting in line at the desk, he asked for any messages being held for Mr Charles Godwin, one of his several identities. The clerk handed him a telegram and Visser read it immediately, deciphering the Guild code without need for pen or pencil:

NAME OF YOUNG FEMALE AGENT OCTAVIA.
STOP. EXPENDABLE. STOP. NO RECORDS FOR
MRS FINCHLEY. STOP. EXPENDABLE. STOP. NAME
OF YOUNG MALE AGENT NOT KNOWN. STOP.
POSSIBLY MODO. STOP. CAPTURE PREFERRED.
STOP. BRING BODY SAMPLE IF KILLED. STOP.
MAIN MISSION IS TO OBSERVE AND REPORT.
STOP. FURTHER ORDERS IN MALTA. STOP.

Agent Modo! Visser had read the young man's file several times. He was described as being extremely strong and with the uncanny ability to physically change his appearance. Visser would have thought it a wild exaggeration if the information hadn't come directly from Miss Hakkandottir herself. Why did they prefer him captured, or a body sample obtained? Was he to dismember him? How much of his body was required? He would need clarification. He shrugged, not interested enough to give it any more thought. Orders were orders. He wouldn't have to kill any of them immediately, which was disappointing. It would be a relatively easy task to stalk them; after all, they wouldn't be leaving the ship until they arrived at Sydney.

He sent the Guild a message saying he had received their orders. When he turned around, he found himself face to face with Mr Socrates.

The old man nodded and said, "I recognise you from the ship. I hope your voyage has been proceeding well."

"Yes, yes, it has, sir, thank you," Visser mumbled, then quickly stepped around him.

Was it just coincidence that he was here at the hotel? After all, it was one of the few telegraphs available to the public. Visser stood at the door long enough to observe that Mr Socrates was receiving messages of his own.

Then he noticed Tharpa waiting outside the hotel—but the servant didn't seem to take any notice of Visser, so he hailed a cab and ordered the driver to take him directly back to the ship. On the way he mulled over his meeting with Socrates, but in the end was satisfied that it had indeed been nothing but an unfortunate coincidence.

CHAPTER 12

An Important Meeting

"Off with your head!" Mrs Finchley rose from her seat at the table in their cabin and stood before Octavia, hands on her hips. "That's the proper pronunciation! Not 'off wit' yer 'ead.' 'H' should never, ever be dropped!"

"Od rot it!" Octavia exclaimed, exasperated after three straight hours of practising her upper-class accent. She'd much rather be training with Tharpa. At least his kicks to the ribs kept her awake.

"Don't use any oaths in my presence, young lady!"

Octavia bit back another curse. Mrs Finchley, normally quite calm, seemed to be in an extremely perturbed state. Angry, even, Octavia thought. Then Mrs Finchley took her hands from her hips and burst into laughter.

"My dear Octavia, I'm reminded of my own youth when I was a budding actress. I was always saying 'werry' instead of 'very.' 'I grow weary of your werrys, you wicked witch,' my old acting master would shout at me." She put one hand on Octavia's shoulder, and with her other, adjusted a lock of her hair. "You are doing exceptionally well."

"Thank you," Octavia said, then added, "Off with my head! Off with my head!"

"Perfect! Perfect!"

As the weeks aboard the *Rome* had passed, Octavia found that she was actually enjoying Mrs Finchley's company. She had never known a motherly type, only the headmistress at the orphanage who believed that the best lessons were taught one smack of the rod at a time. Mrs Finchley would even surprise her with gifts! When the *Rome* had stopped at the island of Malta, Mrs Finchley dragged Octavia off the ship in search of lace and material to make more clothes for her. "A beautiful young woman like you needs a different dress every day," she had explained.

Mrs Finchley calling her beautiful without the slightest hesitation made Octavia glow.

They returned with a steamer trunk of material, and, as each day passed, she sewed for Octavia. Corsets, petticoats, gloves—all fitted perfectly.

"It's late afternoon, Octavia," Mrs Finchley said one day. "Time to switch to a dinner dress. Which will it be? Green? Red? Violet?"

"Violet!" Octavia said, and Mrs Finchley began helping her change into a dinner dress, complete with an impressive bustle.

The number of dresses that had been brought on board for her astonished Octavia: afternoon dresses, dinner dresses, evening dresses and ball dresses. She even had a special green and black dress for Sunday service. Church was a foreign experience, but Mrs Finchley had coached her, so she lowered herself to her knees and rose again at the right times and could recite the Lord's Prayer.

Octavia also attended many of the evening singalongs, each time wearing her best feathered hat. The first-class passengers gathered on the poop deck and sang for the second-class passengers, a gift for those below them. Mrs Finchley had coached Octavia's singing until she sang as clear as a bell. Two lieutenants and even the captain had commented on her pleasant tone. She loved the song "Dream-Pedlary" because of the lines *If there were dreams to sell, merry and sad to tell, And the crier rung the bell, what would you buy?* She liked to imagine what she would buy. More dresses! No. She returned to her favourite fantasy: she would buy an island and wear trousers all of the time. She could run so much faster in them.

Though, she had to admit that while wearing dresses, she did enjoy the looks she got from some of the officers.

She was surprised that Modo sang in a pleasant and rather beguiling baritone. She decided it must be his barrel-like chest that gave it such a rumble. She didn't completely understand why she was spending so little time with him. Yes, she saw him at breakfast and dinner, but their conversations were about the weather or whatever landmark they were passing at the time. This was their third assignment together and she felt quite suddenly as if she didn't know him at all. She often thought of the trick he and Mr Socrates had played on her, having Modo pretend he was a doctor. It made her angry that she hadn't recognised him. He could sit across a table from her and be someone else entirely. But his face was so different from the only other one she'd seen, which had also been handsome! How many faces did he have?

She longed to see his real face, whatever it was!

"Did you really raise Modo?" Octavia asked Mrs Finchley.

Her tutor smiled again, but this time there was sadness in it. "Yes. I've known Modo since he was an infant."

"What … what … ?" She wanted to ask what he really looked like. Instead, she asked, "Where does he come from?"

"I'm not allowed to tell you that. Mr Socrates guards such secrets well."

"But who were his parents?"

Mrs Finchley shrugged. "I believe they gave him up."

"Why?"

"I don't have the answer to that question," she said. "I only wish that they could see him now and know that he is the most exceptional young man I have known."

Octavia nodded. "He is, indeed," she whispered.

There was a knock at the cabin door. They had been speaking of Modo—would he appear just like that? Suddenly she felt that she wanted to beg his forgiveness for ignoring him.

But when Mrs Finchley opened the door, Tharpa stood there, his face impassive as stone.

"Octavia, please come to Mr Socrates' cabin at once. He has called a meeting."

Octavia paused to check her hair in the mirror, then followed Tharpa to see her master.

He was seated at an oak table, papers spread out in front of him, a cup of tea in his hand. Modo hadn't yet arrived.

She took in the room, amazed at how much larger his cabin was than the one she shared with Mrs Finchley; in fact his porthole was twice as large. The lower half of the walls was panelled and the top half was wallpapered with images of intertwined dragons. His bed was perfectly made, not a wrinkle to be seen. Octavia wondered if Tharpa made his bed—or did Mr Socrates do it himself? There were stewards, of course, but she guessed that it was Mr Socrates. He had a military background, after all, and that lot was always fussy about neatness.

She noted a painting of a woman on the dresser. Had Mr Socrates been married? Was he still?

Tharpa pulled out a chair for her and she sat down, her bustle bumping up against the back of it. The damnable things looked nice, but were far too awkward for her liking.

Modo knocked at the door and entered. She was still a little surprised every time she saw this new face. She realised her heart was beating faster. It didn't seem to matter which face he had on—he still affected her.

"You're late again," Mr Socrates observed for the benefit of everyone.

"I'm sorry, Father," Modo answered.

"You may call me Mr Socrates during the course of this meeting."

"I understand, sir, and I do apologise. I had to prepare myself. Though you have trained me well, I still need more than a few minutes to complete my adaptive transformation." He nodded to Octavia. "A pleasure to see you, Miss Milkweed."

She wasn't certain how to interpret his formality. "And a pleasure to see you, Modo," she answered.

"Where's Mrs Finchley?" he asked.

"It isn't necessary for her to be here," Mr Socrates answered. "Now, to begin, I hope you've enjoyed these weeks of rest. And I'm pleased with the progress both of you have made in your studies. We have a mission ahead of us that will test your talents, and perhaps change the course of Britain's history."

Octavia raised her eyebrows. "Really?"

"Yes, well," Mr Socrates laughed, "perhaps I'm exaggerating slightly, but I do confess I'm excited about the potential discoveries that lie ahead of us." On the table he opened a map, the same one Octavia had been given in Westminster Abbey. "I've been receiving telegrams at each port of call, but this is still the most important document we have. The Australian gentleman who brought this map to us was named Ned Land. He had sent me a message through—how to put it?— our sources. He had something very important for the Empire, he said. It came at a price, of course. We paid that price and he delivered the map to England. Very uncouth of him to die before explaining exactly why the map is so important."

"Is it a treasure map?" Octavia asked. She had studied it in the carriage, but it seemed nothing but squiggly lines.

"Oh, it's much more than that, Miss Milkweed. This

map will take us to a temple that holds the key to what could become a significant weapon in Britain's arsenal."

"A weapon?" Modo asked. "What sort of weapon?"

"That's the problem. I don't exactly know what it is."

"Then what does our mad explorer Alexander King have to do with this?" Modo asked.

It occurred to Octavia that he was looking older, somehow. Not so much his face, since that was always changing, but perhaps his eyes.

"Well, this was King's map. Or at least at one time it had been in his possession. It had also been in Dr Livingstone's possession, previous to King's. I have sources in the Adventurers' Club who have heard rumours for decades of this map's existence. Now, it's important to remember that explorers natter like ladies at a tea party, so I take such rumours with a grain of salt. But I wanted to know what had driven King mad, since by all reports he was sane when he embarked on his expedition to Australia."

"Sane?" Octavia said. "But he murdered two men."

"That's not insanity. That is, alas, human nature. Some people can't take too many days in the jungle. It can drive them mad. But the more interesting story stems from an old legend that the Egyptians were once in Australia and built a city, hoping to create a new Egyptian empire. The theory is that they were trying to escape the Persian empire. Or Alexander the Great."

"Is it possible?" Modo asked.

"Anything is possible. It's not probable, but we must investigate every lead. There's a legend among those members of the Adventurers' Club that an artifact exists called the God Face. It's said to be an instrument that induces madness. I believed it was just another fabulous tale until Mr King travelled to Australia, apparently found this Egyptian city, and returned home quite insane."

"But someone else knows about this," Octavia said, "or Ned Land wouldn't have been murdered right in front of me."

"I agree, which is why I wish you had been able to gather more information."

"I preferred to stay alive. I do apologise for that."

"Not to worry. Your description of the mechanical falcons can only mean the Clockwork Guild is at work again. Their failure to secure the map indicates we have a head start. As you can guess, we're going to follow this map, find the ruins and locate the mysterious artifact. Or, perhaps we'll learn there's nothing there at all. Either way it will be an adventure. Any questions?"

Octavia was incensed when Modo put up his hand as though they were in a classroom. He could be so overly keen at times that she wanted to slap him.

"Yes, Modo?" Mr Socrates said.

"What are some of the possible dangers? Besides the Guild, of course. Animals? Plants? Are there natives in that part of Australia?"

"The plants and animals will be little bother for us, I promise that. And as for the natives, yes, there are tribes in the rain forest. But my sources tell me that they've had limited contact with civilised people and they'll likely vanish into the forest long before we see any of them."

"But what if we do see them?" Octavia asked.

"We'll deal with that if it happens. To put it bluntly, if they are aggressive, we have guns and they have spears. But I would prefer to leave them be. In Africa, my policy was to avoid such contact as much as possible. They are like children. We don't want to expose them to too much technology, or force change upon them too quickly. As a society, our role is to lead them gently towards progress."

Modo had his hand up again. Octavia shot him a look, but he didn't notice.

"Yes, Modo, you have more questions?"

"Just one, sir. Why?"

"I believe I just spent the last several minutes explaining the reason."

"Forgive me, sir, but I mean, why are *you* here? I've been playing chess against Tharpa this week and you should never sacrifice the king."

"I appreciate being thought of as a king, Modo, but in reality I'm more of a bishop." He grinned, wrinkles folding around the edges of his eyes. "I've accompanied you on this mission because I want to see this place for myself. I can't just sit in a musty old room pulling the strings. Besides, Tharpa will protect me from any hazards we may face."

Tharpa raised his eyebrows. "I will do my best, Sahib."

"Any more questions, Modo?"

He shook his head.

Octavia was about to get up when Mr Socrates said, "One more thing. Octavia, we have analysed the spider you found on your person. I was correct about it being magnetised. My sources have informed me that our enemies may have been able to follow you using this device and a similar magnet. If this is so, they may be using another such device to follow us. Please go through all your luggage and clothing. And, of course, it's likely that an agent or agents have pursued us onto this ship. Please be extra cautious. You are dismissed."

"Thank you, Uncle Robert," Octavia said coyly. She rose, waited until Tharpa had pulled her chair back, and walked towards the door. "I shall spend the rest of the evening hunting through my clothes. I'm afraid I rather dislike spiders. 'Off with their heads,' I say." And she giggled to herself, then left the men to exchange quizzical looks.

CHAPTER 13

The Horn of Africa Ball

A few evenings later Modo discovered an envelope stuck near the back of the brass mailbox outside his cabin. He hadn't checked for mail in days, assuming no one on the ship would write to him. He opened it to find an invitation for first-class guests to attend "The Horn of Africa Ball." He was glad to have this reminder. The captain had announced the ball over a week earlier, and Modo was looking forward to the event.

Seeing the words "Horn of Africa" in print reminded him just how far they had already travelled. Only two days ago they'd sailed by Alexandria, the city founded by Alexander the Great. Then they had passed through the engineering marvel of the Suez Canal, about which Mr Socrates said, "The French built it for we British to use. Very kind of them." Modo had stared westward as hard as he could, hoping to see the pyramids. No such luck. And now they were chugging across the Red Sea, nearing the Horn of Africa. And to think that they were still only halfway to Australia.

With surprise, he read the date on the invitation. It

was tonight! He rushed back into the cabin and quickly explained the situation to Tharpa, who helped him dress in his finest white shirt with a black string tie, black waistcoat and a dress coat with tails. He combed his newly grown hair vigorously.

"It will fall out if you continue such ministrations," Tharpa advised.

Modo gave him a friendly punch. "Don't tease me! You'll be catching up on your sleep here in the cabin, so no one will be staring at you, but they will be ogling me. After all, I'm the son of a well-heeled gentleman. I assume I shall one day be inheriting his massive fortune."

By the time Modo had fancied himself up, pressed on his silk top hat and made his way to the upper deck, the ten-piece orchestra was already playing on the promenade and some of the passengers were dancing. He stopped dead in his tracks, stunned by the beauty of the scene. The ball had been planned to take place just as they were passing the Horn of Africa, the evening sunlight washing the flat, sandy shores with a red tinge. Even the Indian Ocean caught the warm light, against which were silhouetted gentlemen dressed to the nines and the women in their fanciest gowns. It was all so civilised! This is what Britannia was all about!

One of the cabin boys presented to him a dance card that listed the order of the dances, followed by a directive: *Gentlemen will remove their sabres and spurs prior to the first waltz.*

According to the list, he'd missed the grand march. The orchestra was on to a waltz now. Women in gowns of all colours and styles swayed alongside the men in black suit coats. Modo spotted Octavia on the dance floor and, of all things, Mr Socrates was dancing with her! She wore a dark red gown, her locks tightly bound. He wondered if Mrs Finchley had helped her with her hair; he'd never seen such intricate braids, each held by a red bow. And she carried herself with remarkable poise. She easily passed as an upper-class lady.

When the orchestra began playing a mazurka quadrille, Modo watched helplessly as Octavia accepted a dance with one of the more handsome officers. There was no time to waste.

He ran to the far end of the upper deck and stood breathlessly before Mrs Finchley, asking, "Will you give me the pleasure of dancing with you?"

"Mr Anthony Reid," she said with feigned haughtiness, "'pleasure' is not the proper word. 'Honour' is."

"Ah"—he bowed—"will you *honour* me with your hand for a quadrille?"

She curtsied and offered her hand, and they joined the eleven couples already dancing. Modo had practised the quadrille years earlier with Mrs Finchley. He'd had to imagine the other couples and the intricate pattern of the dance. As they began to move, Modo immediately realised that dancing with a real group would be much more difficult. At first he was awkward and sometimes lost the beat, but with several deep breaths and a few kind compliments whispered by Mrs Finchley he relaxed and his footing became more confident.

"Be the song," Mrs Finchley said quietly. "Feel its rhythm."

The circular path of the mazurka meant that he occasionally found himself next to Octavia briefly. Sometimes he danced close enough to actually say a few private words.

"You look absolutely first class," he said on one of these occasions, as he hooked his right arm through hers and they twirled around each other.

"I know," she replied with a coy smile. "No seasickness on the Indian Ocean, my dear cousin?"

"Not even a smidgen. Bring on the Pacific!"

She spun away, dancing with an officer in a fancy white coat and golden buttons. By the man's insignia, Modo could see he was a lowly captain's clerk! But he was a good six inches taller than Modo.

But the dance soon brought Modo and Octavia together again. "You're looking rather handsome, yourself," she said as she moved away. "Keeping in mind, of course, that you aren't really yourself at all."

The mazurka didn't allow them to speak again, to his great frustration. The orchestra finished and the dancers all bowed to one another. When he looked up, Octavia was already with another officer, a lieutenant this time. Mrs Finchley had been asked to dance by the grizzled captain, so Modo found himself standing alone as the orchestra struck up a painfully peppy polka. He was not feeling the least bit peppy.

Modo threw himself down in a lounge chair. What exactly had Octavia meant by her last comment? Had it been a mistake to use the Doctor's face with her? After all, she really knew him so much better by his Knight face, another from his repertoire. Maybe every time she saw this new face she was reminded of how he could change. She had to get to know him all over again. Was that why she seemed so distant?

But surely she could see it wasn't his fault. This is how he was born.

Already the Horn of Africa was sinking behind the ship. It was certainly warmer this far south, but he still shivered. A waiter brought him a soothing cup of tea and he drank it. He had to admit they did have good tea on the *Rome*.

Modo wanted to go back to his cabin and read, but Octavia would probably accuse him of sulking. So to pass the time he watched the other passengers. He rehearsed all of their names and occupations. Then he matched all the men with their wives. Except for the priest, of course. These were the elite of British society. He wondered if any other members of the Permanent Association were on board. For all he knew everyone on the ship was an agent of Mr Socrates. He laughed nervously. Wouldn't that be something.

And what about enemy agents? With that in mind he surveyed the seated passengers.

The priest would be a reasonable guess as his collar would make him seem trustworthy, but the man was at least sixty and seemed to have had a friendly demeanour the few times Modo chatted with him. He certainly enjoyed talking about birds. No, it would be too obvious to dress up like a priest. A doctor, now that might be a good disguise. Unless someone suddenly became ill—then you'd have to prove you were a doctor.

He noticed that Mr Carpenter was sitting alone, but very near Mr Socrates, who was in conversation with the ship's captain. He leaned slightly towards him as though listening in. Modo ran through his memory of the last month on the ship. He'd seen the man many times and he was usually alone. He'd been sketching out on the deck, so he was some sort of an artist. Modo had never heard him speak. The fact he was alone might indicate he was a solitary agent.

Mr Carpenter glanced at Modo, their eyes meeting for a moment, then he nodded and went back to looking out at the ocean. After a few minutes Mr Carpenter stood and walked down the deck towards the cabins.

Modo waited several seconds, and followed him. He didn't know if he was responding to gut instinct or just looking for an excuse to leave the dance.

Mr Socrates had told him never to put too much stock in gut instinct. "The gut is not the part of the human body that thinks," he'd explained numerous times. And yet, Modo found himself following the mysterious man.

He watched as Carpenter entered his cabin and closed the door. Modo approached it quietly and stood outside, listening. All was quiet. Then he heard a *click* like a hammer being cocked on a pistol.

CHAPTER 14

Interesting Scars

Visser crouched next to his cabin door, a loaded, cocked pistol in his right hand. He waited. The young agent, Anthony Reid, had followed him and that was a bad sign. If he was indeed Modo, then he could assume any face and was immensely strong. His hits at the cricket games proved his strength, but Visser had seen no sign of his transformative abilities. He wasn't even sure what he should be looking for.

What could the young man know about him? Nothing, he was certain. Visser had left no clues about his real reasons for being on the ship. So how had one of his enemies ended up on the other side of the door?

In his mind he quickly ran through various possible outcomes of the situation: if there were conflict and he shot the agent, Visser would be easily captured and put up on charges.

Perhaps before it got that far, in the certain confusion, he could swim from the ship to the African coast.

No, no. A gun was too noisy in any case; it might be heard above the orchestra. And besides, he hated swimming.

He'd tinkered with the falcons, but wasn't sure whether they were wound properly. Contact poison on a knife would do the job, but he hadn't prepared any poison—and what would he do with the body? He glanced over his shoulder to measure the porthole. It was far too small to push the man's corpse through. The cabin was a completely inconvenient place to murder anyone. Of course, Visser thought, he could murder him quietly now, then throw him overboard late in the night. He always had garrotte wire in his pocket; he'd used it many times before.

Why are you crouching here like a child? he scolded himself. *Why not just get to the root of the problem?* He went to his bed and placed the gun under the pillow, removed his jacket and rolled up his sleeves, hoping it would make him look more American. Then he opened the door and pretended to be startled at the sight of the agent.

"Why, good evening, sir."

"G-good evening," the young man said, straightening up as though he'd been listening at the keyhole. "I was just getting some fresh air and paused here for the view. Lovely night for a ball, I must say."

"Yes, it is," Visser replied. The agent was taller than him, his shoulders wider. No matter. The garrotte would still work, so long as he got in proper position behind him. He'd taken down men twice his size. "I must admit I became bored. I'm not so much for waltzing."

"Neither am I, I'm sorry to say. Are you an American?" the young man asked. "You have an accent."

"Guilty as charged." Visser searched the man's face for clues of a facial transformation—stretch marks, wrinkles—anything that would point to his being Modo. But he seemed completely normal. Handsome, even. "I moved there with my family when I was a boy."

"Lovely country."

"Yes it is." Visser had lost count of how many inane conversations he'd had with enemy agents in his lifetime. Next they would be talking about cricket scores.

The young man extended his hand. "I don't believe we've been formally introduced. I'm Anthony Reid."

"Howdy, Anthony, I am Albert Carpenter." Visser wondered if the "howdy" was too much, but the young man didn't react.

They shook hands; Visser found the man's grip firm.

"Carpenter, is it? Do I also hear a pinch of Dutch in your accent?"

Visser was stunned. He thought he'd eliminated any sign of his accent. "Good ears, my man. I do indeed have the slightest accent," he said. "Left over from my youth. My father's last name was Kistemaaker. Quite the mouthful, isn't it? Ha! It means 'cabinet maker,' so he believed it would be easier to fit in with the neighbours if he changed our surname." It was always good to have a story. He'd used the name Carpenter before.

"Wise father. May I ask about your scars?"

"Scars?" Visser replied.

"Yes, on your left forearm. I apologise if I'm being too forward. I'm a doctor and curious about such things. I don't recognise the scar pattern."

The man was certainly observant! Visser glanced at the lines on his forearm, some new and pink, others old and white. Most of them were the result of training the falcons. The birds weren't always considerate enough to land on the leather guards.

"There's a mighty interesting story behind them, my friend." He paused, opening his cabin door wider. "Would you like a whiskey? It's a tradition when telling this tale."

"Whiskey? How kind, but I should return to the ball. I'm supposed to be attending to my father."

"Ah, your father wouldn't deny you a drink with a new friend, would he? I insist, Mr Reid."

The young man smiled. "Well one to 'wet the whistle' as they say. That's very kind of you."

Visser gestured, letting the young man enter the cabin frst, then stepped inside and closed the door behind him.

CHAPTER 15

A Thorny Fence

Modo sat at the small table across from Mr Carpenter, the Indian Ocean visible out the porthole. He scanned the room: a bed directly behind the man, a closed portmanteau on the floor next to it, several books on the shelves. Everything was neat and tidy. A sketchbook sat open on the table, confirming that he was an artist.

Agreeing to the drink, Modo was quickly realising, had been foolish. Carpenter had closed the door, though at least it wasn't locked. The orchestra music would block any sounds of struggle, if one ensued. He was confident he could handle the smallish man if it came to fisticuffs, but there was something agile about the way he moved. He looked older than he'd first appeared, and by the gaslight Modo could now see there were more scars on his cheek. One drew a white line down the side of his neck. Carpenter had blinked hard when asked about the scars on his arm, a sign that the question both surprised and bothered him.

"It's Jameson whiskey—Irish but good," Carpenter said as he half filled two tumblers and set one in front of Modo.

"I'm certain it is." Modo placed his hand around the glass but didn't take a sip. "You had a story to share about your scars. Were you in the military?"

"Gosh, no," Carpenter said. "Not tough enough for that sort of life. I did work on a ranch as a cowhand when I was younger. I was horribly wretched at that, too. Cut myself with thorny fence, I did."

"Thorny fence? I'm not familiar with it."

"A wire fence with barbs that keeps the cattle in. It's tricky to unwind, and we were attaching it to mules to drag it across a coulee. And it wrapped around my arm."

"How unfortunate." Modo heard something ticking in the room. He hadn't seen a clock.

"They fired me the next day," Carpenter continued. "Just one of many reasons I wasn't cut out to be a cowhand. I couldn't ride a horse worth a tinker's damn. It was all for the good. I went to college and became an illustrator. I illustrate for local papers." He pushed the sketchbook towards Modo and flipped the pages. Modo recognised scenes from the ship, recent drawings.

It had been a well-told, perhaps well-rehearsed story, Modo thought. There were even illustrations to prove he was an artist. But there was also a steely determination in the man's eyes. They didn't waver, as though he were watching to see if Modo believed him.

"Now that I look at them more closely, your scars

remind me of talon scars," Modo persisted. He was remembering Octavia's description of the falconer in Westminster Abbey.

"Talons?"

"Yes, from falcons. There are still a few falconers in England; not everyone has those horrible pigeons. Falcons leave a distinctive scar." The ticking, Modo noted, was coming from the portmanteau.

"Curious," Carpenter said, "the only falcons I ever saw were on the ranch in Wyoming. Please drink up, Mr Reid."

Modo brought the glass to his lips. The man was watching him intently, too intently. The whiskey was likely poisoned!

"I'm sorry, sir," he said, "but I just remembered that whiskey disagrees with my stomach. Thank you, in any case. I believe I should return to the ball."

The man slid back his chair and, before Modo could react, pulled a revolver from under the pillow behind him. Modo recognised it as a Galand, small enough to be easily concealed.

"I think we should continue our conversation," Carpenter said.

Modo's heartbeat remained steady and he didn't blink. He even managed to smile. "I'm amenable to that," he said. "You choose the topic."

"What's your name?" the man asked.

"What's yours?"

"May I remind you I'm the one with the pistol." Carpenter waved it nonchalantly.

Modo was hoping he'd come closer so he could swat the gun away.

"Yes, well, my real name is Robert Helmont." It was a character from a French novel Modo had recently read. He drew pleasure from dropping such literary references before the likes of Carpenter.

"Can you change your appearance, Mr Helmont?"

"I—I don't know what you mean." Modo hoped he didn't look as surprised as he felt.

"It's important to me. If you can change your appearance, your shape, I won't kill you. If you can't do so, I will."

"You mean don a disguise?"

"No. I mean a transformation of your actual face and body. I'll count down from ten." He cocked the hammer. "Ten. Nine. Eight ..."

"I don't know what you're talking about!" Modo exclaimed. The man was counting far too quickly. *Think, Modo! Think!*

"Seven. Six. Five. Four. Three. Two ..."

"Wait," Modo said. "I—I'll do it."

Carpenter's eyes lit up with curiosity. Modo cast about in his memory for the right face. The Knight perhaps?

"I'm growing impatient, Helmont."

Then the perfect answer hit Modo and he nearly smiled. Modo began to shift and change, staring intently at his opponent. He made his nose grow longer, his face grow thinner and his hair darken.

"Why, that's unbelievable … it's …" The gun began to waver, as though Carpenter were becoming weak from experiencing the performance.

Sweat was dripping down Modo's forehead by the time he put the final touches on his new face. He'd expended so much energy that his hump was starting to protrude from his back. He ignored it.

"Why … why … You've become *me!*"

Carpenter's eyes were wide with shock. More importantly, he'd lost his focus.

Modo moved quickly, splashing whiskey in the man's eyes and knocking the pistol towards the cabin door, then he jumped forward, aiming a fist at the man's head, a blow intended to knock him out. Carpenter grabbed Modo's arm and yanked, throwing him off balance. Modo struck the bed and the cabin wall beside it. In the moment it took to right himself, he saw that Carpenter had leapt to the opposite side of the cabin, dragging his portmanteau with him.

His portmanteau? Why hadn't he gone for his gun?

Then, leering, Carpenter clicked open the portmanteau and a blur of flashing metal shot out at Modo's face. He threw up his arms, bashing at the spread wings, but the talons ripped through his clothing and into his flesh. He remembered the poisoned talons, and wondered how long he had before it would take effect. The falcon's razor-sharp beak went for his eyes as it let go an ear-shattering screech.

He clamped onto its neck and threw the bird to the floor, so hard that pieces flew off and it lay still. Modo was bleeding, but he didn't feel woozy. Perhaps he hadn't been poisoned.

"Admirable," the man said as he finished winding up the remaining falcons with a key. He snapped his fingers and they attacked.

CHAPTER 16

Flushing Out the Enemy

Octavia saw Modo leave the ball and guilt overtook her. But she was in the middle of a long quadrille and propriety demanded that she stay on the dance floor. Lieutenant Boddle, her dance partner, spun her around, and as she turned she glimpsed Modo halfway down the deck. He appeared to be listening at a cabin door. Then the lieutenant took her hand and spun her again. The next time they danced within sight of the walkway, Modo was gone.

The lieutenant demanded one more dance and, because she couldn't think of an excuse, she was forced to endure another polka. The man had two lead feet. No, steel, she decided after he had twice stomped on her left foot.

When the polka was done she pressed her hand to her forehead and said, "You've twirled me so quickly and with such strength that I'm feeling light-headed." He seemed to take this as a compliment. "I'm sorry, I must return to my cabin."

She turned down his offer of accompaniment and hurried down the deck. Where had Modo been standing exactly? She was considering offering him an apology when a metallic screech released a wave of fear inside her. She knew that sound too well. It was coming from a cabin only a few doors away. She ran to it and clearly heard the struggle going on inside.

Yanking open the cabin door, she found a man dodging two metal falcons; the third bird was on the floor. The man's face was unfamiliar, but he was wearing the same fancy suit that Modo had worn. Modo had changed his face again!

A man with the same face—the real face, Octavia assumed—was on the opposite side of the cabin, waving his arms about. She put two and two together ... the falconer!

She spied a pistol on the floor. As she scooped it up she recognised it: a Galand. She levelled it at the falconer and shouted, "Stop your birds!"

The man regarded her calmly. He made a clicking noise in the back of his throat and one of the falcons turned in mid-air and darted in Octavia's direction. She swung the pistol over and pulled the trigger, and the bullet struck the bird's head and glanced off, sparks flying. The falcon shot past her, smacking her with a metal wing.

By the time she had her wits about her again, Modo was throwing one of the falcons through the porthole and the man was rushing at her. She raised the pistol, but he knocked her over before she could get a shot off. She rolled on the deck and aimed the gun again, just in time to see the man jump over the railing.

She ran and looked over the side of the ship, but he

had disappeared into the water below. It was dark enough now that she couldn't see him even if he were bobbing in the water. The falconer was gone.

Turning, she saw Modo in the doorway of the cabin, his sleeves bloody and tattered—but he was alive. The orchestra was still playing and people continued to dance. No one had noticed the battle.

Modo stumbled over to her, trying to fasten the button on a shredded shirt sleeve.

"You're wounded!" she said, taking his arm. "Good lord, you might be poisoned."

"If I were I'd be dead now," he said, finally getting the button to work. "Assuming it was the same poison he used on Ned Land. Did I really see him jump ship?"

"Yes. He's in the water, soon to be shark food, I hope. How did you flush him out?"

"With whiskey," Modo said with a laugh. It was so odd to hear his voice coming out of a stranger's mouth. Despite his flippancy, he was leaning over and obviously tired. She thought he might have a hunch in his back. "We'd better take a quick look through his room before anyone notices he's gone."

In the cabin, Modo placed the broken clockwork falcon into the portmanteau along with the sketchbook. Octavia found a tin box with three clockwork spiders inside. She quickly snapped it shut.

"We had better inform Mr Socrates," she said, "he'll want to see this with his own eyes."

As they made their way to his cabin, Octavia felt that familiar exhilaration that made her love her life as a secret agent. She could have been killed at any moment during the struggle, and yet she had survived. She had won again!

"My dear Modo," she said, "I must point out to you that for the third time I have saved your life."

"No, no, no," he said, "I had everything under control!"

Then they began to laugh.

CHAPTER 17

An Outlandish Request

Visser landed with a splash in the darkness and immediately kicked off his shoes to begin the long swim towards the coast. The decision to take to the water had been made for him. Perhaps he could have killed one of them, but taking both down at the same time would have been extremely difficult. Inevitably, he would have been captured.

So into the water he went, performing a rather spectacular dive from that height if anyone had been watching. He was pleased that he had angled it well so he didn't go too deep; he still had plenty of air in his lungs when he hit the surface. He flipped onto his back, floating in the darkness, his gaze returning to the *Rome*. The two agents were standing at the railing, searching for him, backlit by the ship's lights.

A good fight. It had been a long time since anyone had tested his skills so thoroughly. Modo had destroyed one of the birds with his bare hands, a feat that Visser found particularly shocking. He'd been told the falcons were nearly indestructible. His masters wouldn't be pleased that the technology was now in the hands of the enemy.

At least he hadn't lost all of them. He made a short whistling sound and two falcons descended on him, one landing on each of his wrists, wrapping their metal-scaled toes around his arm and digging their talons into his skin. The salt water made the wounds burn. He winced only momentarily, then made a *cluck cluck* sound and they flapped their wide wings and began pulling him towards his destination. He kept his head above the water. The birds weren't powerful enough to raise him into the sky, but with their help he moved along with amazing speed.

This was only a temporary setback. There were Dervish tribes near Cape Horn who sympathised with the Clockwork Guild. He would find them, and receive his orders at the next port.

Visser had been employed by the Clockwork Guild for over ten years and had lost count of the men and women he had killed in its service. Each time he completed a mission he demanded something outlandish as part of his payment. A gold stiletto. A red ruby the size of his fist. He would have to think hard to surpass his last request: a human heart. They had brought him one. He didn't ask whose heart it was, but it had tasted good eaten with enough salt.

Perhaps he would ask for Modo's heart. He laughed fiendishly. They had asked only for a sample of the changeling's body, after all. Would they really need his heart?

CHAPTER 18

A Marvellous Piece of Workmanship

Mr Socrates examined the ruined pieces of the clockwork falcon, amazed by the intricacy of the device. No, it was more than a device. There was actual blood and brains in the falcon, as though some living beast had been dipped in metal. But the thing seemed dead. He traced a metal tube that ran from a container inside the bird's chest to the middle talon of each foot. So that was how they loaded the poison.

Mr Socrates had been impressed by Modo and Octavia's work, though he gave no outward sign to either of them. Modo had uncovered the enemy agent, and both had subdued him without alerting anyone else on the ship.

The falconer's disappearance was discovered the next morning when the steward went to make up his room. As soon as his absence was announced, everyone on board began gossiping about Mr Carpenter, all dreaming up theories about what could have happened. There was an unscheduled stop at the next port, where an inspector boarded the *Rome* and sniffed around. Because the captain was an old friend of Mr Socrates, he took his advice that it not be a long investigation. There were a few papers for the captain to fill out, but Mr Carpenter wouldn't be the first passenger to take it into his head to jump into the ocean. Soon the ship was on its way again.

Mr Socrates tried to ascertain what the appearance of this enemy agent meant. The Guild wanted the map, that was clear. So it was safe to assume they didn't know exactly where the God Face was. And if Carpenter had been the only agent in pursuit, then Mr Socrates had put even more space between him and his enemies.

He picked up the falcon again and turned a small key in a slot in the machine creature's skull. The eyes blinked. It leaned forward, snapped its beak and nearly caught his finger. He withdrew the key and the eyes went dead. Amazed, he shook his head. It was simply a marvellous piece of workmanship.

CHAPTER 19

Manning an Expedition

Miss Hakkandottir stood at the prow of a large boat rowed by four soldiers in dark civilian clothing. Her steamship, the *Kraken*, was anchored out at sea disguised as a large transport. She knew better. The twenty-one-pounder guns were hidden under canvas and over a hundred Clockwork Guild soldiers were at the ready below deck. Everyone above deck was dressed as civilian sailors. There was no point in alarming the Australian authorities at Port Douglas. To appear even more harmless, she had pulled a large leather glove over her metal hand.

It had been a long journey from Atticus, the island at the centre of the Guild's operations. A few days earlier the Guild Master had summoned her to his crystal palace and told her to "man" an expedition to discover this temple for themselves. Visser had sent a telegram saying he had been forced to abandon the mission. The Guild had to get one step ahead of the Permanent Association.

They docked and Miss Hakkandottir climbed onto the pier. One man stayed with the boat while the other three followed her into Port Douglas. There wasn't much to the place: several sturdy houses, a general store, a hotel with a pub, and a small church that had seen the bad end of far too many storms.

She knew that the drunkard explorer Alexander King had discovered the legendary temple, then gone mad. That much their agents had been able to gather, before the Australian inspectors handed King over to the British authorities to be transported back to England in shackles. His insanity could be the result of jungle fever, or confirmation of the powerful artifact rumoured to be hidden on the temple site. The fact Mr Socrates was following the map meant it was likely more than a rumour.

She deduced King would have looked for his guides at the pub first, and that's where he would have hired Ned Land. Once Land had stolen the map from him, King would've had to rely on a different source of information. She walked past the pub to the edge of town where the houses became shacks and the skin of the inhabitants was darker. An Indian man cutting a log with an axe paused to watch her pass. Chinese children chasing after stray chickens pulled up short and stepped out of her way. She felt comfortable around such denizens, could practically smell the desperation of the people. Desperation was always useful.

A withered Chinese woman sat outside one of the shacks, stirring a pot of boiling cabbage. Her grey, stringy hair fell loose upon her shoulders and her clothing was a patchwork of rags. Hakkandottir stopped in front of her and the woman didn't look up.

"A white man hired guides or porters from here five months ago," Miss Hakkandottir said in perfect Mandarin. She had learned it during her pirating days in Hong Kong. "They went into the jungle together. Are any of those men still here?"

The old woman looked up, one eye milky with cataracts. With her good eye she examined Miss Hakkandottir for several seconds. "I have no teeth," she stated.

"A pity," Miss Hakkandottir replied. The woman's mouth was indeed a black hole.

"I want teeth," she said.

Miss Hakkandottir reached into her pocket and placed a silver coin in the woman's outstretched hand. "This will be enough to buy wooden teeth."

"Yes, yes," she said. She pointed farther down the lane. "In the red hut is a bad-luck man who went with the white man into the jungle. His name is Zedong."

"May you eat well," Miss Hakkandottir said, and she stepped past the woman.

A dog growled then fled as she approached the red hut, the burly soldiers at her back. She knocked but there was no answer. She pulled open the door, releasing a thick cloud of opium smoke. Three men were crouched around a patch of bare earth, tossing mah-jong tiles. At the sight of her, they stopped playing.

"I'm looking for Zedong," Miss Hakkandottir said.

"That's me," a middle-aged man replied. His thin dark hair was cut short. His eyes looked as if he hadn't slept for a long time.

"Did you guide Alexander King into the jungle?" she asked.

"I no longer guide," he answered, and went back to arranging the tiles.

"That's not what I asked." She stepped into the hut and kicked aside the tiles. "Your game is done. I asked you a question."

"Go away," Zedong said. He nodded at one companion, who drew a knife from his belt; another stood holding an axe handle as a club. "We no longer traffic with foreigners. They are mad."

The soldiers behind Miss Hakkandottir didn't flinch or reach for their own weapons.

"You will traffic with me," she said calmly. With her gloved hand she grabbed the nearest man's knife blade by the sharp edge and snapped it in two, then kicked his knee so hard he collapsed in pain. The second man swung his club and she easily deflected the blow, a move she had learned in Hong Kong, then crushed the man's solar plexus. Both men writhed on the ground between her and Zedong.

"Please, come with us," she said kindly. "We will take care of you and you will give us directions."

Zedong sat for a stunned moment before he nodded and followed her out of the hut.

CHAPTER 20

Slippery Fish and Carrion Birds

A week later, when Western Australia was sighted, Modo was one of the first passengers to run to the port side of the ship and stare over the railings at the sandy beaches and brushy landscape. He sighed—it was so good to see land again after days on the rough, open sea. They had been travelling now for over a month and a half and finally they could see the Australian continent. It would be less than a week before they reached Sydney.

Soon nearly every first-class passenger was lined up along the railing, holding down hats to keep them from being whipped off by the warm breeze. Octavia and Mrs Finchley squeezed in beside Modo. They pointed at flocks of birds—seagulls, Modo imagined. But when the birds circled a bit closer he recognised their shapes: buzzards.

"The water is such a bright blue," Octavia said, "and the sand so white."

Modo squinted, not certain if it was sand or salt.

Mrs Finchley was pressing so hard on her hat that it was losing its shape. "It looks like a savage, uncivilised country," she pronounced. "I hope Sydney has more to offer than this!"

Modo had to agree. All that was visible were rocks and sand and acres and acres of brush on flat dry land. No birds other than the carrions. No kangaroos, creatures he'd been hoping to see since he was a child. No sign of human habitation. In fact, it was the most desolate patch of land Modo had ever seen. Even the sands along the Suez Canal and the Red Sea had some green growth, and numerous huts and villages, along the way.

Gradually, the first-class passengers grew bored, returning one by one to their card games or books or to their cabins to sip tea.

"I have sewing to do," Mrs Finchley said with a sigh. "If all of Australia is this breezy, I'll need chin straps for my hats." She turned to Modo. "Mr Reid, would you be so kind as to escort your cousin back to her cabin when she is finished sightseeing?"

"My pleasure," Modo said, then corrected himself. "It would be my honour, in fact."

Mrs Finchley laughed and left them.

For a time Modo and Octavia watched the landscape pass by silently. It was the first time in weeks that they had been alone together. Modo had spent so much of the journey training or in the cabin that they'd only had time for a few short conversations. Since the excitement of discovering the Clockwork Guild spy, very little had happened and, at times, the trip actually became dull.

"Australia is a hundred times larger than England," Modo said, to break the silence. "A continent unto itself."

"I'm aware of that, cousin," Octavia said. "I'm not a complete dunderhead."

"I wasn't suggesting that you were."

"I know. I know. I'm only frustrated. I've never been cooped up on a ship for so long. Our trip to New York was a lark compared to this."

"I must say that I, too, am tired of the shipboard life, cousin," Modo replied. He really didn't like being her cousin. Then again, he reminded himself, cousins did marry in polite society.

He turned to her and said, sarcastically, "I'm proud, at least, that I haven't yet fallen into the ocean."

Octavia chuckled. He was pleased to see that mischievous light shine in her eyes at this reference to their last shipboard experience. "Yes. That's a habit of yours, isn't it. Good of you to break it." She looked around to be sure no one was near. "Modo, I ..."

"Yes?"

"I've been ignoring you. I apologise for that."

So it hadn't been his imagination. "Well, you've had so many officers to talk to."

"Jealous?"

"No," Modo insisted.

"I'm only playing my part, Modo. A woman of my advanced age must find a husband before she becomes an old maid. Besides, Mrs Finchley has chaperoned every one of those conversations."

"Then, why … ?" He decided it was better to be blunt. "Why have you been ignoring me?"

"I—I will admit Modo that you are more than just a fellow agent. You are a friend. And … well, I'm … I'm just so curious about you. But you're such a big secret … an *enigma* is the word Mrs Finchley would use."

"She called me an enigma?"

"No. But she has been teaching me some big words. Proper words. So many words I could scream, actually. In any case, I feel at times that I don't really know who you are."

"I'm your friend." He thought it was a simple enough statement.

"Yes. But who *are* you?"

What was the answer? he thought, once again confused by her. *I am Modo. I'm just Modo.* He felt like shouting it until all the passengers turned their heads to look at him. *I am Modo! The one who spends hours and hours in his cabin, hiding his ugly body, his terrifying face. I'm the one who lives in fear that Octavia might walk in and see me as I really am. I'm the one who's always on guard.*

This was all about his face. He knew it. She wanted to see it, and had wanted to for months now. She wanted to see his real face—but it was a parody of a face. He would never be able to show it to her.

"I am whoever I want to be," he finally said.

She nodded. "Maybe that's the difficulty. I can't put my finger on it. You're a slippery fish."

Now she was comparing him to a fish. Why did everything always come down to his appearance?

Couldn't she see who he was through his eyes? Had she learned nothing of his character after all they'd already been through? Mr Socrates saw his value as an agent. Mrs Finchley saw talent. But who would ever see his heart?

"I'm more than a fish, cousin," Modo said curtly.

"I didn't mean to insult you."

He sighed. "Nevertheless, it's probably time to escort you to your cabin. This fish is tired."

CHAPTER 21

A Journey Ends

As they rounded into the Heads—the cliffs that guarded the entrance to Port Jackson and the city of Sydney—Mr Socrates rose from his table, pulled on his greatcoat, left the cabin and marched to the forecastle of the ship. He was surprised at his own eagerness and that the aching in his bones seemed to be gone, despite the cool June wind. He'd been to Sydney over twenty years earlier, during the first wave of the gold rush, and had hired a team of ex-military men as prospectors. Within six weeks he'd capped off his personal fortune. He'd had a soft spot for Australia ever since.

The spray was hitting the rocks so hard that it looked as though the lighthouse on South Head was in danger of being washed away, but as they entered the inland sea the water grew calmer. They passed a small village, cottages dotting the wooded hills. Paddle-wheeled steamboats, yachts with their white sails bright in the sun, and other craft plied the waterway. Soon, as they approached Sydney proper, there were more houses and roads. The city had grown. He noted the spires of several churches, rows of large houses with broad terraces and steps that led right down to the water. He spotted the signal station, a four-storey sandstone tower, and the observatory beside it. Somewhere behind it would be the old Rum Hospital that had become Sydney's Parliament House. He had once stood inside that building warning the politicians to guard their young country well.

This is what he needed. To see what the young colonies were doing. He'd been sitting at the old heart of the Empire for far too long.

"We really are in the New World now," an unfamiliar voice beside him said.

He turned and was surprised to see Modo dressed in his jacket and greatcoat. His voice had sounded deeper, which is why Mr Socrates hadn't recognised it. The boy's face was perfectly formed; he really had mastered the transformations.

"Yes, son, we are," Mr Socrates said.

There was lift in his heart coupled with sadness as he called Modo his son. The boy was not his son, of course. His only son had died moments after being born so many years before. But still, Modo was more valuable than any other agent had been. Even more, there was something about the boy's innocence that had got under his skin. If he were honest with himself, there were times Mr Socrates had wanted to shield him from the world. A foolish and unrealistic thought.

"This is one of the most attractive ports in the world," Mr Socrates said. "Picturesque, even. Its description stumped Anthony Trollope. Did you read his work before our visit?"

"There were very few books in our house that mentioned Australia, Father," Modo said.

"Ah, I should have remedied that. We left too quickly to gather the proper educational materials. Well, this is a mariner's and an engineer's dream, so many natural bays with calm water. And gently sloped hills."

"It's more established than I thought it would be," Modo said.

"We civilised this area years ago. The colonies have thrived under the nurturing hand of the Empire. Well, that and the gold rush. There are around two hundred thousand souls here in Sydney. We sent our ne'er-do-wells, our Scots and Irish, our explorers, and look what has been created by British ingenuity."

He waved his hand, and as the boy looked at the city, Mr Socrates glanced at him. At times Modo seemed to worship him. It was both a compliment and a bad habit. He would have to harden the boy's heart. The world out there was tough, unforgiving, especially for one whose real face would frighten children and repulse adults. If there was one thing he knew about British society, it was that it loved to destroy the ugly. He would have to be more disciplined with the boy, for his own good.

Then he took another look at Modo and realised he was no longer a boy. How old would he be now? He'd discovered him fourteen years ago as a toddler. He would be fifteen or sixteen years old now. A young man. He wondered why he'd never given Modo a birthday; he could have picked a date out of the air. Sentimental old fool, he chastised himself. What does Modo need with a birthday? He'd been protecting him far too much. After all, Modo had been ready in time to have gone on several missions in the last few months, but Mr Socrates had held him back. He'd almost lost him last time.

A thought suddenly occurred to him. Could it be that he was really on this voyage to be Modo's protector? The pain he felt shooting through his heart gave him his answer.

No, he thought. He must not attach himself to his subordinates. He'd learned that as an officer in Crimea. He had to apply those rules here, too. Britannia couldn't be protected by bleeding hearts and soft hands.

"Enough sightseeing," Mr Socrates said. "Go prepare. We'll be debarking this ship soon enough."

"Yes, Father," Modo said, and immediately turned on his heel and went back to his cabin.

CHAPTER 22

The Rag and Famish, and Hades Acres

Modo stood outside his cabin next to his luggage and watched as the RMS *Rome* docked at Cockatoo Island. The island's quaint name was rather amusing and a sure sign that he was no longer in London.

"It used to be a prison island," a cabin boy said as he tagged Modo's luggage. Parker. That was the boy's last name. The docks were built by convicts. The prisoners have all been moved to some other gaol, so don't you worry yourself about them dangerous types, sir. Only their bones and restless spirits have been left behind."

Modo tipped him, and soon after that, the porters arrived to carry away his luggage. He was glad to see the last of his cabin. It had been comfortable enough, but he needed to walk farther than the length of the deck. He was tired of feeling like a chicken in a coop.

The rest of his party came out of their cabins and Mr Socrates, with a wave of his hand, guided them down the gangplank. Modo was taken by Octavia's rather fetching green hat and green crinoline dress and noted that Mrs Finchley, too, had dressed up for the city.

They had docked next to a British war steamer *Rosario* and as they walked along the boardwalk Modo was impressed by its size and the guns aimed from its decks. He wondered what the sailors' and marines' lives would be like, with many of their years spent at sea. He'd stick with being a secret agent. He preferred solid earth under his feet.

While Tharpa watched over their luggage and other equipment being unloaded from the hold of the ship, Mr Socrates led the rest of them to a ferry. It transported them over calm waters busy with smaller steamers and yachts. What would the streets of Sydney be like? Modo wondered. Would sheep and kangaroos be stampeding around? They disembarked on the north shore docks and climbed into one of the waiting carriages. Modo sat beside Mr Socrates, gawking out the window as they rolled along the pebbly streets of North Sydney. None of the buildings were as tall or as old as anything in London; in fact it struck Modo how new everything looked, though very dusty. Maybe Sydney was more like New York before the Americans put up so many tall buildings.

"Civilisation at last," Mrs Finchley said. "One more night on a boat and I would have thrown myself to the sharks."

"Our hearts would break with you gone," Octavia said. "And with whom would I be lucky enough to play cards?"

"Aren't you the kindest!" Mrs Finchley patted Octavia's shoulder.

Modo grimaced, wondering why he hadn't thought of some compliment for Mrs Finchley. She and Octavia were getting along famously.

The carriage arrived at the front doors of The Rag and Famish Hotel and everyone stepped out. Modo gave the building the once-over; it was nothing more than an oversized cottage with maybe ten rooms, low trees growing behind it. Two unshaven sailors stumbled out of the front doors, obviously drunk even at midday. They paused to give both Octavia and Mrs Finchley red-eyed stares, then staggered their way down the slate sidewalk.

There were only ground-floor rooms, Modo noted. If necessary he could climb in and out of his room easily, but so could anyone else.

In the lobby were travellers from several nations: Indians, Englishmen, and four French soldiers. Out of a habit that had been drilled into him Modo scanned the room for an exit at the rear and gauged the windows as being large enough to jump through. They approached the main desk, which also seemed to be a bar.

"Are we really staying here, sir?" Mrs Finchley asked.

"Yes, Mrs Finchley. I know it's below your standards, but you'll endure. The owner, Mr Bullivant, is an old friend. Clever of him to name his establishment after Ensign Rag and Captain Famish, isn't it?"

"Who were they, Father?" Modo asked.

"I'm surprised that you ask. They were imaginary characters, after all, and you seem to have an addiction to all that literary nonsense. The Rag is the flag, and

Famish, well, that's what happens to all the ensigns on the sea. Bullivant doesn't think back fondly on his years in the navy."

Mr Socrates handed cash to the innkeeper and in return received three keys. He gave one to Modo. "I do hope you get your land legs back soon, son."

Modo did feel wobbly: keeping up the Doctor face was exhausting him. He'd been overly excited as they approached Sydney and had changed his body into this shape far too early.

"Steady as a rock, Father," Modo said.

After freshening up in their rooms, the four met in the pub and dined on boiled hen and potato. As they were finishing the meal, Tharpa arrived and nodded to Mr Socrates as though a message had been received.

Mr Socrates stood and raised his goblet of red wine. "A toast to the colonies!"

Modo sipped his tea in response as Mr Socrates continued. "I've been in London far too long. One forgets the young energy of the colonies. It invigorates me."

"You'll need a lot of invigorating," Octavia said.

"Ah, Octavia, would you be referring to my age? Well, let me say, I feel young enough that we should all go for a jaunt."

Without a further word of explanation he led them all out of the hotel. A carriage was waiting, the driver a flat-nosed man in a tan coat.

Modo climbed up to the top bench and sat beside Tharpa, while Mr Socrates and the women sat inside. "Where are we going?" Modo asked.

Tharpa shrugged. "Sahib is enjoying keeping this a secret."

He signalled to the driver for them to proceed and they rumbled north through the streets until the houses grew fewer in number. Soon they were in the hills, farms on either side. But these farms were nothing like any Modo had seen from the train in England. They were vast tracts, with hundreds, perhaps thousands, of sheep wandering across them. The road became a line of dust between the trees and hills. Modo was certain he could hear Mrs Finchley complain from below.

A half-hour later they turned into a dusty lane, passing a sign that said Hades Acres. Someone had a sense of humour. They stopped near a brick farmhouse, and Modo followed Tharpa off the carriage, hopping the last few rungs of the ladder onto the ground. They were greeted by three tall, grim men in dusty leather greatcoats and tan slouch-hats, each carrying a rifle. Their boots looked like something from the American West. They had no insignia, so Modo surmised they could be militia. Their faces were stony and all business when Mr Socrates stepped out, but as the women emerged, the men puffed out their chests a little and smiles appeared.

One of them, a man in his mid-forties, stepped up and shook Mr Socrates' hand.

"Welcome back, sir," the man said. "It's a pleasure to see you again."

"Likewise, Clow. We haven't aged a day in twenty years. Is everything in order?"

"Your materials have arrived safely and are being unpacked as we speak. And *she* is here."

The way he emphasised *she* caught Modo's attention. The man had almost spat out the word. But Mr Socrates didn't react in any perceptible way. "Good. Good." He turned to the group. "Come along, you laggards, your mount awaits."

Mounts? Modo wondered if they'd now be jumping in the saddle. He'd never ridden horses, so didn't relish having to learn how in front of all these men. And Octavia.

Soon he'd have to change his shape; he could already feel his face drooping. Fool that he was, he'd forgotten to bring his mask along. He calculated how long it had been since they disembarked. He wouldn't have much more than half an hour before his body began to revert back.

He'd intended to walk with Octavia, but already one of the men was beside her, so Modo stayed a few steps behind. She laughed at something he said, and Modo rolled his eyes.

They carried on to the long, one-storey brick house that looked as though it had been painted white about a hundred years ago. Behind it was a large wood shed and an open area where several men were unloading Mr Socrates' crates. Two of them used a pry bar on the lids.

A lithe, big-shouldered woman with short dark hair, dark skin and a tan greatcoat stood in the middle of all the action. "Not there, but over there!" she shouted.

By the way the men cringed, Modo could tell that they weren't pleased to be taking orders from her.

As Mr Socrates approached, she turned around to face him. Modo had to work hard to disguise his shock at the appearance of her face: it was attractive enough, but her lips were tattooed in a dark blue, and swirling blue lines curled along her lower lip to her chin. Why would she permanently mark up her face like that?

"Ah, boss, you've arrived," she said. She was perhaps forty years old. "Good, you can tell these men how to unpack your precious swag. They don't like taking orders from a dingo."

"It's a pleasure to see you again, too, Elizabeth," Mr Socrates said.

"It's Lizzie and you know it; you're only trying to get my goat." She turned and snapped, "You'd better watch that!" A man holding a wooden box jumped back and glowered at her. "There's an altimeter in there. I bet you don't even know what that is, you worm. You break it and I'll break you."

"I like this woman," Octavia whispered to Modo. She was gazing with open admiration at the tattooed woman.

Modo, however, was a little taken aback and couldn't decide what he thought of her. And Mrs Finchley couldn't hide her horror.

"Leave the men to their work," Mr Socrates said, gesturing for the woman to walk with him back to the group. "I would like to introduce Elizabeth Tompsitt, or Lizzie as she prefers."

She grabbed Modo's hand and squeezed so tightly that he thought his fingers would break. Her palms were rough with calluses. "I'm …" He looked at Mr Socrates for guidance.

"You're Modo, today," he said with a laugh. "Forget your life as Anthony Reid."

"I'm M-Modo," he said. She let go of his hand and he discretely rubbed out the pain.

He wished he could be Anthony Reid again. He would miss calling Mr Socrates Father.

Lizzie clapped Tharpa on the back, saying, "Tharpa, you duffer-dealing digger, it's good to set eyes on you again," and then, without missing a beat, she bowed to Octavia and Mrs Finchley. "I can only imagine what you dainty ones think of me."

Mrs Finchley turned red, but Octavia spat out the words, "I'm not dainty! I'm Octavia!"

"Yes, well," Mr Socrates said. "I know you've all been wondering why we're here and what these crates contain." He pointed at what looked like a long red sheet that had been laid on the ground and folded several times. "All of these parts together will become an aeronautic balloon. Steam powered, of course, which technically makes it an airship." He paused. "And our mutual friend Lizzie will be our pilot."

CHAPTER 23

A Shortcut Through the Sky

As they reached the ranch house, Modo felt his lower lip sag. The hunch on his back was slowly rising and that made his stomach tighten. He couldn't stop it. He pulled on Tharpa's shoulder and signalled him to follow. The two went around the corner of the house as the others walked inside.

"I am ..." he whispered, "losing my shape. And I forgot my mask."

"Ah, young Sahib, this is unfortunate."

"I don't have any way of covering my face."

"There are only friends inside. You don't have to fear displaying your appearance to them."

"I don't want Octavia to see me this way," he said, embarrassed that he was forced to confess it.

Tharpa nodded and placed his hand on Modo's shoulder for a moment before answering, "Then we will solve this." He reached up and unravelled his turban, revealing shoulder-length dark hair streaked with grey.

He carefully wrapped the cloth around Modo's face so that only his eyes were showing. "Undo the collar buttons on your shirt, but keep your coat on," he advised. "That will hide your shape."

"But, are you allowed to do this?" Even though they had shared a cabin, Modo had never seen Tharpa without his turban. "I mean, isn't your turban a religious symbol?"

"I am among friends. And, if it is in aid of a friend, then I am allowed to remove it." He paused. "But be warned, I am told that English women go mad over men with long hair."

They enjoyed a laugh together, then went into the ranch house. Mr Socrates, Mrs Finchley and Octavia were seated at a rough-hewn wooden table. Mr Socrates looked askance at Modo and Tharpa but made no comment. Octavia stared several moments at Modo's mummified head, then even longer at Tharpa's hair. Perhaps Tharpa hadn't been kidding about English women.

Modo carefully brushed the dirt off one of the stools, which got a derisive chuckle out of Octavia.

"Always neat, aren't you," she whispered.

Modo sat down and crossed his arms.

"So you've decided to join us," Mr Socrates chided. He unrolled a colourful map of Australia across the table. "We're going to fly to the Queensland rain forest." He pointed at the northeast part of the country. "By ship it would take us six days of sailing along the coast, but we'll take a shortcut through the sky. At twenty-five knots per hour, more if the wind is in our favour, we'll be there within three days. Why we'll even have time to stop in Brisbane for pineapple, if we so desire. I have a few notes about the geography of the area from a friend of mine, John Atherton, a cattleman and an explorer. It will be the easiest crossing of the Australian jungle in history. We shall have tea and cakes three times a day, far above the earth."

"It sounds marvellous!" Octavia exclaimed. She clapped Modo on the shoulder. "Imagine that, Modo, we'll be soaring like eagles."

He swallowed. "Yes, imagine that."

The idea of being above the earth had always appealed to him, so long as he was holding onto a building. But this was different; they wouldn't be attached to anything at all.

"The Royal Geographic Society would, if they learned of it, be quite envious of our flight," Mr Socrates said. "A trip across the continent like this would take explorers on foot or horseback months."

"But how will we find the temple?" Octavia asked.

"My hope is that we'll spot it from the air, though I realise that's unlikely. The rain forest is particularly dense. Assuming the map Ned Land provided to us is accurate, we should be able to tether ourselves to a palm tree and climb down near the temple. If we're lucky we'll only have to search on foot for a few hours. Any more questions?"

"I hope you don't expect me to ride in that contraption," Mrs Finchley huffed, her arms crossed.

"No, my dear Mrs Finchley," Mr Socrates answered.

"You shall remain in Sydney for the next fortnight or so, longer if necessary. I've already paid for a room at the Occidental Hotel, which you'll find much more to your liking. I've also taken the liberty of purchasing you tickets to the Royal Theatre. For a colony they do have rather good shows, though I don't recommend any of the comedies. A little too common, if you get my meaning."

"You mean belches and farts," Octavia said, demurely.

"How pleasant, Octavia," Mr Socrates said. "Mrs Finchley, please make a note to stamp the last vestiges of the cockney attitude out of Octavia upon our return voyage." He wasn't smiling. "Well, if there are no further questions, it's time to see how they're progressing with our airship."

They followed him outside, where Lizzie was still ordering the men around as they pulled ropes and fit together various mechanical pieces. Modo was glad to see that the car of the airship was as long as a large rowboat and made of thick wicker. Three men were placing an engine in the aft section of the car.

"We have the Clockwork Guild to thank for this," Mr Socrates said.

"How so?" Modo asked.

"Twice they've used balloons or dirigibles, once when they attacked the Houses of Parliament and again on the *Wyvern*. It's important to learn from your enemies. It got me thinking about the possibilities of air travel, so I sought the advice of several inventive military scientists, and with a little of my own tweaking, we've designed this ship."

"I've done some reading, Mr Socrates, about the Montgolfier brothers and their balloons," Modo said, hoping to impress his master. "Which gas will you use?"

"Hydrogen, of course. Yes, it's extremely flammable, but I can't make helium out of thin air."

"But how will we ascend and descend?" Modo asked.

"Ah, you have studied up!" Mr Socrates pointed at the red balloon. "I used your descriptions of the *Ictíneo* as inspiration. As you'll no doubt remember, the submarine ship had two hulls to prevent sea pressure from crushing it. So, there will be a balloon inside a balloon. When we need to descend we allow gas to escape from the outside balloon. When we decide to climb to the heavens, we fill the outside balloon again."

"So you let out the gas to go down," Octavia said. "That sounds rather flatulent."

"I won't even dignify that with a response, Octavia. It's the cutting edge of aeronautic science. With a steam-powered engine and enough compressed coal, we'll be able to travel to our destination and back without resupplying."

He pointed at the framework the men were now assembling, which Modo assumed would house the balloons. "I've dubbed it the *Prince Albert*, after the Queen's departed spouse. If she actually knew about us and our Association, she would be honoured, I'm sure.

"Tomorrow, our little adventure will begin," he continued, "and you, my friends, will be the first to see this country from the air. We're making history, though no one but us will know of it. Now come along, back to our quarters. We'll need a good rest; I'm afraid sleeping arrangements on the *Prince Albert* will be rather dreadful." He paused. "Oh, and don't overeat. We'll be weighing you in the morning to plan for ballast."

Then he laughed in a way that made him seem ten years younger.

CHAPTER 24

Through a Spyglass

Michael Brown had followed the group from Cockatoo Island to their hotel. It had been relatively easy to recognise them from the telegraphed descriptions; no other man on the *Rome* had an Indian servant. He waited outside the hotel as they ate, watched the Indian arrive and, minutes later, followed them on a stolen horse. When they disappeared over a hill, he at first kept his distance, then dismounted and crept up the slope to look down on what they were doing.

He watched through his spyglass as they entered the ranch house. There was no safe way to find out what they were discussing, not with all those armed men wandering around.

At first he wondered what they could be assembling. But he'd been a military man before turning to a life of detective work, and it was soon clear to him that it was a dirigible.

He rode back to Sydney and sent a telegram to his employer.

CHAPTER 25

The Lofty Heights

At sunrise Modo dressed in the khaki trousers and jacket that had been delivered to his room by Tharpa, then wrapped a cloak around his shoulders. He hadn't been given orders about what persona to assume, so he had chosen the Doctor face. This time he didn't forget to pack his mask. He threw his rucksack over his shoulder, closed the door to his room behind him, and went to Octavia and Mrs Finchley's room, where he waited for a full minute, hoping to say goodbye to his governess— but she was likely still asleep. He knew Octavia would already be outside, ready to go.

Shrugging his shoulders, he went down the hall through the dingy pub, left The Rag and Famine Hotel and climbed into the waiting carriage.

"Let's see a little more jump in your step, Modo," Mr Socrates said. "Once again you're the last to arrive." He was wearing khaki clothing, and had a sun helmet on his lap and a particularly robust walking stick in his hand. In fact, it looked more like a cudgel.

"I had hoped to say goodbye to Mrs Finchley," replied Modo.

"No need," Mr Socrates said. "We'll see her again soon enough."

"She was sleeping when I left her," Octavia said as she adjusted the hem of her dress.

Modo was glad to see she'd been wise enough not to wear a puffy crinoline. She was holding a red helmet in her hand.

"So I didn't say goodbye either. She was up late last night working on a secret sewing project."

The door to The Rag and Famine opened and Mrs Finchley came running out, hat askew. She was holding a brown-paper package. Tharpa opened the carriage door and she stood at the step, breathless. Modo wondered what the package could be. *Perhaps it's a gift for me!* he thought.

"Good morning," she said. "I want to wish you all best of luck on your journey."

"Thank you, Mrs Finchley," Mr Socrates said, "though, of course, I never rely on luck."

"I'm aware of that, sir," she replied. "Tavia, this is for you." She handed the package to Octavia. "Don't open it until you're up in the air."

"Why thank you, Mrs Finchley!"

Modo stared at the package. She had called her Tavia. They were that close now. And there was nothing else in Mrs Finchley's hands, no gift for him.

Still, she squeezed his knee and said, "Be a good boy."

"I'm not a boy!" Modo exclaimed.

"Be a good young man, then," she said with a smile. "All of you, farewell."

As Mr Socrates closed the door, Modo thought he could see tears in Mrs Finchley's eyes. His master tapped the ceiling with his walking stick and they started on their way, leaving Mrs Finchley waving on the slate sidewalk. *She likes Octavia more than me!* he fumed inwardly. No gift. What had he done wrong? He allowed himself to sulk for a while, then came to his senses. *Ah, you're being a child, Modo.* He was being a boy, when he wanted her to see him as a young man. He didn't need a gift!

There was a light fog on the ground as they made their winding way out of Sydney and into the hills. They arrived at the Hades Acres ranch house again, where Mr Socrates jumped out of the carriage and led Modo and the others towards the back of the house as though on a charge. He was positively beaming with pride.

The *Prince Albert* sat tethered to the ground, looking like it should have been leading a royal parade. The balloon was as red as any serge on a British soldier; its conical shape ensured it would cut through the wind. Netting encircled it from stem to stern, as did several tin braces.

Lizzie was bellowing orders at the men loading the wicker car with supplies. Modo wondered if she'd been shouting the whole night through.

Mr Socrates stopped right beside the airship. "Twilled taffeta from Lyons," he explained as he poked his walking stick into the outer balloon. "Treated with gutta-percha. It can hold the hydrogen for a hundred years without a single atom escaping."

Three men were lugging a square metal container into the car and Mr Socrates signalled them to stop. They did, but struggled to hold on to the weight as Mr Socrates approached. Two silver metal tubes poked out of the top. Mr Socrates tapped it with his walking stick and it gave off a metallic *bong*.

"Yesterday, Modo, you asked how we would descend. It was a very good question. There are twenty-five gallons of water in this container. But let me ask you, what is water made of?" The labourers faces grew red with the strain.

"Wetness," Octavia answered with a laugh.

"Ah, a layman's answer. Modo, would you care to illuminate Miss Milkweed?"

Modo tried to recall a chart he'd memorised as a child. The answer was easy, but why wasn't it coming to him?

"Modo?" Mr Socrates prompted, tapping the box again.

"Two parts hydrogen and one part oxygen!" he blurted, glad Mrs Finchley wasn't present to witness his slow-witted display.

Octavia rolled her eyes at him anyway.

"Correct, albeit a little slow on the draw. I won't belabour this, but must explain that the Buntzen battery and a few drops of sulphuric acid begin the process of separating the hydrogen from the oxygen. One platinum tube"—he pointed, oblivious to the grunting of the men holding the box—"goes up into the balloon. The other dispels the oxygen. I must say it took a fair bit of tinkering. Thank you, gentlemen, please carry on." The men, now sweating, hoisted the box into the balloon's car.

"You invented this device, too?" Modo asked, incredulous.

Mr Socrates laughed. "Yes, I did, Modo. The understanding of scientific principles comes easy to me. This is the height of technology, Modo, forgive my obvious pun. After this test run, the British army will be so pleased to learn about our success."

"Test run?" Octavia asked, just as Modo said, "You mean this balloon hasn't been flown before?"

Mr Socrates shrugged. "First, a small correction. It's a dirigible—an airship. As you can see it has a steam engine and an internal skeleton. It's self-propelled, therefore it's a ship." He sniffed. "The odds of anything untoward happening to our craft during this flight are acceptably low according to my calculations. Besides, as I've said before, it's the most practical way to travel across this forbidding Australasian landscape."

"As long as we don't end up dead," Octavia whispered to Modo.

When Modo stepped into the wicker car, rucksack in hand, he was surprised that it bounced. The car was twenty feet in length and eight feet wide, so for the five of them there was quite enough room.

Modo spotted two Winchesters and a larger gun in a leather case in a small gun rack near the front of the car. A selection of machetes leaned beside them, bound together. Along both sides of the car were bags of flour and dried meat, biscuits, wine and brandy, and several clay bottles of water.

Octavia climbed up beside him and jumped up and down, making the whole car bounce. "Whee!"

"Stop that," Lizzie shouted, and Octavia froze. "There are springs on the bottom of the car," Lizzie said, her tone not quite so harsh, "to soften the landing."

"All aboard!" Mr Socrates shouted.

Modo wasn't certain where to stand until Mr Socrates pointed at the front and Tharpa joined him. Lizzie took the helm in the centre of the ship, and Mr Socrates hollered, "Tethers off!"

Modo grabbed the railing and watched as the men undid the ropes tethering the *Prince Albert* to the ground. The car jerked as each rope was loosened. He tightened his grip, and his heart sped up. Tharpa looked as calm as ever.

"Are you excited?" Modo asked. "You may be the first Indian ever to take to the skies."

"We Indians came from the sky," he said solemnly, then grinned at the expression on Modo's face. "What will be, will be. This won't be much different than riding an elephant."

"Oh, I don't know about that!" Modo said.

"Anchor up!" Mr Socrates shouted, and Tharpa began to draw the heavy anchor into the car. The *Prince Albert* rose slowly off the ground. Modo's stomach tingled and he wondered if he was going to be seasick, or rather, airsick.

"We're going to the moon," Octavia said beside him. Her eyes lit with excitement, but she maintained a firm grip on the railing.

Though she had tucked her hair up under her sun

helmet, a lock of hair hung down next to her cheek. Modo resisted the urge to brush it behind her ear.

"You'd need bottles of air on the moon," he pointed out.

"Ah, you're such a stickler for facts, Modo. We're going to the moon, I tell you. And the stars beyond. I can feel it in my bones."

The balloon climbed into the sky, cutting quietly through the air. Modo hadn't expected the silence, which made it feel even more unbelievable. To think that they could leave the earth without so much as a bang. And yet, at the moment it felt like the most natural thing in the world. They rose above the short trees, then higher. The men on the ground grew smaller, their upturned faces becoming tiny, featureless dots. None of them waved. The ranch house was a retreating rectangle.

Mr Socrates read his altimeter and looked over the edge. "We've climbed to nine hundred feet above sea level," he said.

Lizzie moved the wheel back and forth, testing the flaps, though it seemed to have little effect. Modo assumed it was mostly the propeller on the back that would decide their direction once they started the steam engine.

Had he ever been this high before? he tried to recall. He'd climbed to the top of Big Ben one night and looked down on all of London. But how high was that? At least when he was clinging to it, the tower was attached to the ground. Here, if the ropes snapped they would fall to their deaths. The *Prince Albert* lurched up about ten feet and Modo grabbed hold. He looked back to Mr Socrates, but he and Lizzie seemed perfectly calm. They were definitely a lot higher than Big Ben now.

"We must find a good northeast wind stream," Mr Socrates said. "Let's get that engine running."

Lizzie tied the wheel in place, then lifted a jug of paraffin oil and began the process of lighting the firebox to heat the water in the boiler. The scent of paraffin wasn't at all pleasant, but more troubling to Modo was the knowledge that a coal fire burned directly below the hydrogen balloon. It took several minutes before the steam and smoke began to drift, then plume, out of the long, narrow smokebox. A minute later the piston was hammering and the propeller began to turn, which caused the engine to rattle and the whole car to shake.

"Do you feel like a bird?" Octavia shouted.

He tried to laugh as he replied, "A bird? No, a rock."

"Modo," Mr Socrates said. "You'll be first on coal duty. Please keep the motor running happily along."

"Yes, sir." Modo walked past Lizzie to his station, grabbed the small shovel and began adding coal to the fiebox. As long as he kept his mind on his job he didn't feel as though he were about to fall out of the sky.

CHAPTER 26

The Solution for Closed Doors

Miss Hakkandottir carried a canvas bag up the steps of the Egyptian temple and paused at the entrance, resting her metal hand on the huge paws of the Sphinx. Despite more than two thousand years of rain that had worn the statue down, and vines that had worked their way into the cracks, she still could make out the lion-shaped head and the eyes that stared out over the ruined city below. The door to the temple was in the mouth of the Sphinx.

The Egyptians were clever builders to carve the temple into the side of a small, black mountain formed from hardened lava. The hundreds of steps leading to the entrance were a wonder. The Sphinx itself must have inspired terror and awe in any who saw it.

She and her company of soldiers had been camped on a flat area of the ruins for over two weeks. Behind her, soldiers continued to cut away the forest to make more room for their white tents, set up in neat rows. Piles of green bush burned along the edges of the expanding territory. They hadn't been bothered by any natives since their arrival. Rifle fire had kept the first group of inquisitive tribesmen away. She'd learned that lesson in Africa. Shoot one and the rest will flee. It would take the natives weeks to regain their bravery, and by that time her task would be done.

Guild soldiers had spent the first week cutting away the overgrowth around the temple, revealing the black stone door that she presumed had once been the main entrance. The door had proven impossible to open; they had smashed it with hammers to no avail, had even worked a team of horses to death trying to pull the rock away. How had Alexander King managed to open the door on his own? There had to be a secret lever to push or some other ancient trick.

Fortunately, in this modern day she was able to bring along her own little trick—dynamite. She opened her canvas bag and tied a bundle of dynamite to the centre of the door, then added two more bundles for good measure. Then she ran the fuse halfway down the long stone stairway and lit it herself, watching as it burned along the stones and towards the dynamite. The soldiers took cover, but she stood out in the open to watch the explosion. The mountain actually seemed to shake, flocks of birds shooting into the sky, and she imagined animals and savages shuddering for miles. It was a beautiful sight; the explosion was immensely satisfying.

Miss Hakkandottir was the first to climb up through the dusty air to where the stone door had been shattered into black shards. *That will teach you for standing in my way,* she thought. She stared into the darkened chamber, then picked up a shard and threw it inside. It landed in shadows.

The Chinese man, Zedong, had likely known the easy way to open the door, and had she realised there would be such an obstacle, she wouldn't have pushed him out of the airship at five hundred feet. She had become frustrated with his inability to remember the exact location of the temple. Less than an hour after the unfortunate tumble, they spotted the temple from the air. Sometimes she was too quick to hand out punishment. It was one of her few faults.

Zedong had confirmed the reports that Alexander King had gone mad after entering the temple. Madness was something she didn't want to fool around with, so she was pleased that Visser had arrived the day before after taking a shortcut through the waterways of the Malayan Archipelago. She signalled Visser to send one of his falcons inside. A few minutes later it emerged unscathed.

She commanded three of her soldiers to enter the temple and find the God Face. With ropes and climbing equipment on their backs, rifles and bull's-eye lanterns held high, they entered the darkness.

She didn't move from her position.

An hour later one of the soldiers stumbled out, his face bloody, and fell at her feet staring directly into the sun.

"What happened?" she asked. "What did you see?"

He moved his mouth uselessly, so she kicked him in the ribs. "What did you see!"

He had scratches all over his face, and his fingernails were broken and stained with blood. Had he gouged his own face? His grey uniform was drenched in sweat, so he stank, and had perhaps even soiled himself.

"Take him away," she commanded bitterly, and two Guild soldiers carried him down to the medical tent.

She stared into the dark, blast-marked mouth of the Sphinx. So the God Face was real. It beckoned her, and she began to feel an emotion she hadn't experienced for a very long time.

It was fear.

CHAPTER 27

The Necessary Mask

The moment the *Prince Albert* left the earth Octavia felt as though she'd bark up her breakfast. But, as with any other time she was upset or afraid, she gritted her teeth and put on a smile. She drew particular inspiration from Lizzie, who wasn't the least bit bothered by the heights or the blustery wind. She was busy at the wheel, handling it as though she were piloting an ocean steamer through calm waters. The fact that it was actually a few thousand pounds of human flesh, metal and wicker floating above the earth this way for the first time seemed not to trouble her. As she stared out at the horizon through her goggles, Lizzie looked as though she had flown hundreds of times.

After a few minutes the butterflies in Octavia's stomach vanished and a sense of exhilaration rushed through her. How many people had ever been above the earth in a balloon? If the pickpockets and drunkards she'd grown up with at Seven Dials could see her now, they'd be yellow-gloakin' jealous to the gills. She was the queen of the sky! Or at least this little bit of it.

She could tell Modo must have felt some fear by the way he'd gripped the guide ropes and the railing when the *Prince Albert* took to the air. She couldn't believe he was the same person who'd climbed some of the highest buildings in London, but she decided not to tease him. He was such a hard person to read sometimes. His body was slim and a little taller now, but she knew that it would gradually widen and he'd cover himself and become more ... crooked. He already looked hunched over as he tended to the firebox. The more crooked he became, the more he retreated into himself.

She distracted herself from thinking about him by looking down at the landscape, marked with rivers and roads like a great map. Mr Socrates had given her the task of making tea using steam from the engine to heat the kettle. "I'm not a bloody steward!" she'd wanted to say, but at least it was something to do.

When the tea was ready, Mr Socrates directed everyone to gather at the bow of the airship. Octavia brought a tray of teacups, graham wafers and a hot teapot. She cursed when the hem of her dress caught on the wicker siding. She had to be so careful in this contraption.

As she served everyone it dawned on her that they were all gathered at the same end. Why hadn't the thing tipped and thrown them to their deaths? It remained perfectly level.

Her ponderings were interrupted by Lizzie grunting, "Is there no coffee?"

"The aroma of coffee would only spoil the view," Mr

Socrates answered, sniffing the air. "I tell you all, I feel twenty years younger."

"You look it, sir," Modo said.

He was quite a quillin' suck-up some days, Octavia decided. A smack to the side of the head might cure that.

"So you're feeling ninety, then, sir?" Octavia asked sweetly.

This got a smile out of Mr Socrates and, more surprising, Tharpa laughed out loud. She'd begun to think the man was as humourless as a stone.

"I appreciate your attempt at cleverness, Octavia," Mr Socrates said. "The truth is I've been out of the field far too long. I'd forgotten how exhilarating it is."

She glimpsed the man he must have been many years ago. A young officer. A conqueror. With thousands of similar men exploring, no wonder Britain controlled most of the world.

Mr Socrates slapped Tharpa's back. "It reminds me of our time in Africa, remember that?"

"Of course I do, Sahib."

"This is Australasia! And to think we're traversing it by air. We've come along much faster than I had expected," Mr Socrates said above the engine's noise. "Thanks to my propeller design! Oh, and Lizzie's piloting, of course. You must sense the wind streams up here, you've done a marvellous job."

"Coffee would have been nice," she huffed, and downed the last of her tea.

They returned to their stations. Octavia, with little to do, just paced the car, watching the sky and ground. She knew they were travelling at a high speed, but it seemed as though they weren't moving at all.

She stole the occasional glance at Lizzie, watching her run the wheel and adjust the levers. Octavia couldn't tell the purpose of much of the equipment.

She found herself drawn to Lizzie's facial tattoos. She would be an attractive, though hard-looking, woman without them. It took a certain amount of courage to mark your face permanently like that; to say, "This is who I am, take it or shove off."

She remembered the package Mrs Finchley had given her, and dug in her rucksack until she found it. When she unwrapped the present and saw the contents, she couldn't suppress a giggle.

It was a pair of trousers, perfectly sewn and softer than any material a man would wear—but trousers! She read the note in Mrs Finchley's tidy handwriting:

> Dear Tavia,
> A dress has no place on an airship. These trousers will make your journey easier and safer. Do change back into your more elegant clothing the moment you see signs of civilisation.
> Sincerely,
> Mrs Finchley

Octavia promised herself she would hug the woman the moment they next met. *Trousers!*

It was another hour before they slowed and lowered the ship to a mountain steppe to "use the facilities" as Mr Socrates so eloquently put it. She climbed out of the car and down the silk ladder, then changed behind a mulberry bush. The air was colder than she'd expected it to be. She moved her stiletto sheath from her left thigh onto her belt. Mrs Finchley had given her handy button-up pockets and loops for attaching things to—even a hidden pocket. With her dress thrown over her shoulder, she appreciated how much easier it was to get up the ladder in trousers. No one said anything about her attire, but she thought she saw Modo give her an amused look.

Soon the airship passed over a town in a green mountainous region. It looked to be little more than a collection of rectangles and squares. "That's Murrurundi," Lizzie said.

"Yes. Of course," Mr Socrates said. "We're doing well and five thousand feet seems a perfect height."

Octavia peered over the side. "Five thousand feet?"

"Yes, Octavia, we're flying higher than most mountains in Australia."

She couldn't even make out any people in the town. She knew there must be some down there, staring up and trying to determine the source of that mechanical noise from above.

Modo, his wooden mask now pulled tightly over his face, joined her at the starboard side of the car. She hadn't noticed him put it on, but could see that he was even more hunched over and shorter than before. His dark hair was thinner now, she was certain of it.

She pointed over the side and down. "Imagine, Modo, the natives look up at us as though we're gods. Of course, if we happened to fall out we'd be flatter than farthing."

"Don't remind me."

She laughed.

"You've put on your mask, Modo. Does it protect you from the headwinds?"

"It's necessary, that's all."

"How did that French spy react when she saw your face?" she whispered. She hadn't intended ever to ask him such a question, but clearly the anger was still lurking just below the surface. She'd thought that she was done with all that.

Behind the mask, Modo's eyes met hers. "She turned away from me."

"I see." Octavia paused, then asked, "Did you show your face to her willingly?"

"I did."

"You did?" she whispered a little too harshly.

He glanced over his shoulder at Mr Socrates, then back at her. "Would you like to see it, Tavia?" he said quietly. "I could show you now."

"No," she said, deciding suddenly that this was the right course. "I don't care if I ever see it."

"Then that's the way it will be," he declared, and returned to his station next to the firebox.

"Yes, it is," she said hoarsely.

She looked out at the skyline; the sun was getting lower. She was surprised to feel tears in her eyes. She wiped them away, relieved no one else could see her.

CHAPTER 28

A Speck in the Darkening Sky

For Modo, the first night in the *Prince Albert* was nowhere near as comfortable as the Langham Hotel or even The Rag and Famine. First, they all had to "use the facilities" one last time before sleeping. That involved lowering the airship close to the ground, hooking the anchor in the grey limbs of a lone snow-gum tree and climbing down the fifty-foot silk ladder. That in itself was an adventure, the silk being such a wisp that it was like grabbing air. Still it held him and the other two men all at once.

When they were finished, they climbed back up into the car and the women took their turns.

Later, when everyone was aboard, they floated a hundred feet above the earth, sleeping in shifts. Modo had first watch, and stared into the darkness below or the sky above, not sure what enemy he should be looking for. He imagined natives climbing up the anchor rope and spearing them while they slept. Or, for that matter, convicts who'd escaped the prison islands could still be roaming around this bush. They might just open fire from the ground.

When he wasn't squinting at the darkened landscape he examined the moon and stars. They seemed closer. If only the airship could travel a few feet higher, perhaps he could reach out and touch them.

He hadn't been joking when he offered to show his face to Octavia. He would have done it. He was tired of her wondering what he looked like. Nor did it matter to him any more that he wasn't supposed to show his face without Mr Socrates' permission. Tharpa saw it every day. Mrs Finchley did too. Why not Tavia? Since he met her eight months ago, always hiding his face from her had been a weight he'd carried. She had been constantly in his thoughts since they'd parted ways, and, in fact, at times it seemed that his every second thought was about her.

Truthfully, when it came to Tavia he was being an impostor. He removed his mask, looked out at the world and let the light of the stars fall upon his face. *This is the real me,* he thought.

Something creaked behind him and, out of habit, he quickly pushed the mask back on and flipped up his hood to hide his tufty red hair. He swung around, only to find it was Tharpa behind him.

"It's my watch now, young Sahib," he said. "You sleep."

Modo rolled up a greatcoat as a pillow and lay down a few inches from Tharpa's feet. It was cold—his breath was turning to plumes of frost, but the buffalo blankets were thick enough to keep the chill at bay. After several minutes he managed to fall asleep.

It seemed only seconds later when he awoke to Mr Socrates poking him with his walking stick.

"You're getting a little too comfortable, Modo. And you're snoring."

"It's his way of frightening away enemies," Octavia quipped.

Modo grinned, blinking away the sleep, shielding his eyes from the sunlight. He eagerly accepted a cup of tea from Octavia, who said, "I added two spoons of sugar, exactly how you like it."

Well, that was an unexpected but deliberate attempt at a truce. "Thank you," he said. And the tea was indeed exactly as he liked it.

After they'd all performed their morning business and climbed back into the airship, Tharpa lifted the anchor. Lizzie lit the boiler and Modo stood at his station feeding the firebox. The steam engine shook and rattled loudly to life, the propeller began to turn, and soon they were sailing north.

The landscape was forested and flat, the mountains now long behind them. If Mr Socrates' calculations were correct, they were travelling at over twenty-eight miles an hour. Not as fast as a train, but then, they never had to slow down for tricky terrain or a town. In yesterday's sixteen-hour voyage, Modo calculated, they would have travelled nearly 448 miles.

For lunch Octavia boiled eggs for the group. They tasted especially good so high up in the air. By evening, the ground below looked like grassland and sandstone, with occasional shrubs tossed here and there. Modo spotted a hut with the spyglass, but there were no roads or other signs of inhabitants.

"It's deserted," Modo said. "We could be floating over the moon."

"There are stock riders and duffers down there," Lizzie said harshly.

Modo couldn't tell if her tone was defensiveness or if she just always spoke that way. "And jumbuckers, too," she added.

"Yes, there are sheep down there and, one must presume, sheep herders," Mr Socrates noted. "Lizzie, you sometimes forget that we don't all know the secret language of the bush."

"I'm sorry, Mr Socrates," she barked, her voice no less harsh. "I shall use fancy talk from this point forward."

"Ah, Lizzie, that would be kind of you," Mr Socrates said. "I should perhaps have told you all that Lizzie is the first of her tribe to be educated. A grand accomplishment."

"But keep in mind, there are many different kinds of education," she said, sounding a little hoity-toity. "And I'm half a breed, as polite society has a penchant for saying. So perhaps it was my British side that took to the kind of education of which Mr Socrates speaks."

"Fancy talk, indeed," laughed Mr Socrates, "but never mind your education. You certainly are one of the most accomplished balloonists I have known. I remember how you'd carry gold from my mine to Sydney via balloon. Not one failed flight or missed deadline."

"You were a miner?" Octavia asked Mr Socrates.

"I was a mine owner and that's a long story. But it was where I first became aware of Lizzie's talent for floating through the air."

"It's where I belong," she said softly.

Modo was impressed by her ability to keep the giant car aloft, and despite a few blustery moments the trip had so far been smooth.

That night they anchored themselves to a spindly tree in a near-barren forest near a giant salt lake. The land around was grassy, sandy and arid, and there was absolutely no sign of human life. The only visible living beings were birds in the water: some sort of stork. Tharpa and Mr Socrates shot two of the black-necked birds and the group dined on freshly cooked fowl. Modo was thankful that the night temperature was much warmer. He dispensed with the buffalo blankets and used only a thin grey wool one.

The next morning Mr Socrates awakened everyone early. "We're going to push right through to our destination," he explained.

Before the sun had crested the horizon, they were sailing through the sky again. With sleep-blinkered eyes, Modo watched as the land slowly became more green. After a couple of hours, mountains rose out of the earth and blue rivers flowed between them. Modo felt as though what was passing under him wasn't real. How could a mountain look so small? he wondered.

As each hour passed Mr Socrates was clearly becoming more excited. He kept checking his instruments and staring through the spyglass. "We're nearing the Pacific!" he shouted finally, and at that moment the humid scent of the ocean wafted through the air. Modo was warm enough that he was tempted to take off his cloak, but that would have left his hump visible.

By late afternoon the land below them was a beautiful shade of dark green, lush and thick. So thick that Modo couldn't imagine how they'd land. Other than the occasional river, there didn't seem to be even the slightest break in the foliage. He'd read about the creatures that lived in the rain forest. It must surely teem with life!

The firebox was set for the next half-hour, so Modo went to the bow of the ship and tried to glimpse the Pacific, but it wasn't visible yet. He also kept his eyes on a grey wall of forbidding clouds that had gathered in the west. They looked powerful enough to blow the airship out over the ocean.

Mr Socrates unfolded the map to the Egyptian temple and Modo shivered in anticipation. After all this time and travel they were finally that close!

"Follow that river," Mr Socrates directed Lizzie.

She turned the ship and they were soon floating over a river that ran through a gorge.

"Everyone watch for lightning," Mr Socrates said. "We don't want to be pinned on the end of Zeus's bolts. We'd be blown to smithereens!" He said this with a chuckle, and Tharpa began to laugh.

"They are reliving their youths," Octavia whispered to Modo, elbowing him in the ribs as though they were sharing a joke.

"So, see anything interesting?" she asked a moment later.

He saw her, that much he knew; her slightly upturned nose, her look of guile, the eye-catching freckles on her cheeks—he saw all these things. Despite lack of sleep and no proper washing facilities, her beauty had not diminished in the slightest. And the trousers just made her more ... he searched for a good word ... jaunty? Daring?

"All I see is the green earth and the blue—make that grey—sky," he said.

"Are you feeling more comfortable at this height now?"

"I was never uncomfortable!" He kept his voice steady.

"Ah, I know you better than that, Modo. Remember, I crossed the Atlantic with you, all wobbly-legged from seasickness. Your legs look steadier today."

"You judge me by my legs?" he said.

"Well, the mask hides your face, so I cannot judge you by your smile. Besides, they're a fine example of legs."

He blushed behind the mask. She was always playing games with him: one moment angry, the next joking, the next his closest friend and a confidante. Their conversations felt like chess games and he was constantly three moves behind.

"Nice of you to notice," he finally said. "Do you see anything out there?"

"Well …" She turned her gaze away from him and it was like someone had turned off a spotlight. "There's a bank of dark clouds on our left."

"On the port side, you mean," he corrected.

"Yes, yes, the port side. My apologies, Captain Modo. Ensign Milkweed can be such a dunce at times! There's no lightning that I can see." She squinted. "How high did Mr Socrates say we were?"

"Right now? Three thousand feet above sea level."

"Do you know how high hawks can fly?"

"No," Modo said.

She pointed at the clouds. "What's that?"

He followed her finger and for several seconds he thought she was seeing things. Then he spotted a black speck moving within the grey mass of clouds.

"Mr Socrates," Modo said, his voice quavering a little. It couldn't be a hawk. The shape was all wrong. "Uh, Mr Socrates, there's an object in the sky. Directly to port and forty-five degrees up."

Mr Socrates grabbed his spyglass and looked through it. His face grew grim; his jaw tensed. "Tharpa, unlash the carbines!" he commanded. "We're about to have visitors."

CHAPTER 29

The Sparrow and the Hawk

In the few moments it took Tharpa to load his rifle and join them port side, the object had disappeared into a fold of clouds.

"What is it?" Modo asked.

"Adjust our course, Lizzie!" Mr Socrates shouted as he folded the map and placed it in his rucksack. "Thirty-five degrees starboard." He loosed the flap on his pistol holster. "An airship, Modo. Hard to tell what type from this distance."

"Were they flying a flag?" Octavia asked.

"No. Enough questions! Octavia, grab a carbine. See if your target practice has paid off. Modo, run up the Union Jack. It may be another vessel in Her Majesty's service. Snap to!"

Modo snapped to, leaping to the starboard side of the car. The flag dangled on a pulley rope that would draw it to the bottom of the *Prince Albert*'s car. He quickly pulled the rope and the Union Jack flapped in the wind, clearly visible about ten feet below the car. It seemed like flimsy protection.

"Bring us up to four thousand feet," Mr Socrates commanded. Lizzie opened the valve that sent hydrogen into the outer balloon and they started to climb. "Keep your eyes peeled, all of you."

"More coal!" Lizzie bellowed.

Modo went over and dumped coal directly from the pail into the firebox. He looked out the aft of the airship, scanning the clouds. There was no sign of the other vessel. He assumed the *Prince Albert* was climbing so that they'd have a better view of the sky, but if the balloon was pierced or otherwise damaged they'd have even farther to fall. Then again, three thousand feet or seven thousand. What would it matter? Either way they were dead.

"Higher, Lizzie!" Mr Socrates shouted. "Push the beast to her limits!"

She adjusted a lever and the engine went from a chugging roar to an ear-splitting thunder, steam and smoke spewing out of the stack, the propeller spinning madly. Modo had studied steam engines enough to know that the boiler could explode from too much pressure, and he wondered how close they were to that. He'd be the first to be blown to pieces. Or at least thrown over the edge of the wicker car.

Mr Socrates alternated between reading his dials and staring through his spyglass, while Tharpa and Octavia held the carbines, scanning the sky. The green rain forest below looked deceptively soft.

After several minutes of full-speed travel, the wind pulling at Modo's hood and the ground growing farther and farther away, Mr Socrates lowered his spyglass. "Octavia," he shouted, "make some tea, please."

"Tea?" she replied, dumbfounded. "Now?"

"Yes, Octavia. We seem to have lost our guests, or they have fled at the sight of us. So, tea, it is. Now, dear girl. Now."

She set her Winchester against the side, and took her place next to the motor, dropping the teapot over the steam vent. "High society madness!" she grumbled.

"It'll calm our nerves," Modo whispered.

The hissing of the kettle grew to a higher and higher pitch, eventually becoming a whistle. Modo shivered. It was getting colder the higher they ascended, so tea would be nice.

He heard a reverberating rumble and wondered if the *Prince Albert*'s engine was slowing down. He shovelled in more coal. The engine was running as quickly and loudly as it ever had. What was the unusual noise?

"Do you hear that?" he asked Octavia.

"Hear what?" She lifted the pot from the steam vent and it stopped whistling.

A low bass grumble could be heard clearly, louder than their own engine.

"Shut down the engine," Mr Socrates ordered. "It's hot enough that we can start it up with a moment's notice."

Lizzie pushed a lever and the engine clunked and clanked to a stop, along with the propeller. The thundering was directly above them, and it made Modo's very bones rattle. Only one thing could be making that noise. He leaned over the railing to crane his neck and see what was out there.

A shadow loomed over the *Prince Albert*; he could make out the edges of a massive conical balloon at least twice as large as theirs. Their pursuers had manoeuvred themselves perfectly so that they were directly above the *Prince Albert*.

"Tharpa! Octavia! Ready your guns!" Mr Socrates pulled his pistol from its holster.

Octavia set the teapot on the floor, swept up her rifle and leaned out of the car.

A hawk-like screech echoed from below, and before Tharpa or Octavia could fire, the carbines were torn from their hands by two clockwork falcons. His last hope, that this somehow wasn't the Clockwork Guild above them, was gone.

"Start the engine now, Lizzie!" Mr Socrates commanded as he charged over to twist dials on the hydrogen machine. "Hang on, everyone, we're going to dive!"

Even as he spoke, a grappling hook swung down and hooked the wicker side of the car. It was followed by two more hooks, then four, and then there were at least six that Modo could count. The *Prince Albert* dropped a few feet and began to lurch back and forth. Then they were rising! The ship above them actually had enough power to prevent them from diving!

Tharpa cut the rope of one hook and Modo grabbed a

machete and cut another, then looked up to discover that the grappling hooks had jabbed into the exterior of the balloon itself, catching the netting. Hydrogen hissed out of several gashes.

Modo climbed up the side of the *Prince Albert*'s balloon, clinging to the netting as he hacked at the grappling hook ropes. Above him, the enemy car was studded with metal, a sharp spur sticking straight out the front. If they had rammed the *Prince Albert* it would have easily punctured both the exterior and interior balloons. That could only mean they wanted them captured alive.

Goggled faces peered over the edge of the car above as they threw down more grappling hooks. Modo heard a bang and a bullet that had just missed him punctured the balloon instead. He nearly dropped the machete. Perhaps they *didn't* want them alive! He chopped through the last rope and the *Prince Albert* dropped and jerked so hard he was flung into the open air, releasing the machete and letting out a shout. He was surprised when his fall stopped suddenly and he was hanging upside down, swinging beside the wicker car. He twisted his neck to see that his legs were tangled up in the netting. Octavia grabbed him by the cloak and with Tharpa's help yanked him into the car.

"Good to have you aboard again," Tharpa said.

"Modo, man the firebox!" Mr Socrates shouted.

Modo took his position, not daring to even think about how he had nearly fallen to his death. He looked over the side; they were getting closer to the earth; they were at two thousand feet, perhaps.

Lizzie cranked the wheel, turning the ship this way and that. Wind and heat from the engine began to dry his eyes, so he grabbed a pair of goggles and placed them over his mask.

"This may be an inappropriate time to mention this," Octavia said, "but goggles over a mask looks rather silly."

They both laughed, so hard Modo worried Mr Socrates would yell at them. Fortunately he was busy shouting orders at Lizzie.

"We are smaller so we should be able to outmanoeuvre them," Mr Socrates said. "Sixty degrees to port! Now, Lizzie! Crank it hard. More steam, Modo! Let's see what their top speed is."

The *Prince Albert* was fleeing at such a velocity that the outer balloon rippled, and yet they continued to sink. Their pursuer dove to their level and snuck up behind them like a giant shark following the scent of blood, gaining quickly. Modo swallowed hard as he watched the spar on the end of their airship glittering.

"Tharpa, get out the elephant gun."

Tharpa nodded and removed the double-barrelled gun from its leather case. Modo had seen that same gun on the mantle of Victor house and knew it was dear to Mr Socrates. Beside it had hung his trophies from hunting some of the largest game on earth: Cape buffalo skulls, elephant tusks and rhinoceros skulls. All had fallen victim to that gun.

Tharpa took up a position at the aft of the *Prince Albert*, and calmly poured black powder down each barrel. He dropped a large round bullet into each one, then packed it all down with the ramrod. *Hurry up!* Modo wanted to yell, but he knew Tharpa was moving as fast as any man could.

"Give them both barrels," Mr Socrates shouted. "Aim at the balloon, not the car. Pretend it's that elephant who charged us in Mozambique, old friend!"

Friend? Modo had never heard Mr Socrates refer to Tharpa as his friend before. Nor did he understand the jaunty tone in his voice; neither he nor Tharpa seemed frightened at all.

Tharpa grinned, raised the gun to his shoulder and took a moment to aim. Modo was relieved that he was pointing the barrel over the propeller; just one of those bullets would knock the spinning blades right off. Tharpa pulled the trigger and both hammers struck at the same time. The gun went off with the sound and force of a cannon, knocking Tharpa back against the steam engine. A cloud of smoke filled the car, and when it cleared they couldn't see any obvious damage. The bullets had ricocheted off the metal plates that protected the front of the balloon. Their enemy lunged closer, as if they'd found a higher gear. Modo could now make out the arrowslit openings at the front of the car and the glint of goggles behind them.

"It's called the *Prometheus*," Mr Socrates said. The name of the ship was clearly emblazoned on its side. "Another Greek name! The Clockwork Guild does have a fondness for Hellenic names." He sounded as though he were teaching a lesson. "Load again, Tharpa. Faster this time. I do believe you've slowed down in your old age."

Tharpa raised one eyebrow as he began to load, then got off another volley. This time Modo saw the bullets ricochet off the front of the car. The goggled heads in the window slits disappeared, then reappeared.

A fire flared on the starboard side of the *Prometheus* and Modo nearly raised his arms in celebration; perhaps a bullet had hit home or their steam engine was bursting into flames. But then the fire began to dart, arrow swift, towards them and hissed by the wicker car, trailing smoke and sparks as it arced its way down to the jungle floor. Any closer and it would have caught the hydrogen leaking from the balloon.

"Chinese rockets!" Mr Socrates shouted. "I do believe they meant to miss us. Rest assured the next shot will be true. They'll expect our surrender."

A woman's voice blared out of a voice trumpet at the front of the *Prometheus*. "At any moment we can knock you from the sky. Stop your engine, put down your guns and prepare to be boarded. We promise to spare your lives."

Modo knew that voice, the slight Scandinavian accent.

"It's Miss Hakkandottir, sir!" he exclaimed.

Mr Socrates nodded and said, coolly, "It's been many years since I've heard it, but I'd know that flat tone anywhere."

Modo was impressed at how calm his master sounded. Mr Socrates turned to the altimeter, flicked it once with his finger. "We're at one thousand feet," he reported. "Turn off the engine, please, Lizzie."

"Off, sir?" Modo asked, as Lizzie began shutting several valves.

"Yes. We can't outrun them and we can't pierce their armour with our gun. If we dive they'll only grapple us again or they could easily rocket us out of the sky." He holstered his pistol. "Better to meet them face to face and see what we're dealing with."

Modo doubted there were any weaknesses in the floating behemoth behind them. The *Prince Albert's* propeller thudded to a stop and the engine noise of the *Prometheus* grew louder as the enemy ship caught up with them. A black flag, with the Clockwork Guild symbol, flapped from a pulley at the bottom of the car.

The enemy pulled up alongside them, their steel-plated car looking more like an armoured galleon. Two rectangular doors fell open like drawbridges, revealing eight Guild soldiers, rifles pointed at them. Behind them was the falconer, with a falcon on either wrist. Miss Hakkandottir, her red hair loose and blowing in the wind, stepped out from between them in her usual dramatic fashion.

"Alan," she shouted with a wry smile. "A distinct pleasure to see you again."

Alan? At first Modo didn't know whom she was addressing, but she was looking at Mr Socrates. Of course, that was his first name!

"Yes, Ingrid. It's been fifteen years. Must your men point their pea-shooters at us?"

"At ease," she said to the soldiers, and they lowered their rifles.

"I see you have a new hand," Mr Socrates noted.

Miss Hakkandottir raised it to the sun and the metal sparkled. Modo imagined her polishing it day and night. She had once poked a sharp metal finger into his eye, nearly blinding him. "Yes. Extremely useful. I should perhaps thank you for removing my original one."

"And you have a new master?" Mr Socrates asked. "Did he come with the hand?"

"I would rather not shout such scintillating repartee across ship bows," she yelled. "I will tell you all about us in time. First, we will attach a towing rope and send over a boarding crew. Our own pilot will ensure you arrive safe and sound with us at our base. There we can have a proper conversation. I see you still have the Indian with you. Oh, and that's Modo, is it not? Who else would wear a mask. I have been hoping we would meet again."

Modo didn't like her cruel eyes on him. He stood as straight as he could and glanced over at Mr Socrates. Would he order an attack? He was concentrating, staring at the *Prometheus*, seeming to be searching for weaknesses. But all Modo could see were the soldiers, rockets and metal armour plating.

"We welcome your boarding party," Mr Socrates shouted. Then he turned his face slightly and scratched at his cheek, hiding his next words from Miss Hakkandottir. "Better to take our chances falling to the ground. On my order, Tharpa, fire the flare gun into our outer balloon. The force will blow them out of the air. We'll fall, but hopefully the forest floor and the springs of the car will save us."

Modo exchanged glances with Octavia, then peeped over the edge. They would surely die.

"Alan," Miss Hakkandottir shouted. "Please bring your ship closer."

There must be another way. Looking up, Modo saw one of the grappling ropes hanging above them, the hook still firmly caught in the balloon. The rope was just long enough.

As he took a step back to make a run at it, Tharpa grabbed his arm. "No, young Sahib. It will not work."

Modo nodded to Tharpa. "You're right, teacher," he said, and let the air out of his lungs, making himself look deflated and resigned to their fate. Then, with a twist of his arm—a move Tharpa had taught him years ago—he broke his trainer's grip and launched himself through the air shouting, "Fly! Fly! Save yourselves!"

He grabbed the dangling rope and swung, increasing his momentum. Halfway between the two ships he let go, arcing majestically towards the *Prometheus*.

CHAPTER 30

Stupid, Stupid Fool

It was the bravest and stupidest act Octavia had ever seen. One moment they were all standing still, hoping not to get shot, and the next Modo was shouting and leaping through the air like a circus acrobat.

"Modo! You stupid, stupid fool!" she couldn't help screaming at him. He'd misjudged and was dropping like a stone, plunging towards the forest floor. Octavia sucked in a panicky breath as he passed within arm's reach of the bottom of the enemy ship and managed to snatch the Clockwork Guild flag with both hands and hang on. His weight actually rocked the *Prometheus'* car like a pendulum. Immediately, he began to climb up to the bottom.

Bullets ripped through the air and Octavia was knocked to the floor. At first she thought she'd been shot, then realised something was holding her down. Tharpa!

"Do not stand up, Miss Milkweed," he said. As he lay on his side, he began to load the elephant gun.

"Start the engine, Lizzie!" Mr Socrates shouted. It fired up, the boiler still hot enough to produce steam. "Now dive, dive, dive!"

Octavia crawled over next to Mr Socrates.

"We can't just leave Modo!"

"Nor can we stay in their line of fire," he answered. "Get to the bow and guide us."

"But he'll die!"

"I won't leave Modo," he promised. The determination in his voice surprised her. "We're going to pass under the *Prometheus* so he can drop onto our balloon. That's the new plan. The little fool didn't follow my orders, so you had better!"

She crawled to the bow of the ship, pausing to check for Modo. He'd made it to the underside of the *Prometheus* and was working his way towards the back, but there were already soldiers crawling down the sides of the car to rid themselves of their parasite.

Her stomach performed a somersault as the *Prince Albert* suddenly plunged towards the earth.

CHAPTER 31

A Swan Dive

About halfway between the airships, Modo discovered that he'd miss the enemy car entirely. As he arced below the *Prometheus*, fear overtaking him, he reached out and grabbed the huge flag flapping at the bottom of the airship. He clung to it, stunned, thanking the Fates that it held his weight. The enemy's cursed flag had saved his life, for the moment anyway. He wondered, briefly, what Tharpa thought of this horrible display of acrobatics, then he began to climb. He didn't dare look down.

After he'd gone a few feet it occurred to him that he had no plan. In any case, it wasn't like he had options. Up was the only way to go. He would give them something to remember him by. The longer he fought, the better the chance his companions would escape. He focused on getting to the metal springs on the underside of the *Prometheus*, climbing hand over hand until he reached them.

The *Prince Albert* dropped down past him with such speed that he only got a glimpse of his fellow agents lying on the floor. Were they deserting him? Or maybe one of his companions had been shot. Or all of them! But Lizzie must be alive because the ship was spiralling down on an exceptionally well-controlled path.

Hakkandottir would know he was down here. There were eight soldiers in the car armed with rifles, a pilot, or two maybe, an engineer, and Miss Hakkandottir. Each would be armed and all he had were his bare hands. Why hadn't he thought to bring a machete?

Then he remembered the clockwork falcons. Fool! He scanned the sky for their shapes but they were either pursuing the *Prince Albert* or waiting on their master's arm above him.

The *Prometheus'* steam engine roared as the ship dove in pursuit of the *Prince Albert*. He looked down to see the *Prince Albert* circling a few hundred feet below. They seemed to be keeping pace with the enemy, and it dawned on him that they might be waiting for him to jump. How long they could maintain their position, he had no idea. He could just wait here for them to ascend close enough. Then, once he landed on board, he could grab the netting on the exterior balloon. But that would mean the chase would just begin again and they'd be no further ahead. No, the *Prometheus* had to be disabled, one way or another.

He swung along under the car, clutching the springs and hoping that the bolts were strong enough to bear his weight. The best way to stop the enemy, of course, would be to bring the whole thing down. But it wasn't like he had a stick of dynamite.

Don't focus on what you don't have! he told himself.
The most logical thing was to damage the engine. He
could jam the propeller, a simple enough concept, but
how to accomplish it? A stolen rifle would be chopped in
half. If he could just see the engine itself, maybe he'd have
his answer.

The *Prometheus* turned to starboard and a blast of
wind caught him, blowing his cloak around, so his hood
became tangled in a spring. He tried to extricate it with
his left hand, holding tight to the ship with his right, but
the spring had poked a hole through the fabric.

His right hand suddenly stung so painfully that
he opened it and found himself hanging by his hood,
swinging back and forth in the wind. A Guild soldier was
right behind him, arm raised for another smash. Modo let
out a yelp and caught the pipe wrench, absorbing a bone-
shaking blow. He pulled himself up using the man's arm,
tearing his hood free. He was eye to eye with the enemy.
Modo got a grip on a spring and yanked the wrench out
of the soldier's hands. The soldier tried to grab Modo,
but he slipped, falling head first through the air. Modo
turned his face away.

A bullet ricocheted off the metal undercarriage.
Another Guild soldier was twenty feet away, hanging
by one arm, aiming his pistol with the other. Modo
tucked the pipe wrench in his belt and scrambled as
quickly as he could to the aft of the car, then swung
himself up and was nearly decapitated by the propeller.
He pressed hard against the side, hoping the wind
wouldn't blow his cloak into it. But as he edged around

the side of the car, the blades caught the hem of it. With all his strength Modo yanked it out—a section was now in tatters. *Why did I wear a cloak!* he wanted to scream.

Several gyroscope-like instruments stuck out of the ship beside him, spinning madly; he imagined they somehow measured airspeed. A bullet struck one and it fell from the ship. The soldier was now climbing up the side of the ship for a better shot. Thankfully, the swaying of the *Prometheus* made it difficult for him to aim while clinging with one hand.

No sense hanging out here, Modo thought. He swung his body around, caught a corner of the partly extended gangplank with his hand, and, with an acrobatic leap that included a great flip through the air, threw himself into the *Prometheus*.

He landed firmly on his feet, face to face with Miss Hakkandottir. Before he could react, she had her metal hand around his throat and had pushed him down on the floor, against coils of ropes. He tried to pry her fingers but they were as strong as the determination in her eyes.

"I was hoping to capture you, Modo," she said, almost gently. "The Guild Master wants to know what makes you tick."

The air in his lungs was disappearing. She'd soon crush his windpipe! He'd never break her viselike grip. But Mr Socrates' voice came to him: *Fear attacks rational thought.* He'd said it a thousand times. She was only human. Her hand was strong, perhaps stronger than he was. But the rest of her was flesh.

He booted her in the knee and she spat out a curse, but her metal hand still cut off his airway. He grabbed her hand with both of his and pulled it away from his throat with all his strength, hoping he didn't rip out his windpipe in the process. He sucked in a long breath. Success! He flung himself up to his feet and stumbled against the side of the car. Bullets cut through his cloak, missing his body.

In a flash he took in the scene before him: six soldiers with pistols aimed at him were spread out through the car, behind them were a pilot and co-pilot madly working the controls, and next to them the falconer.

Modo raised his arms in surrender, which momentarily stopped the shooting. If he could get to the pilots he could toss them overboard. That would put an end to the pursuit.

Miss Hakkandottir stood up, holding her knee. She was about to say something, but he leapt forward, grabbed her by the hair and spun her around as a shield between him and the Guild soldiers, pinning her metal hand against her side. He dragged her along so that his back was pressed against the steam engine. The red-hot boiler burned through his clothes, the misty steam and smoke making his goggles fog up. He pulled out the pipe wrench and held it high.

"I'll brain her if any of you makes a move."

"Dimitri," Miss Hakkandottir shouted. "You are the best shot. Aim between his eyes."

One soldier raised his pistol, his hand steady. Modo jerked to the left, dragging his hostage with him, and the bullet pinged off the boiler. Miss Hakkandottir ripped her hand from his grip, screamed in rage and swung it back behind her, so that he had to use the wrench to deflect the metal hand. It struck the boiler, making it ring like a bell.

"Shoot again, you idiot!" Hakkandottir commanded.

Dimitri's hand was trembling, the pistol barrel wavering. Modo suddenly realised that Miss Hakkandottir didn't care whether or not the bullet went through her before it hit him, so he shoved her into the soldiers, knocking Dimitri and two others down. Then he turned, grabbed a metal rod on the ceiling and swung to the opposite side of the steam engine and began smashing at it with the wrench. Dials shattered, hoses broke, spraying out water and steam, but the engine continued to roar. It would take hours to dismantle the machine!

He dropped the wrench and grabbed the bottom of the red-hot boiler, struggling to lift it, ignoring his burning hands. The metal bands that held it to the floor snapped and, to his own surprise and the surprise of his enemies, he lifted the engine and tried to heft it over the side. It was too heavy and he fell back, dropping it, but pipes had snapped and began to smoke and clatter. The whole car lurched to starboard and Modo slipped over the side, reaching out at the last moment to cling to the railing.

He looked down, searching. No sign of the *Prince Albert*. He glanced up to find Miss Hakkandottir, bleeding from the forehead, shaking a sabre at him.

"Die!" she grunted. "Just die like the rat you are!" She swung the sabre.

The excruciating pain in his hand made Modo let go.

He closed his eyes, not wanting to see death coming for him. *Don't be stupid, Modo,* he thought, and opened them again just as he struck something. He had a moment to realise it was the balloon on the *Prince Albert* before it burst, hydrogen shooting out of vast rips in its side. He bounced off, flailing his arms and finding nothing to grab. He glimpsed the car, a blurred vision of Octavia's horrified face, and then the beautiful green of the rain forest floor.

CHAPTER 32

A Sudden Descent

M r Socrates heard the thud as though a huge rock had slammed into the *Prince Albert*'s outer balloon. It burst with the impact and the airship plummeted towards the ground.

"Lizzie, guide us down!" he shouted.

She grunted as she pulled a lever and tried to steer the ship.

As Mr Socrates turned to examine the damage, he saw a figure fall through the air, a cloak flapping around him. Modo! Good Lord! It would be impossible to dive the *Prince Albert* fast enough to catch him.

"Was that Modo?" Octavia shrieked. "Was it?"

"Yes," Mr Socrates said. He couldn't bring himself to watch Modo fall any farther. He looked up. The *Prometheus* was smoking in the sky and going in circles. "He accomplished his goal."

"But I thought we were going to get closer to him!" she yelled. "We were supposed to rescue him! That's what you said!"

"We got as close as possible!" Mr Socrates bellowed back, disappointed with himself for letting her set him off like this. He paused to take a deep breath. "Now get a hold of your emotions. We're descending with some speed and need to lighten our load. Find anything you can that's not necessary and toss it overboard."

Octavia stared at him, anger burning in her eyes. He almost gave her a slap to snap her out of it, but feared he'd only make things worse. Besides, with all Tharpa had taught her, she might just flatten him.

"Deal with what's before you," he said to her calmly, "then respond to what you cannot change."

She blinked, then said through clenched teeth, "Fine, I will!" She threw the teapot, of all things, over the side.

He bit back a curse.

The darkest of thoughts hit him: *Modo is dead.* His knees nearly buckled. His stomach lurched and he gritted his teeth. *No, it can't be! That boy, my boy, my agent, can't be counted out so soon. Modo has more lives than a cat.* He would believe the boy was dead only when he saw his lifeless body with his own eyes.

He lifted a sack of flour and cast it over. "Help me with the engine, Tharpa!" The *Prince Albert* was getting dangerously close to the treetops, Lizzie steering them left and right to avoid the taller ones. They hefted the motor then and heaved it over the side. The airship popped up several feet.

The primary balloon was deflating, too, but at least they were falling more slowly now.

"My dear Lizzie, I would appreciate it if you'd now find a clearing for us," he said, as though he were ordering crumpets.

She nodded in agreement.

He wished he'd chosen a green balloon rather than this red one that would stick out in all this foliage. Sometimes he was far too patriotic, he thought, and it would be the death of him.

"There?" Lizzie pointed to a small gorge where a branch of the river ran through a rocky bed. It looked almost peaceful.

"Yes, put us down!"

"Hold onto your teacups," Lizzie warned. The wind bashed them around, but she was able to steer them closer and closer to the ground, the wicker car cracking and buckling as it snapped off treetops and branches. They dove into the clearing, bounced twice across the water, hit a pile of rocks, and came to a stop so abrupt that Mr Socrates flew across the car and smashed his head on the hydrogen machine, burning his scalp.

He stood up groggily and felt around until he found the emergency valve rope. He gave it a good tug and the valve on top of the balloon opened, releasing the hydrogen into the air before it could blow them to bits. He shoved the balloon skin out of his way and looked up. No sign of Hakkandottir. Yet.

Tharpa had been tossed from the car, but was splashing through the water towards them. Octavia and Lizzie were both in the car holding their heads, but seemed unharmed otherwise. "Any broken bones?" Mr Socrates asked, barely giving time for a reply. "Good! Quick! Drag everything into the forest before they spot us!"

They each grabbed hold of a section and wrestled with it, pulling desperately until the balloon and the car were well hidden under the ferns and palm trees. All the while Mr Socrates glanced up at the bits of sky he could see. No sign of their enemy.

"Please, let's start searching for Modo," Octavia said.

"No," Mr Socrates replied forcefully. He'd already thought this through. "He's a smart young man and I trained him well. If he's alive he'll find us."

"And how will he do that?"

"Because, Octavia, he will go to the temple. That's his mission and our greatest hope. If we're going to find him anywhere, it will be there."

CHAPTER 33

Looking Death in the Eye

For Modo, the fall from the sky and the events that followed had all happened with mind-boggling speed. He'd smashed through the pine and palm trees and landed on his back on the rain forest floor. A missing finger, his pinky, was his only major injury. He couldn't believe his injuries weren't worse.

Moments later, before he'd even had a chance to gather his wits, he was fleeing from a gang of tribesmen.

And here he was falling again, this time into a deep pit. Time had slowed down, as though the grains of sand in an hourglass were dropping one by one. He counted the stakes. Sixteen in all. Sharpened bamboo.

He could relive every moment of his life if he so wished; he pictured the first time he'd seen Octavia in her green dress; the way she had looked as he clung to her arm about to fall from the *Hugo*; her horrified face as he dropped past the *Prince Albert*. Did this slowing down of time happen to everyone before they died?

He concentrated. Impossible to avoid hitting the ground. Unfortunately, his weight and speed would ensure the stakes would pierce him through. *Unless,* he thought, *I twist myself.* He'd seen cats fly through the air. They were always able to turn and land on their feet. If he landed on his side there was a chance he'd fall into the gap between the stakes.

Time was speeding up, so he twisted his body, only to find he was now falling back first. He glimpsed the natives at the edge of the hole, angry faces glaring down as they waited for his death. Desperate, he twisted again. He'd die with his murderers being his last sight. At the last moment he rotated—and fell between the stakes. One stake glanced off his mask, knocking it askew, then he thudded against the ground on his right shoulder.

He lay there for several seconds, trying to catch his breath. His attackers let out a disappointed groan. Objects poked into his flesh. He couldn't see, so he pulled his mask down to his neck. He shuffled around, creating a clatter. By the light flooding in the opening of the hole, he saw he was lying on a bed of bones! He couldn't tell if they had belonged to human beings or animals. Beetles ran here and there and a green scaly lizard scampered away, its tail zagging wildly.

One native shouted, and Modo fully expected to feel a spear puncture his vital organs. Better to look death in the eye, he decided. He turned over onto his back, his bones aching, and stared up at his soon-to-be murderers.

The tribesmen let out a uniform cry of terror. One began wailing and pulling at his dark, curly hair. Another flung away his spear, covered his eyes and fell to the ground.

What is it? Modo looked over his shoulder, expecting some tiger or monstrous creature to be standing there. He turned back just as the remaining tribesmen dropped to their knees and then, he assumed, to the ground. He could no longer see any of them over the edge of the pit.

After a moment's pause, he stood, legs shaking. The pit was at least twelve feet deep, and the natives appeared to be gone. Maybe they'd all silently backed away. Or it was a trap! They might all spring on him at once.

Sturdy vines hung down one corner of the pit over the reddish-brown soil. They must have been used by the natives to descend and butcher their kills. He yanked two of the stakes from the ground, tucked them in his belt and climbed up the vines, his mask swinging on his neck like an oversized necklace. Near the top he held the sharpened bamboo in front of him, and poked his head out warily.

He was stunned to find the tribesmen still on the ground, some of them shivering and kneeling, their dark skin painted with white lines and handprints. Others were prostrate, their flaps of leather clothing barely covering their backsides. One looked up at him, his face marked with a series of white leopard-like spots. He muttered a cry of alarm and lowered his head again.

Modo pulled himself out of the hole and dropped the stakes. He could make no sense of it. Only moments ago they had been hunting him like a wild beast and now they were bowing before him. What had changed?

He wiped the sweat from his eyes and his hands felt his fallen-in nose, the mangled chin, the bumps across his cheek. They were all seeing his face for the first time.

He stood there, absolutely stupefied, and it was all he could do to not fall over: they'd actually been brought to their knees by his ugliness. To their knees! He wanted to pull out his hair. He felt a scream building deep inside him, a scream that had been waiting in his soul, in his heart, since birth.

Instead, he let out a sudden hiccup of a laugh that was tinged with madness. Several of the warriors shivered visibly and covered their ears.

"Am I so ugly?" he asked them.

He picked up one of their spears, saw that its shaft sat inside another wooden instrument to improve the throw. A clever device! They'd been carrying wooden shields, too. He picked one up. It was carved with an image that had been outlined in white lines—a representation of a supremely ugly face. He nearly dropped the shield. The features on it looked similar to his own!

"'Alas, poor Yorick!'" he quoted, "'I knew him, Horatio, a fellow of infinite jest, of most excellent fancy.'" He paused, and let out another bark of laughter that echoed in the forest. "Don't you know Shakespeare?"

He tossed the shield aside. Was there nowhere on earth that he wouldn't be seen as ugly? For a third time he laughed, then cut it short. *Modo, you self-pitying fool! Behaving like a madman won't help you—you'll just be dragged off to Bedlam.*

He didn't stop to consider just who would actually

take him to Bedlam from here. Once again he looked down in disbelief at the prostrate natives. None even dared to peek at him!

But one pair of eyes didn't look away. A girl, no more than ten years old, stood about twenty paces from him, mostly hidden in the folds of a fern. She straightened her back, pushed aside the leaves and walked towards Modo, even though the warriors whispered admonishments and waved her away from him. The girl's curly hair was white as snow, her dark skin painted with intricate spiderweb lines. She strode fearlessly between the men, not taking her eyes off Modo. She stopped in front of him.

"Who are you?" he asked.

She replied with several words that made no sense. Seeing that he wasn't understanding her, she paused and pointed at the canopy of trees with her little finger and said what sounded like "*Jiri, jiri.*" Then she pointed at him with the same little finger.

"What do you mean?"

She pointed skyward again. "*Daray.*"

"I fell from the sky, yes, that's right." He wondered if that was it. Had they seen the airship battle? They would have heard it, at least. All that strange thunder above them, then a man falls from the sky and lands in the middle of their hunting grounds.

No, not a man. A god! After all, he fell from the sky. He chuckled to himself. *Me, a god? Hah!*

But the warriors remained cowering before him, had been this way for some ten minutes now. It was the way emperors and kings were treated not so long ago, according to the history books he'd read.

Modo pointed at his chest. "Modo," he said. "Me, Modo."

The girl had a brilliant spark of intelligence in her eyes. She pointed at herself with her little finger. "Nulu" it sounded like. She pointed at him again. "Meh Moh-Doh."

"Modo," he repeated.

"Moh-Doh." She nodded and let out a little huff of satisfaction. "Moh-Doh. Moh-Doh." She pointed at herself. "Nulu."

"Nulu," he said. The smile that appeared on her face was so large that Modo wanted to hug her. She started babbling ever so quickly, gesturing at the sky and then at him and the forest and back at the warriors. Then she made a circle with her hands.

Modo held up his hand and she stopped babbling.

"I have no idea what you are saying." He spoke slowly, and louder than usual. "Tell them to get up," he said, pointing at the warriors. She stared naively at him. Then it dawned on him—she was looking at his face without grimacing. In fact, he would have described her as looking blissful, as though she were looking at something she'd wanted to see for her whole life. Blissful? He really was going out of his mind.

He gestured upwards several times, saying, "Get up! Get up!"

Nulu stood beside him, imitating his actions but speaking in her language. One warrior raised his head and looked at Modo and Nulu. He whispered to his companions and they all got warily to their feet. They were taller than Modo, much taller than he'd expected them to be. He'd always thought of these uncivilised tribes as being short and stout, but these men were even taller than Mr Socrates. White handprints ran along their bodies and faces. A few had clearly dined a little too often, but most of them were slim and muscular. They kept their eyes cast down as though they had been chastised.

"What am I to do with you now?" Modo asked.

CHAPTER 34

A Perfectly Fine Trophy

Miss Hakkandottir scanned the sky and the rain forest below the airship with her spyglass. She had been presented with a chance to swoop down from the heavens and scoop up her lifelong enemy and a handful of his key agents. It had all been coming together so perfectly until, in only minutes, that hunchback had shattered her plans.

He'd moved with more speed and agility than she'd dreamed would be possible, and his strength was truly staggering. To actually lift the steam engine! It had taken a crane to lower it into the car! Her only consolation was that Modo was dead now, though even that represented a failure of sorts. As much as she'd wanted Socrates and Tharpa and all the information inside their brains, she wanted Modo more.

When she'd told the Guild Master and Dr Hyde about meeting Modo on the deck of the *Wyvern*, and explained how he had the ability to change his physical appearance, the possibilities staggered both men! They wanted him captured alive so they could study him. Perhaps his talents could even be duplicated.

And she'd almost had him, right here on the very deck of her airship. But now he was a shattered corpse on the rain forest floor, the buzzards and lizards and whatever other creatures down there feeding off him, consuming all his secrets piece by piece.

A piece. A piece! But that's all she needed! Just a piece of him. An earlobe. A toe!

Then she remembered that furious swing of her sabre, so she ran to the place near the railing where his blood had spattered. Below that, curled up next to several spent shells, she discovered his little finger. She picked it up with her metal hand and called for a tin box. Gently she placed the finger inside, then slid the tin into her trousers and buttoned the pocket. When they landed she would bottle it up with formaldehyde. It was something at least; a perfectly fine trophy. The good doctor could work with this, she hoped.

"Hurry with that engine!" she commanded. "Time is of the essence."

She returned to surveying the sky and the rain forest. Mr Socrates had certainly landed somewhere. The tribes or the crocodiles would likely destroy them, if they had even survived their crash. But she knew from experience that one should never take chances by assuming such things, and when it came to her old enemy, one could never count him out. If he lived he would likely scurry towards Port Douglas. She would dispatch patrols and cut him off.

CHAPTER 35

A Touch, a Word

Modo waved his arms, then put his nine fingers together in a gesture that he hoped looked like a temple. It was where he needed to go. If only Octavia and Mr Socrates could see him now. Then with a pang of panic he wondered whether they were alive. Did he succeed in preventing the *Prometheus* from capturing them? If so, they may have darted back to the coast. But would they leave him here? Or, more importantly, would they leave the temple in the hands of Miss Hakkandottir? He doubted that. He would have to find them.

While they couldn't have landed too far away, the most logical place to find them would be the temple. Even if the worst had happened and they were all dead, Modo could still complete his assignment and extract his revenge, if necessary.

These men standing before him would surely have seen the temple at some point. Perhaps they'd even explored it. He pointed in the direction he believed was northwest and performed the temple gesture again, saying, "Egyptian temple! Egyptian temple."

They wouldn't even know what Egyptians were. It was useless. He dropped his arms. His missing finger throbbed, an odd and painful sensation. Every once in a while it dripped blood.

He felt a tug on his sleeve, then Nulu grabbed his good hand. This caused a hiss of surprise from the surrounding warriors who, Modo guessed, expected her to vanish or explode. She pulled gently and led Modo through the group and beyond. The warriors began following several steps behind. She found a clear path through the foliage.

"Are you taking me to the temple?" Modo asked as he ducked under a vine.

Nulu nodded, and they walked silently for several minutes. To his surprise, he saw that her white hair was not dyed that way, but had clearly grown out white as if at birth she'd seen something frightful. She walked with a confidence he wished he possessed, as though she saw strangers such as him every day.

There was movement in the brush ahead and Modo was tempted to grab his knife, but three young girls and two boys stepped out of the forest and joined the girl and Modo, falling in line behind them as if on parade.

Perhaps I have a concussion? Is all this a dream? He continued walking with her warm hand in his; no one had ever held his hand this long before, other than Mrs Finchley when he was a child. He glanced back. The warriors looked braver now, staunchly carrying their spears, yet none would meet his eyes. Everyone was silent, though occasionally Nulu would whistle an odd tune between her teeth.

Nulu led him up an incline, which involved circling around the trunks of large palm trees. There, quite suddenly, was the tribe's village, a small clearing marked with several worn pathways and ten round huts built of banana and palm leaves, each big enough to sleep a few people.

The children behind him let out a cry and took off through the bushes so quickly that Modo thought at first it was in fear, and looked over his shoulder. The warriors averted their eyes again. There was no lurking danger that he could see. Then it dawned on him that the children had decided to become the heralds of his arrival. They raced to the centre of the village and called out so that by the time the group entered the settlement, men and women of all ages, pregnant mothers with extended bellies, and more children came out to stand at the firepit in the centre of the village and gawk at him as he approached.

A large, round-bellied man in an animal-fur robe limped out and stood at the centre of the village. His beard was grey and his white hair stuck straight out. In one hand was a club and around his neck hung a kind of wooden breast plate. One eye was grey with blindness, the other open in shock.

Nulu led Modo directly to the elderly man. "*Ngaji,*" she said, "*jiri-warra.*" She offered up Modo's hand.

The old man hesitantly took it. Modo found the man's hand to be warm, the fingers rough. He was trembling visibly, from age or fear, Modo couldn't tell. He was a leader, Modo guessed, a shaman or a chief or something— he wondered if there had been anything written about this tribe. The old man was staring at him with that one eye. There was something familiar about his face. Then it came to him: this man was Nulu's grandfather.

"Moh-Doh," Nulu said, pointing at Modo. Then she pointed at the old man and spoke slowly. "Runyuji."

Modo gave a slight bow. "Hello, Run-You-Gee, I'm pleased to meet you." The man shuddered again, as though each new revelation was almost too much for him. His hand, though, gripped Modo's tightly.

Everyone, even the warriors, were now staring openly at him. He'd never had so many eyes on him at once. They didn't seem frightened; in fact he would have sworn that they actually *wanted* to look at him.

Without any warning, Modo began to weep.

CHAPTER 36

A Now Dream

Nulu didn't know that gods could shape tears. She stared up at the one who fell from the heavens and watched the tears trailing down his perfect face. She expected them to burst into flames as they fell to the ground and bring the ancestors to life. She wouldn't have been even slightly surprised to see her grandmother, mother, father, and all those who had gone to the spirit world, suddenly rise up from the earth. It was that kind of day.

"The one with the God Face must be happy," she said to her grandfather, the cleverest of all the men in their village.

"They are tears of joy," her grandfather announced to the tribe. "The God-Faced One cries with joy to see the Rain People."

The one called Moh-Doh wiped the tears from his face and mumbled something in his strange god language. It was very much like the language of the grey ones who had come to the forest a few weeks earlier, but they were always shouting. A long silence followed and Nulu wondered if this was a *now* dream or a *then* dream. Or could it be a *future* dream? No, it was *now*. It was really happening. She knew that because of his tears, the warmth of his hand when she had held it, and because, at this very moment, his stomach was rumbling.

"We must feed the God-Faced One!" she whispered.

Her grandfather gave orders to the Rain People as Nulu again took Moh-Doh's hand and led him down to a large log lying near the firepit. She patted it and sat down.

"Quickly, a feast, a feast!" her grandfather called.

What does a god eat? Nulu wondered.

A white cloth was wrapped around his left hand, soaked with blood. A god who weeps tears and could bleed?

When her grandfather joined them on the log, she pointed at Moh-Doh's hand. Then, following her grandfather's quick commands, she ran to his hut and returned with the healing leaves and a bowl. Her grandfather ground some of the leaves into a paste and removed the bandage. Nulu gasped when she saw he was missing his little finger. Moh-Doh winced as the paste was applied, but seemed thankful when they were finished. Nulu bound the hand carefully with the remaining leaves.

As they waited for the food, she marvelled at how this normal day had turned into a dream day. In the morning she had followed the hunting party, who were alarmed by the roaring and thundering in the skies. She was not supposed to leave the village, but she had done it before and, after all, she was the granddaughter of the wise one and her parents had died fighting the crocodile, so she could do things that other children couldn't, without fear of punishment.

One warrior had climbed a tree to discover there were giant birds battling in the heavens. Then a grey man with a white face had fallen to the earth, dead. The Rain People had encountered the grey men and their clinking dogs at the stone place and knew they were killers. They had already lost three warriors to their death sticks.

So when a second man fell through the trees and lived, they decided to pursue him and be certain he was dead. His face had been covered with a mask. Nulu had only caught a glimpse of him, then the chase was on, the calls driving him towards the hunting pit. But he survived the pit where all animals die. She heard the cries of confusion and fear from the warriors, had then seen Moh-Doh climb out of the pit with his face revealed.

The question was: why had the God Face come to them? Was this the end of time? Would everything change from this moment on? These questions were too big for her mind. She had no idea what any of it meant; that was for her grandfather and the other elders and the ancestors to figure out. No, she could only be humbled by the fact that she had actually seen the God Face after a lifetime of stories by the fire. He was real! The eyes looked warm, the smile kind, and it had seemed entirely natural for her to bring him here.

And now the one with the God Face was sitting among them eating the food they offered and nodding and speaking in a language she couldn't understand.

CHAPTER 37

Freshly Chewed Meat

Modo was enjoying a handful of berries from a woven palm-leaf basket. The basket was still wet, as though the berries had been soaked. They were both bitter and sweet, bursting on his tongue. Next the women brought cooked meat on a large wooden platter. The meat was pale in colour and tasted something like salted and smoked duck or chicken, he couldn't decide which. There was also fish.

The tribe didn't seem to want to boil him alive or slice him into ribbons. They had chased him through the forest, but they couldn't be blamed for that; after all he'd fallen out of the sky and invaded their land.

He had wept, of all things, with all those eyes on him. And aside from their initial hesitation, they didn't seem to be staring in revulsion. Quite the contrary. They seemed to adore him. He smiled and shook his head.

"This is all very lovely," he said. "Very, very lovely." He patted his stomach to signal his happiness and one of the pregnant women rubbed her own and giggled. Of course they didn't understand a word he said, but he hoped the tone of his voice conveyed his friendliness. They'd likely never seen a civilised man before.

The young girl, Nulu, was the one who fed him first and he instinctively trusted her. The remainder of the tribe were growing more comfortable and muttering among themselves, again pointing at him with their baby fingers.

He'd read so many accounts of savages and how ruthless they could be. The men had weapons, of course, but he saw that there were frail and vulnerable tribespeople too: a few old men, a toothless hag, small children. If they were savages, why hadn't they abandoned the old and crippled ones to the crocodiles?

"Please join me." He offered the food around. "Please."

Nulu was the first to take something off the platters, choosing a long piece of cooked, stringy flesh. She chewed it, then removed it from her mouth and handed it to an old woman who swallowed it. How revolting! Many of the other children were doing the same thing for other aged tribespeople. These elders were clearly toothless and wouldn't survive without the aid of their grandchildren's good teeth. Revolting, but kind, too.

He pictured doing the same thing for Mr Socrates when he got old, and chuckled. Several children giggled along with him.

Remembering his master reminded him that he had a mission to complete. He needed to finish eating and get on with the assignment.

Modo examined his wounded hand and was pleased to see that the stub of his little finger had stopped bleeding thanks to the leaves wrapped tightly around it. The pain had softened to a dull throbbing.

It would soon be dark; best to move along as far as he could before nightfall, much as part of him wanted to stay here forever. "I thank you for your food and hospitality, but I must go now."

They gawked at him as he brought out his compass and held it to see which direction was northwest. Thank goodness he'd memorised the map. They hadn't crossed the main river by air, so he would still be on the east side of it. If Mr Socrates was anywhere, he'd be heading towards the temple right now.

Unless he'd crashed and they were all dead or captured. If that was so, it would be impossible to say where they were. If Modo found the temple, at the very least he could later find the nearest port, for the map had shown its location clearly.

"Again, I thank you." Modo bowed towards the tribe, turned and walked away. They parted for him and he wondered if it would be that easy to leave.

Sure enough, as one, they rose and walked silently behind him in a long line. Modo stopped. This wouldn't do. He couldn't have them tramping through the forest behind him. But wait—was there a way to get them to take him to the temple? The warriors were armed and there were fifteen of them. They could find Miss Hakkandottir's camp, if she had one, and fall on the Guild soldiers and kill them.

And how many of these tribesmen would die? Just to rescue him?

He waved his hands and said, "You must stay. Go back."

No one moved. He went to the nearest one and pointed him in the opposite direction. Then he pointed another. Finally Nulu came up to him with a basket of food. She held it up to him and he stood there because he was already stuffed, feeling dumb as a post, until it dawned on him that she wanted him to take the food. He filled his pockets. Then, as one, the tribespeople turned away.

Modo trod through the forest. It wasn't until he'd walked for two hours that he was certain he'd left the tribe behind. With each step it felt as though he were walking away from a dream. That was all it could be. Though at first there'd been some fear, mostly those natives had looked at him with joy and without revulsion. How could they be real?

It began to rain. Soon he was a soggy mess, his tattered cloak a weight on his back. He took it off and squeezed it dry, then carried it under his arm. He crossed a small stream, watching for serpents or any sharp-toothed animals. He wished again that he'd been able to learn the flora and fauna, especially the creatures that would either eat him or poison him or both.

He'd stay away from toads. He didn't know if it was here or in Africa where there were poisonous toads whose touch alone would kill you. And then there were the alligators. Or was it crocodiles? One or the other lived here.

"Maybe you can ask them to introduce themselves when they bite your leg off," he whispered.

He munched on a few berries from his front vest pocket, followed it with some smoked meat. The sun set quite suddenly, as though someone had just blown out a candle. He couldn't see much beyond all the vines and leaves.

Modo worried he hadn't thought this through very well. For one thing, where would he sleep? On the forest floor? Up in a tree with the snakes and the monkeys? One of those huts he'd just left would be handy now.

He didn't dare light a fire for fear of alerting Hakkandottir to his presence, so he slept with his back up against a tree, legs pressed as close to his chest as possible for warmth. It was a horrible, fitful mockery of sleep, but when he awoke as the light appeared in the east, shining yellowish green through the leaves, he found a fur blanket had been laid over him and someone had placed a basket of berries at his feet without making a noise or leaving a footprint. He whispered his thanks and ate his breakfast. Then he got up, stretched his aching muscles and began to follow his compass.

CHAPTER 38

Cutting a Path

The first night in the rain forest had dampened Octavia's enthusiasm for being alive. It had been a grand adventure while they were in the air, but on the ground among the hooting animals, chirruping insects and the wet chill, she loathed it. Rats she could take; London had millions of them. But scaly things that slithered, creatures that made odd growling sounds, others climbing in the trees; bats the size of owls, and a pestilence of insects biting and crawling on her skin—it was all a little much for a girl from Seven Dials.

A night of no sleep had been followed by a cold breakfast of canned meat and water. Then Mr Socrates barked commands like an infantry general and they packed up camp and marched on, tracing the path indicated by the map in his hand.

"Miss Hakkandottir will expect us to make a beeline for the nearest port," Mr Socrates explained. "I'm guessing that she's now got her soldiers patrolling the paths leading to Port Douglas and Cooktown. She may even have created allegiances with whatever natives inhabit this area. So, we will circle westward and approach the temple from that direction. Nothing like the element of surprise."

"I don't mean to be impertinent, sir," Octavia said as she stomped on one of the millions of ferns carpeting the forest floor, "but how can we be certain that the artifact is actually still in the temple?"

"We can't. The only way to be certain is to enter the temple ourselves. My guess, and I admit this is only a guess, is that Miss Hakkandottir is still here because she wanted to revel in my obliteration or she's still attempting to steal the relic. After all, we don't know for certain what it was that drove Alexander King mad. Perhaps whatever it is, is proving to be a bulwark against her."

It was now clear to Octavia that it was the jungle that drove the explorer mad. She followed Tharpa as he swung the machete, cutting a path through the hanging vines. *We'll have to hack our way back to London!* Octavia thought as she struggled under the weight of her haversack—it was stuffed to the top with smoked meat, biscuits, ammunition and any other useful supplies they had retrieved from the *Prince Albert*'s wreckage. Mr Socrates held his elephant gun as if he were waiting for a charge, and Lizzie brought up the rear.

After three bug-bitten hours they stopped for lunch, sitting on a fallen tree trunk and munching hard biscuits with marmalade. Tharpa sharpened the machete between bites and Mr Socrates made notes in his journal.

Lizzie sat staring into the forest. Octavia drank water from a tin cup and studied Lizzie's tattoos. In the jungle light they made the woman look less civilised.

"Lizzie, do you know this area very well?" Octavia asked her.

"Been here once or twice," she grunted.

"Ah, and you lived to tell the tale, that's a good sign," Octavia quipped, but Lizzie didn't smile. She was on par with Tharpa for humourlessness. "You're of native blood—is your tribe from here?"

"No. This is the land of the Rain People."

"And what are they like?"

"They live. They hunt. What more do you need to know?"

Octavia shrugged. It was like conversing with a python. "Well, where are your people?"

"In my heart," Lizzie said with a hint of bitterness.

Octavia nodded and fell silent.

A few minutes later they were back on their feet. Mr Socrates marched ahead confidently, but Octavia had lost all sense of direction. With all these leaves it was impossible to tell whether the sun was in the east or west! She'd never understood the use of a compass; it was the streets, their curves or straight lines and landmarks, that made sense to her.

According to Mr Socrates, humanity had risen out of a jungle just like this one. As she slapped at a mosquito, she found it very hard to believe. Humans built cities and ships to get away from these uncivilised places. It was insanity for any English citizen to return willingly to the jungle.

She trudged over the moist earth, catching her foot on a thick vine and biting back a curse. Lizzie was walking along like it was Hyde Park, for pity's sake. *You should try to be half as graceful as her,* Octavia told herself. A lock of hair slipped in front of her eyes; humidity made her hair unruly with curls. She shoved the lock back under her sun helmet and looked over at Lizzie, envious of her cropped hair. At least they both had trousers on. Octavia didn't even want to imagine what it would be like trouncing through this green hell wearing a dress.

Her thoughts turned to Modo, as they had a thousand times already that day. He might be dead. She'd been trying to keep her spirits up by dreaming of other more cheery scenarios in which he had hit his head and lay unconscious somewhere, or had landed on two feet and was right now doing jumping jacks to keep warm. All the scenarios ended with the emotional reunion of the two of them.

He may have lived. He was much stronger than any man she'd known, and he could, as her old gang would have said, "take a beatin.'" But the fall was from such a great height that his body would have been shattered. She pictured him lying on the forest floor, his body splayed out, his mask lying several feet from him. His face is turned towards her. Of course, it's featureless. Even in her imagination she can't put a face to him.

What does he look like? In death he could still be a stranger to her; would always be a stranger to her.

And now she would give anything to see him again, with or without a mask. Even if he was the ugliest man on earth, she wanted to look into his face again.

CHAPTER 39

A Swollen River

Throughout the day, Modo watched and listened carefully, but the tribe no longer seemed to be following him. He felt relief and fear; if they weren't watching over him, then he was very much on his own. With each step he wondered if his encounter with the natives had gone exactly as he remembered it. He'd lost blood and was still a little woozy from his fall. Could the whole thing have been a dream? His pocket full of berries told him otherwise.

The deep thundering of a steam-powered engine could be heard in the sky. He scrambled to the topmost branch of a pine tree, so high that the tree began to wave back and forth, hoping to see the *Prince Albert*. To his dismay, he spotted the *Prometheus*. The airship had been repaired and was travelling northwest. Perhaps they were searching for him. He ducked behind the branches. Well, if they were going back to their base, he'd been heading in the right direction.

He climbed back down to the forest floor and followed his compass. After another hour of trudging he came to the river that he was sure had been on the map. The map had led Modo to believe it would be a relatively minor river, but instead it was a deep body of green water that cut through the bottom of a gorge. Using vines as handholds, he carefully climbed down the gorge wall and stood on a large flat rock, staring at the surface of the river. He wondered what demonic jungle creatures lurked below. A school of piranhas, which would consume a man one razor-sharp bite at a time? Water snakes that swallowed their prey whole? Several gigantic smooth rocks jutted across the river, looking as though they'd been tossed there by some capricious god. They were so far apart, it would be impossible to hop from one to the other, and he wasn't going to risk swimming across. At the very least it was heartening to find the river, for it meant he was closing in on his destination.

Along the bank, he hopped from stone to stone, searching for a way to cross and keeping his eyes open for predators. The gorge provided a break from the overhanging forest so there was a lot more sunlight here, so much so that he had to squint at times.

He began to give up hope of finding an easy way to cross and once again contemplated swimming the river. He eyed a few of the fish he could see in the clear water, small, backs speckled black and white. Piranha? Or perch? Once again he admonished himself for not memorising some of the naturalist illustrations he'd seen as a child. His education was lacking!

He finally found one lone tree at a bend in the river that had grown in an arc towards a tree on the opposite shore. Something moved in its foliage and, as he approached, an animal that looked half-kangaroo and half-monkey hopped and climbed through the branches, using its long tail to steady itself. It swung from the tree to the one on the opposite side, making the feat look relatively easy. Moments later it had jumped to another tree and vanished in the forest.

Modo inspected the unusual tree. Its bark was grey, its narrow roots well exposed above ground, buttressing the tree. He shimmied up the trunk to the closest leafy branch, beginning to feel the exhilaration he'd always felt when climbing, but kept a wary eye out for snakes. When he was near the top, the tree started to bend. In his excitement about finally crossing the river he'd forgotten he was a lot heavier than the monkey creature. Nervously, he inched farther along the branch. The tree on the opposite bank didn't look so close now, but he was pretty certain he could still make the leap.

And so he grabbed a branch above him and swung back and forth, building momentum. Just as he was about to let go, it broke! By pure luck he hit the branch below with both feet and pushed off of it, launching himself over the water and catching a branch on the opposite tree. It snapped and he fell, crashing through several branches, latching onto one only a few feet above the water.

It promptly snapped and he dropped into the water with a great splash, falling so hard and deep that his buttocks hit the rocks on the bottom. Piranha! Snakes! He shot up in a wild panic, only to find he was standing in waist-deep water. He charged the short distance to the riverbank, gasping and panting in relief that nothing had bitten him.

Laughter could be heard in the trees on the other side of the river and Modo wondered whether it was a human or a kookaburra bird. They were known for a bird cry that sounded like human laughter.

Modo straightened himself, squeezed the excess water from his cloak, and climbed up the gorge and back into the rain forest. According to the map, the temple wasn't far from the river, but it wouldn't be easy to spot; after a thousand years or more of growth, the forest would have claimed it back. That said, if Miss Hakkandottir were already there, then he would hear them before he saw them.

As if on cue there was a metallic clanging in the distance. Modo shook his head. Such a coincidence had to have been his imagination getting the better of him. He listened intently. Nothing. He pushed his way through the vines until—*clang! clang!* There it was again. It wasn't a noise animals would make and so far as he knew the natives didn't have metal. He moved toward the sound, working his way up an incline. The map had indicated that the temple was part of a small mountain, looking down on the surrounding forest.

He came to a clearing and there it was, at the far end of a great plateau, jutting out of a small mountainside.

The temple.

CHAPTER 40

The Temple

Octavia was awakened by a tickling sensation on her leg. Still in a dreamy fog she wondered if it was Modo, then thought: he'd never tickle her leg. He wasn't brave enough.

She opened her eyes, lifted her head from her rolled-up blanket, and caught her breath. A spider the size of her fist was crawling up her leg, the hairs on its dark body white in the moonlight. She held still, out of wisdom, not fear. *You've seen worse things in London sewers!* she told herself. The problem was, she didn't quite know what to do; she wanted to swat it away but couldn't remember what Mr Socrates had said about spiders. Would hitting it make it sting her? They bit, that much she remembered. Best to just lie still and hope it would go away. It reached her thigh and rambled, almost drunkenly, towards her midsection. Would the thing leap at her face? She held her breath.

Then a hand appeared out of the darkness and lay, palm up, on her stomach. "Don't move," Lizzie whispered. The spider crawled onto her fingers and up her arm. "This one ain't poisonous," she said, guiding it onto a palm-tree frond. The spider crawled away.

"Thank you," Octavia said. "Just so you know, I wasn't frightened."

Lizzie smiled. "No, you weren't. For a London Town girl, you're doing well enough." She extended her hand and helped Octavia to her feet. "Pack up. Mr Socrates has already given orders to move out."

And before she was really awake, Octavia found herself marching along in line. She wolfed down a few biscuits on the go.

"No speaking above a whisper now," Mr Socrates instructed. "We're likely in the area of the temple now and we'll no doubt be running into patrols."

Since it would be too loud to hack a comfortable path, they were forced to follow the natural trails of the jungle, sometimes having to crouch and crawl through the overgrown vines and leaves. Octavia promised herself that when they got back to Sydney she'd give Mrs Finchley a big hug for making the trousers. And she'd buy her a glass of wine, too. No! A whole bottle.

As they crossed a narrow, rocky stream, Octavia slipped on one of the stones and caught herself before she went head first into the water. She was getting exhausted and Mr Socrates showed no sign of wanting a break. The old man was a slavedriver! But she had to admit he was a lot tougher than she'd imagined he'd be.

On the other side of the stream she spotted a human footprint in the mud. "Psst!" she said to the others, and pointed at it.

"The Rain People," Lizzie whispered. "Three days old."

"You can tell just by looking?"

Lizzie smiled for the first time that day. "No. But if I say it with enough confidence, you sterling believe it."

Octavia had to stop herself from laughing. "What do you mean by sterling?"

"In Australia, we call ourselves by currency, so you English are sterling. Understand?"

"But I'm only a few farthings," Octavia quipped.

Mr Socrates shot them both a perturbed glance, so they climbed on quietly.

The path gradually became steeper. Here and there stones jutted out of the earth. Octavia had never sweated so much or been bitten by so many insects. She itched. She was tired. And she wished she hadn't thrown the teapot out of the *Prince Albert*. She couldn't even take comfort in a cup of tea.

Tharpa had scouted ahead and now returned, quiet as a cat. His eyes were bright with excitement. He led them up to a rocky ledge and pushed aside the vines and fronds. Octavia was surprised to discover that they'd actually climbed quite high. They were looking down at a plateau where there was still evidence of the foundations of an ancient city! Beyond these ruins the sun shone bright on the face of a small mountain. Grey-clad soldiers were working in the distance, busy as ants, carrying supplies up a set of stone stairs that led past something that looked like a great stone lion.

"So the temple exists!" Mr Socrates whispered. "Marvellous! And judging by the colour on the Sphinx, the Egyptians actually carried limestone all the way here. I presume it's from the coast. They were amazingly industrious!"

"Uh, sir," Octavia said, "you do see all the soldiers over there, don't you?"

Mr Socrates shrugged. "A minor nuisance."

She couldn't tell if he'd gone mad or was just playing her.

Even from this distance Octavia could see that the sides of the doorway into the temple were ragged, as if it had been blown apart. Many of the trees around the temple had been chopped down and there were a few dozen Guild soldiers right below them, their white tents bright against the dark green. All were armed. The *Prometheus* was docked on a large flat rock, tied down with ropes.

Several soldiers patrolled the perimeter of the grounds, large hounds at their sides. Octavia had encountered the four-legged monsters before—part metal, part flesh. She didn't want to get near them again.

"Looks like they've been camped here for weeks," Mr Socrates said. "Enough time to get well set up."

"And to die." Tharpa was pointing at a small graveyard located this side of the settlement. No crosses, but each mound was marked with large black stones.

Mr Socrates pondered. "Sickness, perhaps. Or conflict with the natives."

"The Rain People are peaceful," Lizzie explained.

"Yes, perhaps, but the Guild are not. Sometimes these conflicts occur despite our better natures," Mr Socrates replied.

Octavia spotted the red hair of Miss Hakkandottir, who was walking alongside a row of crumbled stone buildings overgrown with vines and small trees.

"Miss Hakkandottir is right there," Octavia said, pointing her out to Mr Socrates. "With one shot from your elephant gun we could end this now."

"Yes and then, within a few short minutes, we would be swarmed and killed," he said. "Besides, the gun is only effective at close range."

Octavia watched Miss Hakkandottir helplessly as she strode through the camp. The soldiers' attention seemed to be drawn to her. She signalled to one and he immediately began to do her bidding. *That's what power is,* Octavia thought. *Powerful people attract followers; they're decisive.*

"We'll have to travel farther around the site," Mr Socrates said. "We don't want to take them head-on."

"When will we enter the temple?" Lizzie asked.

"Tonight," he answered. "When it's dark we'll sneak in."

"You'll have to be a lot more quiet," a voice said from above.

Octavia whipped her stiletto from its sheath. Mr Socrates aimed his elephant gun towards the voice and cocked the hammers on both barrels.

"You should know I have you in my sights," he said. "Now, who said that?"

The leaves rustled and a figure lowered himself, then swung from the tree to the ground in front of them. The familiar stocky shape, the crooked back, the wild African mask.

"Modo!" Octavia exclaimed, dropping her knife and running to throw her arms around him.

But she was stopped in her tracks when three muscular men dropped out of the trees behind Modo, weapons at the ready.

CHAPTER 41

Scope of Duties

Pure joy filled Modo's heart as he lowered himself down and swung to the ground in front of the group. Yes, Mr Socrates still had his gun pointed at him, Lizzie had raised her machete, and Octavia was holding her stiletto, but it was the look on Tharpa's face that Modo loved the most. He'd surprised his teacher! He'd snuck through the trees above them without even the slightest creak of a branch or rustle of a leaf. Tharpa's smile grew ear to ear, and Modo believed he even looked proud. Mr Socrates shook his head; was that pride on his master's face, too?

It was all so perfect!

Octavia ran towards him and he prepared to catch her in his arms, but just before she reached him he heard a rustling above him and behind him, the soft thud of feet landing. He turned to see three of the Rain People, their spears out and aimed at his companions. The warriors had followed him the whole way without his knowledge!

Tharpa lifted his machete as Mr Socrates raised his elephant gun. The warriors prepared to launch their spears.

"No!" Modo shouted, standing between the two parties. Then he remembered their situation and whispered, "No! They're with me." He pointed at the spears, gestured to throw them down, but no one understood him or perhaps they weren't willing. Modo claimed a spear from one warrior and tossed it to the ground. The other two followed his example.

"They're friends," he said, pointing towards Mr Socrates. He clasped both hands together as though shaking hands with himself, trying to get the message across. "Good friends."

One of the warriors mimicked his hand gesture, so Modo hoped that meant they understood.

"You little devil!" Mr Socrates grabbed Modo by the shoulder.

For a moment he thought his master was going to hug him, but Mr Socrates slapped Modo's back.

"You're alive!" he whispered. "How is that even possible?"

"I have the rain forest to thank for that," Modo whispered. "And my training, of course."

"But where were you?" Octavia seemed to have got her nerve up again and she gave him a brief hug, then backed away quickly.

Modo was breathless. She had hugged him in front of everyone! It was so wonderful to see her face again.

"What happened?" she asked. "Tell us, you scoundrel. Tell us now!"

He took a deep breath and told them. When it came to the point in the story where he climbed out of the pit, he hesitated. Should he mention that he thought the tribe was worshipping him? Would Mr Socrates think he'd grown vain? But he could only give them his interpretation of the facts. It was what he had been trained to do.

"It has to do with my face, sir," he said to Mr Socrates, and then looked at Lizzie briefly.

"Your secret's safe with Lizzie," he said. "I've known her for over twenty years. She's rock solid. Carry on."

And my secret is safe with Tavia, he thought. Otherwise Mr Socrates would have had him debrief in private. All his secrets were safe with her.

He explained the events with the tribe with as much detail as possible. The presence of the tall warriors standing silently behind him added credence to the tale.

"Stunning!" Mr Socrates said.

The shocked tone of his voice made Modo proud of how he'd handled himself.

"How many of them were there?" Mr Socrates' measuring eyes were on the tribesmen.

"Fifteen warriors, sir, maybe forty tribespeople in total," Modo replied. "There may be other clans. This was the only one I saw."

"Can you command them?"

Modo hesitated. "Command them?"

"Do they listen to your orders? They dropped their spears for you. Can you communicate effectively with them?"

"Yes, to some extent." Though now that he thought of it, the girl, Nulu, had helped to interpret much of what he'd said. The other natives had seemed too much in awe of him to comprehend what he wanted.

"Perfect! With fifteen warriors on our side we could, in the dark of night, sweep down and fight our way into the temple, if necessary. These Rain People look to be fine physical specimens and certainly have tremendous knowledge of the forest. They'd be a great asset in our cause."

"Our cause?" Modo echoed.

"You said they worshipped you."

"Worship? No, I misspoke. They were affected by my appearance, that's all."

"A small distinction, Modo. This is one of those odd intersections of life. They probably worship an idol or a spirit god with a face they see as being similar to yours. We must take advantage of this."

"But back on the ship you said we shouldn't interfere with these tribes; they were children." Modo reminded him. "'As a society our role is to lead them gently towards advancement.' Those were your words."

"Thank you for quoting my own words back to me." Mr Socrates narrowed his eyes. He spoke deliberately and coldly. "All right then, you listen well, Modo. But listen to this: in optimum conditions we should proceed with a policy of non-interference. But at the moment we're in a desperate situation." He gestured towards the temple with the elephant gun. "The Clockwork Guild is right there in front of us. Perhaps even as we discuss these niceties, they are uncovering a weapon that could turn the tide of any battle. Do you want the Guild to own that weapon?"

"N-No." Modo cursed his stutter. Mr Socrates seemed to be the best at bringing it out.

"Then command these warriors to become our allies."

"They're not mine to command." Even as he spoke he knew there'd be terrible consequences. But Modo had managed to stop his voice from wavering, and even straightened his back.

"Are you refusing me?" Mr Socrates asked so quietly that Modo barely heard him.

"No. Never."

"Then you will have these natives return to their tribe and bring the rest of their warriors here?"

Modo tried to swallow, but his mouth was dry. He imagined the men being cut down by rifles, the tribe having no one left to protect them. All this just to retrieve some ancient trinket.

"With the greatest respect, I cannot do that, sir."

Out of the corner of his eye he saw Octavia stiffen, preparing for a blast. Tharpa's face was unreadable. Mr Socrates gave Modo a look of such fury that his eyes seemed to glow.

"No?" His whisper was hoarse. "It was an order, Modo."

"I cannot obey, sir. I don't believe following that particular command is within the scope of my duties."

"Your duty is to me and to me alone," Mr Socrates shouted so loudly that everyone seemed to cower a little, and exchange concerned looks. The natives picked up their spears again and began whispering to one another.

"I know that, sir. I'll do anything you command with my own person. I would die if you so require."

"Modo," Octavia said.

"You stay out of this," Mr Socrates commanded without turning his eyes away from Modo. "So, you are disobeying a direct order?"

"If you see it as such."

"I do see it as such."

Modo couldn't bear seeing the disappointment in his master's eyes. Mr Socrates had always been so calm and logical, but now the livid look on his face made him appear maniacal. Only a few short days ago Modo had been calling him Father. Only minutes ago Mr Socrates had celebrated Modo's return. Why did it have to come to this?

"I cannot go against my conscience, sir."

"If this were the infantry I'd have you tied to a cannon wheel and flogged." Mr Socrates' hands were gripping the elephant gun so tightly that Modo wondered if he were itching to shoot him. "But we need you to complete this assignment. I'll tell you now that when we are back in England you'll no longer be allowed to be an agent in the field. You'll return to Ravenscroft for retraining and reeducation regarding your duties."

"I will accept any punishment you deem fit, sir."

"Yes. You will. Now send your minions away. The rest of you, follow me up this ridge." Mr Socrates trudged past Modo, whose eyes were downcast.

Modo didn't dare look anyone in the eye, especially Octavia.

After his companions had disappeared into the foliage, Modo turned to the warriors. They were brave and they'd proven they could be fierce. Was he wrong? If they died willingly, wasn't it their choice?

But who'd look after Nulu? Who'd feed the children who in turn chewed the food for the elderly? No. It wasn't right. He took the nearest warrior by the shoulder and pointed him back towards their village. "Go! Go, home. This is not your place."

They stood there and stared at him, their faces solemn. Then finally Modo pointed again, this time with his remaining little finger, and the warriors, still facing him, nodded, backed quietly away and became shadows.

CHAPTER 42

A Visage Revealed

It began to rain gently as Modo followed Mr Socrates and the rest of the group up a ridge and through the thick growth of ferns and trees. He felt heavier, was heavier, actually—his clothes weren't drying since he'd fallen into the river. His master had been completely silent for the last twenty minutes.

Modo exchanged glances with Octavia, but her face was hard to read. Was she upset with him? After all, without the help of the natives, their lives were more at risk. Had he betrayed his friends as well as his master?

Mr Socrates stopped dead and gave several hand signals, instructing them to set up camp. Using a section of the balloon fabric they'd salvaged, they built a shelter. They shared a tin of meat and Modo produced the remainder of his berries. He longed for one of the Rain People's baskets full of food.

"We'll enter the temple at 4 a.m.," Mr Socrates said. "At that hour, there'll likely be the least number of guards on duty. I'll give you each a specific assignment just before we begin our mission. Until then, I suggest those of you who aren't on watch should sleep." He pointed at Modo. "You'll take first watch. Go to the north end of that path. Don't fall asleep; that's an order. Tharpa, you take the south."

Modo nodded, but before he'd taken two steps, Tharpa grabbed his shoulder. "You are wounded."

"Yes." Modo lifted his left hand. "Miss Hakkandottir cut off my little finger." He said it loud enough for Mr Socrates to hear, but his master didn't look up.

Tharpa took Modo's hand and examined the leafy bandage. "The natives bound your wound, I see. They did it well, better than my own work. Is it painful?"

Modo shook his head.

"Good. Go to your station and keep your eyes and your wits about you, young Sahib."

"I will."

Modo walked about twenty yards away from their camp. He thought of climbing a tree, but the leaves would block his sightlines back to the camp. He found a place on the path where the foliage wasn't too thick and he could actually see stars and a part of the moon. He stood in the shadow of a tree, his only movement an occasional blink. He listened. For all he knew the whole tribe of Rain People might be sitting above him.

He'd disappointed Mr Socrates, and Modo felt shame right down to his very marrow. He'd never directly disobeyed his master before. Yes, months ago he'd taken it upon himself to charge after that giant monstrosity that had attacked the Parliament buildings, but that was in the heat of battle. This had been a calculated decision to not follow an order. He couldn't picture the Rain People dying for whatever lay inside that temple. It was a British concern, probably some bauble that would end up in the British Museum. What did the natives know of a treasure in an ancient temple, left there by Egyptians who had vanished thousands of years ago?

And Mr Socrates didn't know the tribe; he hadn't met Nulu or seen the pregnant women, the children and the elderly. Nor had he shared food with them. If he had, then perhaps he would have understood what he'd been asking Modo to do.

He would somehow have to explain all of this much better to Mr Socrates.

The rain stopped. The stars were brighter here, not faded by gaslight as the stars above London were. They'd been shining down on this jungle for millenniums. And here they were, a little ragtag group about to go to war over some ancient artifact. People would die, the struggle would end, bones would turn to dust and the stars would still shine. It was insanity—the same insanity that had put Alexander King in Bedlam.

Modo remembered the words of King: "You should never touch a god." What did that mean? And what about the fragments of rhyme he'd blathered? They—

His thoughts were interrupted by the soft tread of feet behind him. He'd been taught how to guess the weight and size of a person just by their sound. Without turning, he whispered, "It's not your watch yet, Octavia."

"You are a clever boy, aren't you?" she replied.

She stood next to him. He could see her clearly in the moonlight; her hair was bedraggled, her clothes muddy and wrinkled. He'd seen her shine like a jewel in her finest dress, but he'd choose to remember her this way over any other memory. The moonlight made her pale skin even paler and more perfect, with the exception, perhaps, of the few welts from mosquito bites.

"Come out of the light," he whispered. "The enemy could spot you."

She did, stepping closer to him.

"This is a good vantage point," he explained. "The way is clear in all directions."

"Yes, I see."

"You can't sleep?" he asked.

"Who can sleep? I'm soaking wet. Every insect on this forsaken countryside has taken a chunk of my flesh. And later tonight we will likely die trying to steal an imaginary treasure from under the nose of a woman who probably sleeps lying on the skulls of babies."

"You never could give a short answer," he said, grinning.

"Yes, well, not everyone can be as overly short in words as they are in height."

He had to admit he enjoyed her teasing.

"I'm proud of you," she added.

"Proud?"

"Yes, you faced down Mr Socrates."

"Ended my employment as an agent, you mean."

"Ah, this isn't employment, it's a grand lark, Modo. You are too valuable for our mutual master to throw under the wagon. Besides, he was wrong."

"Wrong?" Modo shifted his position, leaning against the tree.

"Yes. Those rainy people, whatever they're called, aren't servants of the Queen."

"We are in Queensland, so they are, technically, her minions."

"On a piece of paper in London, yes. Here they wouldn't even know there was such a bumblebee as Queen Victoria."

"You shouldn't speak of Her Majesty that way." He tried to sound incensed, but he couldn't suppress a chuckle.

"Sorry, I meant busybody, not bumblebee. Where are my manners? And, about Mr Socrates, you know you agree with me in your gut at least, even if your mind hasn't caught up yet." She paused. "I have missed our reparting."

"I believe the word you want is *repartee*," he said.

"A French word? You do like the French, don't you?" She let out a derisive sniff. "Just rest assured that I'm proud of you. I do have a question, though. Did the natives really react that way to seeing your face?"

"Yes."

"But which face was it? Either of the ones you have shown me?"

"No. It was the face I was born with." *The abomination,* he wanted to add. And yet, even as he thought that bitter thought, for the first time he wanted to correct himself on that count. The Rain People had looked at him with adoration. Even Mrs Finchley couldn't summon much more than caring pity when she gazed upon his twisted face.

"Well then, it must be something to see," she said.

"It's what evolution decreed would be mine." He pointed towards the mask. "This face."

"If you believe in such stuff."

"Science is not belief. It's science. Truth."

"The truth is in the believing."

Now what was she on about? Under the circumstances he wasn't up to arguing the difference between science and belief. Not tonight. He cleared his throat. "Once, not too long ago, I offered to show my face to you. You refused."

"I was jealous. You'd showed it to that coquette agent from France. And you'd kissed her."

"Not on purpose."

"Which wasn't on purpose? Showing her your face or kissing her?"

"Kissing her."

"Still, it was a rather traitorous action."

"Showing her my face?" Modo scratched his head, honestly confused by the conversation.

"No, kissing her. The Queen wouldn't be proud. Alarmed, I would think. A crime punishable by the gallows."

"I don't understand your point, Tavia."

"It's this, Modo." Her voice had begun to waver. "I'd like to see your face. I swore I would never ask again, but here I am, asking."

Should he show her? It seemed a hundred years had

passed since they had finished their first assignment, and shortly after that, she'd asked to see his real face. In actual fact it had only been nine months. He was so much younger then, he thought.

She was watching him, smiling, almost as though this were all a joke. But he knew her well enough now. That humour, that sarcasm, was what she held up as a shield against the world.

"It isn't much," he whispered. Then he undid his mask and lowered it, grateful that the darkness would soften his disfigurements. *Coward,* he thought, and he moved slowly into the moonlight. He closed his eyes, not wanting to see her reaction.

He knew exactly what she was seeing; he'd memorised his face—the jutting jaw, the flattened crooked nose—and on his head the reddish clumps of hair, really more like moss. He could point out every imperfection; how one eye was slightly larger; how one particular mole drew a person to look at his twisted lips and crooked teeth.

"Modo," she said softly, and he opened his eyes again.

She smiled an alabaster smile that he expected to shatter at any moment. Her lips became a straight line, but she didn't grimace nor did she turn her eyes away.

"It's not so bad, Modo," she whispered. She drew in a deep breath as if she were about to dive into a deep pool. "It's not the worst face I've seen."

"You've seen worse?"

"Truthfully," and she let out a little chuckle, "no. But your eyes do shine without the mask."

What did that mean?

"Would you like me to cover it up?" he asked. Did it sound like he was begging? He so wanted to slap the mask back into place.

"No. I ... I feel as though I'm meeting you for the first time." She reached out and he flinched. Her fingers floated close to his cheek, but then she put her hand on his shoulder. "There are worse things in life, Modo."

"I don't need pity. Or consolation, either."

"Yes. I understand. I do understand."

Then he saw something move over her shoulder. Lizzie was several feet away, frozen, staring at his face. Hard, tough Lizzie, who never seemed phased by anything, looked truly shocked. She backed away into the shadows.

Modo slipped the mask back on. "It's not a face for the world to see. When you return to camp could you please tell Lizzie that it's her watch."

"Yes, Modo." Octavia took a couple of steps, then stopped and turned back. "Thank you," she said. "I mean it. Thank you."

Then she returned to their camp.

CHAPTER 43

The Thrum Inside Her Mind

Miss Hakkandottir stood near the burning torches at the doorway to the temple. She opened and closed her metal hand, watching her fingers very closely. They were definitely moving more slowly. The little finger at times actually became stuck in position and she would have to unlock it with her other hand. It was the humidity in this horrid rain forest! The constant dampness was reaching into her metallic joints. She should have brought Dr Hyde with her. He had created this appendage and knew the intricate mechanisms that made it work. This was the first time in years that she had had any difficulty with it. Well, Visser, with his little keys and clockwork knowledge, could fix it temporarily at least.

She gazed into the darkness of the temple. Each hour that passed without discovering the God Face grew more frustrating. The Guild Master had expected her to land at Etna with their prize weeks ago. Whenever the *Prometheus* returned from their ship with supplies there were new telegrams asking about progress. Progress! Progress! It was impossible in this backwards, overgrown hellhole.

She had sent three soldiers into the temple in the last three days. One had been driven so insane that he climbed as high as he could up the cliff face and threw himself, screaming, to his death. The second had fled into the forest and they'd found his body hours later, a spear in his back. The third was in the medical tent tied to a cot and singing lullabies. Lullabies! There was no point in sending another soldier inside; they had weak minds. The tincture that kept them obedient affected their brains in too many ways.

And where had Mr Socrates gone? To the port. Now that she thought about it, she couldn't conceive of his giving up. But she had lost sight of the enemy airship during the battle with Modo. She didn't think he could have limped his pitiful airship back to port. He would have had to set down—but the rain forest hid its secrets far too well.

She stared through the rectangular doorway into the dark passage that led inside the mountain. It taunted her now, had done so for weeks. Somewhere, beyond whatever traps the Egyptians had left, was the God Face. She believed she could hear a low thrum coming out of the darkness, a sign of whatever power lay hidden in the tomb. Or was it her imagination? Was she also becoming unhinged?

Not likely. She was stronger than that.

"Visser," she shouted. "Visser!"

A moment later he bounded up the stone steps. The man never slept. He was such a small fellow, his spidery fingers always drumming on his sides. His eyes and bird-like movements reminded her of the falcons he carried around. Rows of keys jangled along his belt.

"Yes, Miss Hakkandottir," he said.

"Please, make my hand perform properly. Tomorrow morning we shall make the appropriate preparations and I will enter the temple."

He was silent for a few moments. "If you don't emerge, or return incapacitated, do you have orders?"

"You won't need orders," she said, "for you and your lovely falcons will be accompanying me." She was pleased to see him shiver a little. So, the cold-blooded killer wasn't so fearless. "We will emerge sane and healthy," she promised as she held up her hand. "Now make these fingers work."

CHAPTER 44

Married to Adventure

Octavia returned to her bed—a spot on a buffalo blanket under the shelter next to Lizzie. She sat down, trembling. It had taken all of her willpower to not turn away from Modo's face; to not let out a little cry of surprise or revulsion, and, this was the most important part, to not cover her eyes. In the past several months she'd pictured his possible face ten thousand times, but had not anticipated what he'd revealed moments earlier—a face well beyond her imagining.

If not for their friendship she couldn't have held herself together. The look in his eyes—not begging, but fearful that she would turn away—kept her strong. She steeled herself and she looked back at him. How could he have grown up with such deformities? To see it in the mirror every day? But he could bear it. So should she.

In some corner of her mind she had believed he'd only been imagining the extent of his own ugliness; that it would prove to be some small bump, or birthmark, or perhaps crooked teeth. If that were the case, he would still have one of the several handsome faces she'd seen so often. But this was more than any singular deformity, and there was nothing familiar about his appearance except his eyes. He'd needed her to look at him, and so she had.

She had wanted to go a step further, to touch his face and soothe the pain he so obviously felt. She had lifted her hand to do so and instead had squeezed his shoulder. Like a chum! Like he had just scored in cricket! She had given in to the fear that touching his face would undo all of her strength.

Octavia had already forgotten what she'd said to him, but she hoped that she had at least consoled him. A great pity welled in her heart, though Modo had made it clear he didn't desire pity.

"You must sleep," Lizzie whispered.

Octavia stiffened. Lizzie was now sitting up and looking at her.

"No, not yet," Octavia said. She closed her eyes and Modo's face was still there, burned inside her eyelids.

"He is not a handsome man." The words were said without sarcasm or pity—just a statement of fact.

"You saw him?"

"Yes. I heard whispers and investigated. It was private. I apologise for interrupting."

That was the greatest number of words Octavia had ever heard her string together.

"I—" Octavia couldn't find any words. "It's all right. But I—Do you ever—? Were you ever married?" The question came out of nowhere to Octavia's great embarrassment.

Lizzie laughed quietly. "A half-breed such as me? No."

"But surely you have dreamed about it."

"No. This is all I dreamed about."

"This? This what?"

She gestured. "A life of adventure. Of travel. In the sky. That's my marriage."

Octavia nodded. It was the most logical thing she'd heard in days. "I understand, Lizzie." She paused. "I guess I should sleep now."

"Yes. You will need your strength," Lizzie said. "I will relieve Modo."

Octavia closed her eyes, but listened until she heard Modo's soft footsteps. He lay down a few feet away, mask on. She watched him through half-closed eyelids.

Sleep well, my friend, she thought to herself, knowing full well he would not.

CHAPTER 45

The Horus Stone

Modo slept fitfully, curled into a hunched ball. He sweated so much that he felt naked, which wasn't a wonderful sensation in a rain forest. At one point he was asleep long enough to dream he was imprisoned in Bedlam, except the room was overgrown with vines. Every few minutes or so, he would wake up and look at his pocket watch, reading it by the moonlight: 2:00 a.m. ... 2:15 ... 3:00 ...

At 3:25 he decided to stay awake, lying still. In thirty-five minutes they'd be climbing down the ridge and sneaking past the metal-jawed hounds, the mechanical birds and the Guild soldiers. Or at least, that was the plan. Their chances, he knew, were slim, and he wondered if this was what all soldiers felt like the day before an attack.

The vision of Alexander King's room had been so clear. Even now he could picture it as though his mind were a copper plate and the memory had been etched there. And then, just as clearly, he could recall his interview with King, the way the man had gouged and bloodied his own face, the crazed look in his eyes. Something in the temple had caused that mania. Something so powerful that it seemed to be holding Miss Hakkandottir back.

What had King said to him in that odd doggerel?

"The mountain keen, the forest green, the God Face burns inside ..."

Modo could still recall with great clarity the dementedness in the man's eyes. It was as though he were here with him in this rain forest.

"The west at your spine, the face divine."

Modo thought about this. If the west was at his back then he would be facing away from the entrance to the temple. So how did King enter? Walking backwards?

"Through the doorway go, beneath the Horus stone. The face it waits, it waits, it waits!"

Modo pictured the entrance of the temple, his well-honed mind adding each detail. The doorway was guarded by the Sphinx statue. It looked as though the vines surrounding it had been stripped away by the Guild soldiers. He hadn't seen anything that represented the Egyptian god Horus. Modo, as a child, had been particularly drawn to etchings of the Egyptian gods. Horus was the one with the human body and a falcon head. There were blast marks at the door, a sign that it had been opened with dynamite. Even with all her cunning and manpower, Miss Hakkandottir had had to stoop to blowing up the door. *So how had Alexander King entered?*

And, quite suddenly, it all became clear.

In the same moment he heard soft footsteps and, without opening his eyes, Modo swung out his arm and grabbed the hand that was about to touch his shoulder. He looked up to see Tharpa and smiled in relief.

"I know how we'll enter the temple," Modo said, getting to his feet.

When they'd all risen and gathered in a circle, Mr Socrates nodded at Modo, saying quietly, "Tharpa says you have information." He looked as though he hadn't slept a wink; his eyes were red; his white hair, normally shorn short, had grown during the trip and was poking in several directions. He put his sun helmet on.

"Yes, remember that rhyme King was murmuring during my visit to Bedlam? It's only now that it's making sense."

"Enough prelude if you please—spit it out," Mr Socrates ordered.

The tone of his voice made Modo's stomach turn, but he pressed on. "I've realised there must be another entrance on the west side of the ridge. If Miss Hakkandottir isn't aware of it then it won't be guarded."

"And how did you come to this conclusion?" Mr Socrates asked.

"Alexander King repeated a rhyme to me. *'The west at your spine, the face divine. Through the doorway go, beneath the Horus stone.'* If the west is at our backs then we would be on the opposite side of the temple. I couldn't see any symbols of the god Horus at the front entrance."

"Are we to trust our mission to the rhymes of a madman?" Mr Socrates asked. "I taught you to use logic."

"This *is* logical, sir," Modo said defensively. "I don't believe King could have entered through the front. He had a much smaller party than Miss Hakkandottir and she was forced to blow her way in. I believe he must have stumbled across a back entrance."

"Do you expect us to waste hours searching for it?"

"No. It should be relatively simple. We only need to find the Horus stone he mentioned in his rhyme." Even as he spoke, he could hear how silly his words sounded. A rhyme? He was trusting a rhyme? It had seemed so logical when his eyes were closed, but now that he was awake with the whole party looking at him, he began to doubt himself.

"It's the safer path," Tharpa said, bolstering Modo's hope.

"If you say so," Mr Socrates said, a slight bitterness to his tone. He took a deep breath. "You may be correct, Modo. And if so, this would be a safer choice for a small raiding party like ours. We'll attempt to find it. If unsuccessful we'll have to create a diversion and use the front door. We leave immediately."

They cleared their camp and quietly continued their hike around the shoulder of the mountain. As they moved higher, there were more rocks, but the trees still clung to each crevasse and gave them cover. Mr Socrates led them around the ridge using his compass, and when the west was at their backs, they began to walk straight east.

Modo checked his watch. It was five o'clock now. The sun would rise in an hour, and along with it, the rest of the Guild soldiers who weren't already on watch.

The group struggled to get their footing on rocks and foliage made slippery by the rain. The sun began to rise, heating the jungle. At this altitude, the heat and humidity still made him sweat, especially with his mask on. Occasionally, Mr Socrates would give him the eye, and Modo felt himself shrivel inside. This was taking too long.

Then, just as Modo was about to give up, Tharpa pointed at something that looked at first like nothing more than a shadow. They stopped at a sheer cliff and Modo now saw a carved column that had been attacked by vines, rain and time. But at the top he could make out the falcon-headed Horus! The god of life, Modo remembered, and that's what he felt as he looked at it—a sudden burst of life. This was the entrance!

"Is that it?" Octavia asked.

"It may be," Mr Socrates answered, a lightness in his voice.

They walked past the statue and arrived at an area where large rocks had fallen over. Behind these, they found the entrance to a cave.

"This is the route King took," Modo said. "It must be."

"Then lead us, Modo," Mr Socrates commanded.

The interior was black. Modo immediately took a few steps into the darkness. Though he worried that he was about to fall into an abyss, he didn't want to disappoint Mr Socrates.

"Wait, you overzealous fool!" Mr Socrates hissed. He'd followed Modo into the cave. "Take this." He rummaged in his haversack and pulled out two bull's-eye lanterns. He struck a match and lit the wick of one of them, then slid open the blind. A bright light, magnified by the bulging glass, lit his face, accentuating his wrinkles. He handed the lantern to Modo. "We couldn't use these outside. They would have made us easy targets. Here we should be free from prying eyes. Don't drop it." He lit the second lamp.

Modo held his lamp as high as he could. The walls were rough hewn by human hands and weeping with water. He stooped over to avoid banging his head and walked deeper into the cave. Judging by the bones and offal and guano on the floor, several different types of animals had used the cavern as a shelter. As he moved forward, the walls gradually grew narrower and smoother.

He turned a corner and had to duck as several large grey bats flapped a few inches above his head. Octavia gave a bit of a shriek, which was followed by Lizzie's laughter. Modo wanted to turn around to tease Tavia, but given Mr Socrates' serious demeanour, he thought better of it.

The tunnel grew so narrow that Modo had to get down and crawl on hands and knees, a tricky thing to do with the lamp in one hand. He was reminded of the London sewers, but at least there he didn't have the entire weight of a mountain sitting above him. His shoulders brushed either side of the tunnel. If he got jammed inside would they be able to pull him out?

The passage widened and Modo emerged into a large square chamber, where he was able to stand, and soon everyone was there, gawking along with him. The room had been carved into solid black igneous rock, once lava, the floors and walls now as smooth as glass. The ceiling, several feet above them, was embedded with hundreds of glittering jewels. He raised his lantern and the reflection from the gems blinded him. They were almost within his grasp. He reached up and took a step without looking down. Someone grabbed him from behind and pulled him backwards, nearly knocking him over.

"What the blazes," Modo muttered, staggering to maintain his balance.

"It's a long fall," Mr Socrates said, releasing Modo's shoulder and pointing at the floor. "You're much more useful to me in one piece."

Modo now saw that he was standing at the edge of a deep chasm, about three feet wide and stretching the length of the room. It was very difficult to differentiate it from the black polished rock floor.

"Thank you, sir," he said.

"Don't thank me," Mr Socrates grumbled. "Please, pay attention to everything around you. The Egyptians designed this room to entice you to look up when you enter, thus distracting you from the crevasse and certain death. There'll be more clever traps like this one."

"So the hole is here to defend against grave robbers?" Octavia asked.

"That and, I presume, it prevents any rainwater from entering the main chamber of the tomb. Instead, it all runs into that crevasse. Who knows how deep it is."

"So you believe this is a tomb?" Modo asked.

"It's always about tombs with the Egyptians. They were, how shall I put it, obsessed in that way. I can guarantee you that there'll be a king's chamber somewhere in this mountain, and there we'll find the God Face."

He pointed his lantern at the wall on the other side of the crevasse and the light suddenly brought to life white hieroglyphics.

"Well, well. What have we here," said Mr Socrates. "It says, '*Any man who shall enter this my tomb, an end shall be made for him. I shall break his neck like a bird's.*' Well, that's good news for Octavia and Lizzie. Being women, not men, they should be safe from this curse and any neck discomfort."

"You can read hieroglyphics?" Modo said.

"I've dabbled in Egyptology. A little hobby of mine." Mr Socrates sounded wistful, but then he looked down at Modo and narrowed his eyes. "That's enough talk. Lead us forward."

"Yes, sir." Modo jumped the chasm easily, then walked into the tunnel on the other side of the room, followed by Mr Socrates and the others. He was beginning to feel like the canary in the coal mine, but an order was an order. He would follow it.

The sides of the tunnel were just as smooth as the entrance chamber. Every few feet brass torch holders poked out of the rock, the wooden torches long since rotted to dust. After a few minutes they arrived at an open space where the tunnel branched off in three directions. Modo stopped and looked back to Mr Socrates for instructions.

"The middle one," he said without hesitation.

Modo led the way, wondering exactly how the Egyptians had been able to cut these passages through pure igneous rock. It would have taken a thousand years! It seemed like a crazy thing to do. Not to mention boring and dangerous. The tunnel gradually became smaller and once again Modo and the others were forced to crawl on hands and knees. He sensed that the path was declining very gradually. They'd calculated that the cave was directly opposite the main entrance, and it was safe to assume they were travelling towards the front of the temple.

The passage soon opened into another chamber. Just inside it, Modo stood up and walked down three stone steps. He shone his lantern across the room, and what he saw left him breathless. A sphinx carved out of solidified lava watched them with two gleaming lapis lazuli eyes. The blue stones made its eyes appear alive in the most uncanny and unnerving way.

Even Mr Socrates let out a surprised "Oh!" when he saw the Sphinx. "We'd be the envy of all the world's Egyptologists if we could just ..." His voice trailed off, then he snapped back into action again. "Forget the sightseeing. The room doesn't have any obvious exits. Everyone feel along the walls. Let me know if you find anything unusual—levers or off-centre stones—depressions—anything that might open a secret door."

Modo shone the light directly on the floor to be sure he was on something solid, then took a few steps into the chamber. He swung the lantern around and ran his free hand up and down and along a section of the wall. The ceiling was low enough that Mr Socrates could explore it. Tharpa was kneeling on the floor, exploring there.

Some time later, Mr Socrates looked at his watch and put it back in his pocket "This is taking too long. It must be a dead end! They always make a number of these to confuse grave robbers. We have to double back."

Frustrated, Modo led them back, but when he emerged at where the tunnels had branched out, he was confused. There were now four tunnel entrances!

"Are we back where we began?" Octavia asked.

"We must be, but there's an extra passage now," Modo replied.

"Ah, it just wasn't visible until we approached from this direction," Mr Socrates explained. He looked at his pocket watch again. "It's well past sunrise now. Miss Hakkandottir will most likely be making her next move, I'm sure. We'll have to split up. Modo, Lizzie, Octavia, you take that tunnel. Tharpa and I will explore this one." He handed his lantern to Tharpa. "Let's synchronise our watches," Mr Socrates said, and Modo did so. "Go as far as possible as quickly as possible and return here in twenty-five minutes."

Tharpa and Mr Socrates took the wider passage. As Modo was about to enter their cramped tunnel, Lizzie grabbed the bull's-eye lantern from him and said, "I shall lead this time. I'm the oldest."

Octavia and Modo glanced at each other, but before they could say anything Lizzie had grabbed the lantern from Modo and was crouch-walking into the tunnel.

They followed her, having to hurry to keep pace. They advanced for a distance, splashing through pools of water, before they could stand up again. The passage ended near a ten-foot-square pit that seemed to have no bottom. On the other side was a plain igneous-rock wall with a foot-wide ledge. To get there was a longer and more dangerous jump than Modo would dare try.

"It's another dead end!" Octavia said.

Lizzie shone the bull's-eye lantern so that the opposite wall was clearly lit. "There are no hieroglyphics," she observed. "So far it's the most ordinary chamber we've encountered."

"We should go back," Modo suggested. "We still have time to explore the last tunnel." He turned to leave, but what he heard stopped him cold.

"'All that glisters is not gold; Often have you heard that told: Many a man his life hath sold. But my outside to behold: Gilded tombs do worms enfold.'"

He couldn't believe the words were coming out of the mouth of this tattooed woman.

"You know Shakespeare?" he said, trying not to sound incredulous.

"My father's favourite play," she answered. "This wall isn't gilded on purpose. They wanted us to turn back."

Modo felt stupid for not coming to that conclusion himself. "But it's still too far to jump the pit safely. Perhaps they brought their own ladders. Or a plank."

"Or they just pressed this," Lizzie said. She'd been examining the wall beside the tunnel. Near the ceiling, set in the wall, was a small boulder. She pushed on it.

The sound of scraping stone echoed up from the bottom of the pit. They looked down into it, but nothing seemed to have changed. It wasn't until Modo turned back to the tunnel that he saw what they'd done.

"We've just blocked the passage!" he cried out, and dove at the boulder, hitting it over and over, to no avail.

CHAPTER 46

Thinking Like an Egyptian

Modo finally gave up on thumping the boulder and went to the door, shoving it so hard that he slipped and nearly fell backwards into the pit. "We're stuck," he said, out of breath.

"Do you think the pit's really that deep?" Octavia asked. Lizzie pointed the lantern into it, which allowed them to see that the walls were lined with shiny black, jagged rock. A collection of white sticks lay on the bottom, about forty feet down. White sticks? Then it became clear to Modo what they were.

"Those are bones," he said. "We're not the first to be trapped here."

"Bones?" Octavia's voice cracked slightly. "What a horrible way to die."

"It's quick at least." Lizzie pointed the light away. "We won't end up like them," she said simply and with such confidence that Modo desperately wanted to believe her.

"There must be a way across," Octavia said.

"We have to think like the Egyptians," Modo offered.

"Old and dusty?" Lizzie asked.

It was the first funny thing she'd said, and both he and Octavia shared a look, then began to laugh.

"Perhaps the answer is another trick," he said. He bent down and felt along the top of the pit.

"There's a flat rock here. Could you shine the light on it?"

Lizzie did, but even with the light he couldn't actually see what he was touching. He leaned over, so far into the pit that Octavia gasped, "Don't slip!"

It wasn't until he sat up again, and the light fell at a particular angle, that he could see what was right in front of them. "There's a bridge!" he exclaimed. "The stone is so dark that it doesn't reflect light." He stood up and moved towards it.

"Wait, Modo!" Octavia said. "How do we know it won't collapse?"

"I'll test it out," Modo said, shrugging. "Just one of us at a time."

"You're far too heavy," Octavia countered. "I should go. I'm light as a feather."

"No. I have better balance and—"

Their light was gone. Lizzie had slipped past them and was already halfway across the bridge. She looked as though she were walking on air.

"Well, if she's light enough …" Octavia said, stepping onto the bridge

Lizzie set down the lantern at the opposite side, where

it dimly lit the outlines of the bridge. "Come along, children," she chimed, as Octavia took several tentative steps across.

When she'd reached Lizzie, Modo took his turn. It was relatively easy to cross so long as he stared straight ahead.

Lizzie was already searching out possible lever stones. Finally, she found one and gave it a shove. The rock blocking their way slid aside quietly, revealing yet another tunnel.

"How long has it been?" Octavia asked.

Modo nearly slapped his forehead. Mr Socrates had wanted them back in twenty-five minutes. He looked at his pocket watch. They'd been gone for thirty-five! It felt as if they'd been wandering for hours.

"We were supposed to be back by now."

"But there's no way back," Lizzie observed calmly. "We'll have to hope we find them by going on."

So they followed the passage. It narrowed and for a while they were forced again onto their hands and knees. Suddenly the tunnel turned into a smooth slide and Lizzie slipped down it at great speed, acrobatically turning so she was travelling feet first, holding the lamp away from herself with one hand.

Modo slid down next, digging in his hands but gaining more speed than he would have thought possible. Going so fast face first wasn't smart, so with all his strength he pushed his legs apart until he'd slowed down enough to swing his body around. Then he heard Octavia, right behind him, screaming, "Ooooohhhhhhhh!"

Next thing he knew he was falling a few feet and smashing onto a rock. Lizzie was moaning on the ground next to him, her lantern somehow still burning a few feet away.

Lizzie was on her feet first, and she gave Modo a hand up as Octavia came shooting out of the tunnel. She managed to land on her feet, then tumble to the floor.

"Well, that was more excitement than I was looking for," Octavia said, letting them both pull her up.

It was another obsidian chamber, this one at least fifteen feet tall. On either side of them were golden statues of Horus. The room seemed even more majestic than the one with the Sphinx, and the walls had numerous brass torch holders, perhaps indicating some sort of ceremonies were conducted here.

"We're getting closer," Modo said.

Then they heard a bird-like screeching from behind them that sent a chill down Modo's spine. Lizzie spun the bull's-eye around, the light catching the clockwork falcons as they swooped down at them, talons gleaming.

CHAPTER 47

Too Many Days Behind a Desk

Mr Socrates followed Tharpa down the passage, carrying the elephant gun in his right hand. The engineering of the temple's burial tomb was stunning and indicated the city outside must once have been thriving with trade and teeming with labourers. Perhaps at one time there'd been farms and villages surrounding the temple—the beginning of a new Egyptian empire. He had no idea what had become of the Egyptians—disease, failed crops, war—there were many things that could reduce an empire to ruins. Perhaps they just grew tired of jungle life and returned to Egypt in their barques.

He had more important things to think about than long-dead Egyptians. There was, of course, the problem of Modo. The young agent was growing too much of a spine and at the same time was too soft. Worried about the lives of a few savages? Had it been a mistake to have Mrs Finchley raise him? Had Modo had contact only with men throughout his youth, perhaps he wouldn't have turned out this way. Mr Socrates thought Modo had been taught that sacrifice was what brought the British Empire to greatness. Clearly a review of the lesson was in order. Such sensitivity as he'd shown to the tribesmen was not how empires were built.

As the tunnel narrowed, he spotted more hieroglyphics and wondered, briefly, if Modo had been right to refuse him. *Perhaps the chance to launch a surprise strike on Miss Hakkandottir blinded me,* he thought. The blow could have cost the warriors, and all of them, their lives.

At least Modo had come up with this second plan. The boy's brain was worth something. With luck and a bit of pluck, they could remove the God Face and be gone before Miss Hakkandottir was any the wiser. But it was bothersome that she hadn't already secured the artifact. What was holding her back? Perhaps it was as simple as not finding the right tunnel. He couldn't imagine what else would have delayed her.

Tharpa stopped and held the lantern up high so that Mr Socrates could see a smooth wall, handholds carved deep into the stone.

"We will have to climb, Sahib," Tharpa said. "Would you like to wait here?"

"Are you suggesting I'm too old to climb, Tharpa?"

"I would never suggest that, Sahib. I should have said, would you like me to go first?"

"Yes, lead the way." He handed him the elephant gun. "You carry the gun. Do try to resist firing it in a small space or we'll go deaf. All right, let's see if these two-thousand-year-old footholds will take our weight."

Tharpa slung the gun over his shoulder, took the lantern and began climbing easily. Mr Socrates was impressed that he still had such agility. The man didn't seem to age.

He followed, slowly, digging his hands and feet into the holes. After about twenty feet he had to stop to catch his breath. Too many days behind a desk, he admonished himself.

"Are you well, Sahib?"

"Just keep going, Tharpa!" Mr Socrates snapped. "I never know whether you are teasing me or generally concerned about my health."

"I am always concerned about your health, Sahib."

It was another ten minutes of climbing before they found a ledge to climb on to. He accepted Tharpa's help to get over the edge of it and lay on the smooth, cold rock, wondering if his heart would burst. He wheezed a few deep breaths in and out until he saw that Tharpa was staring at him.

"Don't say a word," he said raggedly. "I'm in perfect health. Now, where are we?"

Tharpa lifted the light and they could see that the ledge was just outside an opening into a small corridor that descended farther into darkness.

"Carry on," Mr Socrates said, then followed Tharpa.

Soon Mr Socrates was crawling on his hands and knees, cursing the rheumatism in his joints. The Egyptians must have had knees of stone, he decided. Or they didn't live long enough to develop rheumatism.

The passage led into a large square chamber and Mr Socrates was relieved to stand again. Tharpa waved the

bull's-eye around, and there in the centre, was, of all
things, a chariot, surrounded by clay jars, shields, dry
flowers and an ostrich-feather fan. A few of the jars had
been broken; he and Tharpa weren't the first to enter this
room. Perhaps Alexander King had been here. If so, that
was good news.

"They kept the pharaoh's intestines in a jar," Mr
Socrates said.

"A good place for them," Tharpa answered, making
Mr Socrates laugh. It was so rare to hear humour from
Tharpa that it always came as a surprise.

They walked through the room to a short passageway
ending in a flat stone doorway. Tharpa easily pushed the
door aside and it moved silently into a gap in the wall.

"They were brilliant engineers," Mr Socrates said.

They stood side by side as Tharpa held the lantern
high, the light reflecting off rows and rows of what
seemed to be mirrors, which had the effect of multiplying
the bull's-eye's light many times over till it was almost
as bright as day in the chamber. Mr Socrates saw then
that what he'd thought were mirrors were in fact rows of
white sapphires reflecting the light in all directions. In the
centre of the room was a gold-plated sarcophagus.

"The king's chamber," Mr Socrates exclaimed. "We've
made it, Tharpa!"

And at that moment, he heard the echo of pistol fire.

CHAPTER 48

Promises Worth Nothing

Modo stood completely still in the dark. On their first attack the clockwork falcons had knocked the bull's-eye lantern from Lizzie's hand, smashing it on the floor. The only light in the room was emitted by the glowing red eyes of the birds.

"Their beaks or talons are poisonous," Octavia yelled.

A falcon dove at her. Modo followed the blur of its ruby eyes, then heard her grunt.

"Ah, one got me."

"Octavia!" He swung his hands out and followed her voice until he found her. "Are you bleeding?"

"Yes," she hissed, "but my sun helmet saved me from the worst of it."

She was still speaking, so she hadn't been poisoned. Yet Mr Socrates had said there was a vial inside the creatures; maybe it took time for the poison to work.

A falcon screeched again and Lizzie let out a shriek of pain, then swore like the blazes. Modo was now convinced the birds could see in the dark, so perfect were their strikes.

Without warning this time, a falcon's talons slashed Modo's head. The bird flapped away and Modo held the wound, his fingers wet with his own blood. He felt as though half his scalp had been torn off.

"We have to get out of here!" Modo shouted, but he had no idea how. He'd been spun around and wasn't certain which way was which.

Then a light appeared at the far end of the chamber. Modo hoped it was Mr Socrates, but when a second and third light came around the corner, his hopes were dashed. Six Guild soldiers approached and stopped about twenty paces away, pistols raised. Two of them were struggling to control mechanical hounds straining against their leashes. Modo had nearly lost his arm to one of those hounds and had no desire to tackle one again.

A soldier aimed his lantern so that Modo had to cover his eyes momentarily. When he looked again, the falconer was rounding the corner, making a clicking noise with his tongue. The mechanical birds darted back and landed on his arm.

Miss Hakkandottir strode between the soldiers and pointed at Modo. "You're alive!" she exclaimed, staring incredulously.

"So far," Modo offered, feeling a tinge of pride in having fooled her.

"You do amaze me, but I doubt you can survive bullets through the heart. It would be best if the three of you surrendered now." Her voice grew softer. "We will not harm you. I promise."

"Her promises are worth nothing," Octavia spat out.

"Ah, but they are. My word is my bond. We will feed you and make you comfortable. It will be a peace treaty between us."

Lizzie, who was slightly behind Modo, whispered, "Whatever you do, don't move a muscle." He felt something slide between his arm and his body. His heart skipped a beat as she continued to whisper, "Be prepared to run. There's a tunnel behind us."

He heard the smallest of clicks, recognised that it was the hammer on a pistol being pulled back. Good Lord, she was using him as cover.

"I want your answer right now," Miss Hakkandottir said.

"Have your men lower their guns," Modo said. "Immediately."

"You are not in a position to make demands! Give me your answer or we will shoot Octavia first."

Out of the corner of his eye, Modo saw Octavia stiffen.

"Enough talk," Lizzie whispered, and there was a *pop* right beside Modo.

The bullet ricocheted off Miss Hakkandottir's hand. She had raised it in time to deflect the bullet! Lizzie's second shot smashed one of the lanterns a soldier was holding.

"Ah, blast the luck!" Lizzie said. "Run!"

Modo grabbed Octavia's hand, ducked to the ground, then turned and darted to the tunnel Lizzie had spotted.

Behind them, Miss Hakkandottir shouted, "Shoot them! Shoot them! Release the hounds, you fools!"

Bullets zipped around, but none found its mark. Lizzie paused at the tunnel opening to push Modo and Octavia onwards, bellowing, "Go! Go!"

He looked back to see her reload her two-barrelled Derringer. The gun was tiny, meant only for shooting someone across a card table, so he knew it wouldn't do much damage.

"Go!" she screamed again, and let off a round.

Modo took Octavia's hand and pulled her along the passage, thankful that it was wide enough and tall enough for them to run upright. He glanced back again to see that Lizzie was only a few steps behind them, but closing in on her were the mechanical hounds, their metal claws clicking on the stone.

"Faster!" Lizzie screamed.

They burst into another chamber and Modo stopped, turned and eyed the pillars that had been placed on either side of the doorway. Just as Lizzie passed through the entrance he put his back against a pillar and, straining mightily, pushed it over to block the door. He had just enough time to push the second one into place before he saw the glowing eyes of the hounds through the space between the pillars. The beasts threw their massive bodies against the pillars and moved them an inch.

"We have to keep going," Octavia gasped. "They'll be through that in no time."

It was nearly pitch black, again, though the passage ahead of them seemed to emit the faintest bit of light.

"This way," Modo ordered. "I just hope it's not a dead end."

"Yes, a dead end would be bad," Lizzie quipped, then laughed.

As they ran on, the light up ahead of them grew brighter. Was it possible that Miss Hakkandottir had somehow circled around them? They had no choice, in any case, so they dashed on into a grand chamber, where they were suddenly blinded by the brightness.

When his eyes adjusted, Modo found himself looking at a large, golden sarcophagus. Behind it stood two familiar men.

"Ah, Modo, you are late again, I see!" Mr Socrates said.

CHAPTER 49

The God Face

Modo's eyes were wide as saucers. Mr Socrates was standing there with his index fingers in his ears. Tharpa was pointing the elephant gun with one hand, a finger of the other hand stuck in his left ear. They looked absolutely ridiculous.

Octavia elbowed Modo in the ribs and he suppressed a guffaw. Lizzie laughed, hard.

"Well, we didn't want to go deaf from the blast of the elephant gun," Mr Socrates tried to explain after he pulled his fingers out of his ears.

Tharpa lowered the gun.

"But never mind, we've found it!" Mr Socrates exclaimed triumphantly. "I don't quite know what to make of it, but it's here. It's here!" He pointed at something behind the sarcophagus.

"Mr Socrates ... Miss Hakkandottir!" Modo made a move towards the passage behind the sarcophagus. "She and her men and her dogs are pursuing us. Their way will only be blocked for a short while."

"Ah, that's the gunfire we heard," Mr Socrates said. "Then we better be quick about this. Come along."

Modo and the two women walked around the sarcophagus, and found a statue of a man at least twice the size of a human, his imposing figure seated on a throne carved from what looked like obsidian. It had been set into the wall, facing the sarcophagus.

But what really took Modo's breath away was the figure's pitch-black head, its lapis lazuli eyes glowing like stars, the facial features twisted grotesquely.

"It's my face," he whispered.

He'd stared at his own ugly mockery of a human face for so many years that it was shocking to see something so similar, especially set in stone.

But there was something else about the God Face. Looking at it was making him queasy, as though it exuded a powerful force. The blue stone eyes were glaring directly into his own, as if searching out his darkest thoughts, his deepest doubts. He began to shake.

"Tharpa and I have been studying it for the last little while," Mr Socrates said. "It certainly does have a disconcerting effect—it seems to bring about nausea, doubt, and even saps confidence. Tharpa and I experienced all these things. I cannot say what it is about the shape, or perhaps about what's in the rock itself, that causes this reaction, but I'll admit it's already made me tremble."

"It's my face," Modo said again.

"What did you say?" Mr Socrates replied.

"The face on the statue … it's almost exactly like my face."

"No, Modo. I don't see it. There's something primeval about it, that's all. Some symbol that makes our minds react the way they do."

Octavia turned to Modo, looking pale and frightened. "I don't see the resemblance either, Modo. It's very hard to look at for any length of time."

All along, Lizzie had chosen to keep her back to the statue. "I can't look at it," she hissed. "It's cursing us!"

She took a few steps towards the tunnel, and Modo worried that she would flee. Instead, she stood there, her arms crossed.

"Why haven't we been driven insane like King?" Octavia asked.

"Perhaps we're all made of stronger stuff than Alexander King," Mr Socrates suggested. "We're able to overcome the effect the image has on us."

And I, Modo thought, *I can look. In some way I know this face. It cannot overcome me.*

A stone-on-stone grinding echoed down the passage. "It sounds as if we will soon have unwanted company. Well, I've grown tired of running. Tharpa, set up behind the sarcophagus. Lizzie, you join him. Modo, fetch the God Face and be quick about it. I have an idea."

"You mean remove it from the statue?"

"Yes, those are my orders."

"Yes, sir," Modo said.

He climbed the side of the throne and stood on the legs of the statue. The sapphires encrusted in the walls reflected light directly onto the statue's face. He averted his eyes as he climbed closer to it; nonetheless, his muscles began to tremble and he grew weak, feeling he might fall at any moment. In order to find a way to pry the head off the body, he was forced to look at it.

For some reason he stopped trembling, and something like hope began to creep into his heart. Someone with a similar disfiguration had perhaps become a great pharaoh. Maybe that's why he had left Egypt. He'd come here to carve his own kingdom in the jungle. *It could be that I'm not such an oddity after all,* he thought.

"It's me," Modo whispered into the statue's ear.

"Modo, don't be superstitious," Mr Socrates called, "just bring the God Face down. And hurry."

"There was another person like me," he babbled to the face. What was making him speak to a rock this way? "He might have been a pharaoh."

"Don't jump to such conclusions! What if the Egyptians just hired a sculptor to create a stone guardian, a statue whose sole purpose was to frighten away grave robbers? Now, bring it down to me, Modo."

Modo twisted the head a little and it moved. He turned it again and pulled it from the socket. It gave Modo an awful feeling to remove the head from the body, as if he'd committed a sin. He imagined the ghost of the pharaoh and all his slaves suddenly swirling around him, shouting their anger.

He shook his head and climbed down, surprised at how heavy and cumbersome the God Face was.

When he stepped down onto the floor and turned, he wasn't surprised to see Miss Hakkandottir at the tunnel entrance, her soldiers lined up behind her. Still, he trembled at the sight of her. He hugged the God Face against his chest, hoping to hide it from her sight.

"Ah, Modo. Mr Socrates. It is so kind of you to save us the trouble of discovering the God Face," she said. "Please be so good as to give it to me. *Now*."

CHAPTER 50

The People Who Fell from the Sky

Nulu stood beside the warriors and watched as the fire-haired woman, her dogs and the grey men went into the mouth of the god home. The Rain People kept their distance, for they knew that the fire sticks could poke a hole in a man from far away. But this was dream-time and now-time, and they wanted to see what was unfolding.

The warriors had returned to their village and hustled her back to the god home because they knew she could understand Moh-Doh. He was in that mountain; two warriors had come running to tell them they had seen him enter. And now the grey ones were entering, too.

For generations only the bravest of warriors and shamans had entered that place, for all emerged changed after seeing the spirit world and the God Face. Sometimes they would return only speaking spirit words and would never speak the Rain People's language again. It was the true test of any chief, warrior or shaman. And now these people who had fallen from the sky would face that test.

None of this had been predicted in the stories and dreams of the elders. These people who came out of the sky and walked like gods on the earth were here, but for what purpose?

The Rain People clutched their spears and waited. There were big things happening, clashes between gods and the servants of gods. And they were the little Rain People. The man with the God Face would signal them if he needed their help.

Until then, they would watch.

CHAPTER 51

A Horrible Whisper

Twelve soldiers pointed carbines at them. Two more soldiers held the leashes on the mechanical hounds. The falconer carried the mechanical falcons on his arms.

Tharpa pointed the elephant gun directly at Miss Hakkandottir. She looked right through him.

"Ingrid, it's only a stone head," Mr Socrates said. "A talisman. Useless. Not even made of gold."

"I shall be the judge of that, Alan," she answered. "Thanks to that head, I have lost several men to madness. Some have died. And yet you have seen it and you remain your old obstinate self. I wonder why?"

"We're English," he said.

Modo was impressed by his flippancy.

"Your Indian slave is not. Neither is your pilot. Perhaps the men I sent in here were just weak."

Mr Socrates shrugged. "We seem to have reached an impasse. Lower your gun, Tharpa."

Tharpa did.

"Ah, these last many years have given you wisdom," Miss Hakkandottir said. "Now, please, Modo." She looked at him, almost pouting. "Stop trying to hide the head. Please deliver it to me."

Modo looked at Mr Socrates, who nodded, and Modo took a step forward. He lifted the head of the statue so that it was caught by the sapphire light. A soldier approached with his hands out to take it, but when Modo turned the face towards them, the man went white. He raised a hand to cover his eyes, then whimpered and stumbled backwards.

"What is wrong with you!" Miss Hakkandottir shouted. But when she looked squarely into the carved face, even she fell silent. "Horrible," she rasped, lowering her gaze.

Modo took another step forward and they all moved back. More soldiers covered their faces. Miss Hakkandottir tried to raise her head, but failed. One soldier dropped his pistol and ran screaming back down the tunnel. He was followed by another, and another. Even the falconer cried out, and turned, carrying his birds with him. The hounds, confused, followed.

Miss Hakkandottir stood there, alone.

CHAPTER 52

An Uncontrolled Retreat

Miss Hakkandottir had been taken by surprise. The God Face, perfectly caught in the light, seemed to have some otherworldly power. The ghosts of the dead Egyptians were speaking to her. Looking into the blue eyes of the God Face, she suddenly felt all the weight of the tomb above her. The past, her own past, began to sprout and grow wings inside her head.

In her peripheral vision she saw the first soldier flee. Then the next and the next, followed by Visser. But their minds were weak. Her own constitution was much stronger. She would win!

And yet, as she continued to look at the God Face, her mind began turning around like a gyre—*fear, flee, fear*. As Modo approached with the artifact, more and more voices in her head began to speak. The people she had killed, they were all still there in her memory—soldiers, pirates, a multitude raised their voices. Then a childhood memory of the raised hand of her father. Her crippled grandmother with a serpent's tongue. Her sister, whom she had drowned in an icy river near her family's sheep herder hut. All of them screamed at her in a maddening chorus.

Despite her attempts to stand her ground and prove herself brave, involuntarily she stepped back. And once she'd stepped back, her body responded on its own and continued backing away. It terrified her. Modo, that masked creature, was following, holding that horrible severed head. The voices were growing louder. This, then, was the madness she'd seen in her men—it had found a way to get inside her head too.

CHAPTER 53

Driving the Enemy Before You

M odo strode after their enemies, holding the head high, taunting them with it whenever they turned around.

"It's working!" Mr Socrates exclaimed. "The God Face is driving them away. Step aside, Modo, and let us get a clear shot at Miss Hakkandottir."

Modo heard the order, but couldn't obey. He was too caught up in the moment to stop. "I'll get her!" he shouted. "I will!" He had relished the fear in Miss Hakkandottir's eyes. *I hope you go completely insane,* he wanted to shout after her. His wounded hand throbbed as though urging him on. He dashed after her and the soldiers. *You cut me! You hurt my friends! Murdered my colleagues! Go mad, you evil woman!*

"Modo! Stand aside!" Mr Socrates commanded, but his voice was already distant.

Miss Hakkandottir was running now, over the fallen pillars. Modo matched her step for step. If his companions were following, he was unaware of them. At one point

Hakkandottir turned to face him, a snarl on her lips, but her eyes were immediately drawn to the God Face and her strength waned again. She fled.

The remaining passages and stairs were a blur. At one point Modo jumped a crevasse without even stopping to gauge the distance. The God Face was guiding him, was pulling him towards the destruction of his enemies.

Once he was outside in the sunlight he saw Miss Hakkandottir running pell-mell down the temple stairs. He stopped cold, gasping for air. It was his own face he was holding up to the world. His own face he was using to drive them away.

But a triumphant thought followed: his face was a powerful weapon.

A pack of Guild soldiers were running up the stairs, rifles raised, but they were shocked to see their leader and fellow soldiers fleeing the cave. Modo removed his mask and walked towards them. *What are you doing?* he asked himself. There were over fifty of them.

They took one good look at him and bolted, their rifles rattling to the ground.

Modo stopped beside the paws of the Sphinx and looked down at the ruins of the Egyptian city. With great satisfaction he watched as Miss Hakkandottir scurried down the hillside below the temple and through the ruins of the city.

A loud blast at his side barely made him shudder. Tharpa was firing the elephant gun. A second blast and sparks flew near Miss Hakkandottir. She didn't pause, was pulling at her hair with her metal hand as she ran past the *Prometheus* and disappeared into the cover of the forest. In less than a minute the temple and the city had been abandoned by the Guild soldiers.

Modo put his mask back on and turned around to find his companions standing behind him in the doorway of the temple, the mouth of the Sphinx. The lion-like statue was looking directly at Modo. Did it approve? He wouldn't have been surprised if it had lifted its stone paws and shaken off a thousand years of waiting. It felt as though anything could happen on a day like this.

Mr Socrates' lips were moving, but he wasn't making a sound. Then he felt a sharp pain in his ears and the sound flooded in. He'd been deafened by the report of the gun.

"... she'll be dead soon enough. But that was a stunning display!" Mr Socrates exclaimed. His eyes had a glow that disturbed Modo. "To drive the enemy back like that. Such a powerful, powerful weapon! We'll have to study this God Face. There must be a way to duplicate the effects."

"Don't you wonder why *we* weren't driven mad?" Modo asked.

"Mad?" Mr Socrates' eyes were focused on the God Face, so Modo tucked it inside the folds of his cloak. "Yes, that's an oddity, but with enough experimentation we will get to the bottom of that, too."

Modo looked from Mr Socrates to Octavia, Lizzie and Tharpa. What was the one thing they all had in common? The reason was clear. "Don't you see?" Modo asked.

"See what?" Octavia asked. "Modo, are you feeling unwell?"

"I am feeling perfectly fine," he said. "All of you had seen my face before. Our enemies hadn't. That's why you weren't driven insane by the God Face. You saw *me* in that stone head."

"Hmm." Mr Socrates scratched his head. "You do seem to have a penchant for self-aggrandisement, Modo. You cling to these notions of your own importance—perhaps it's a lingering effect of being abandoned as a child."

Modo gritted his teeth.

Mr Socrates raised a hand. "This is not the place or time to argue. Let me hold the head."

Modo didn't want to give it up before he had to do so.

Someone in the distance began beating a drum, and Modo wondered if it was the first sign of a counterattack. A choir began to sing in an obscure language.

Modo and the others looked around, perplexed, until Octavia said, "Look—down there!"

Crossing the ruins and climbing the long stairway was a group of half-naked people, moving in single file. As they approached the steps to the temple, Modo recognised them as the Rain People—fifteen warriors followed by Nulu and her grandfather.

One warrior was pounding on a hand drum. The remaining warriors carried spears, and shields painted with the God Face image. They continued up the steps towards Modo.

* * *

"They're friends," Modo said to his companions. "Please, no guns."

Nulu pointed at him with her little finger and said, "Moh-Doh." Then she said several more words.

"Nulu," he replied. Seeing her calmed him and he was moved by the way the tribesmen gazed at his face with such reverence.

She tugged on his cloak until he got down on one knee in front of her, then pushed back his mask and touched his face. Her fingers were warm.

"*Walu. Ngulkurrijin. Yulu*," she whispered as she stroked his cheek.

He didn't know what any of the words meant, but listened intently. She repeated them softly several times.

Then, gently, she took the God Face from him, so heavy in her little arms that she nearly dropped it. She bowed slightly and turned away handing the God Face to her grandfather. Then the warriors and her grandfather bowed and followed her down the steps towards the rain forest.

"But … but …" Mr Socrates pointed at the tribe. "They can't take the God Face!" He took a few steps after them, then turned to Modo. "Command them to return it! Now!"

"I can't, Mr Socrates. I don't speak their language. Besides, it belongs to them, more than it does to us."

"*Belongs* to them?"

"You saw the symbols on their shields. We'd alter their lives if we took it."

"That God Face could end wars!"

"Or start new ones," Lizzie said.

Modo was surprised to hear her speak. Her face was solemn.

Mr Socrates was equally shocked. "What does that mean?"

Lizzie shrugged. "Weapons are meant to be used."

"Of course they are," Mr Socrates replied.

Modo saw that the Rain People had gone back into the forest. "It's too late, either way," he said. "We can't get it back now."

Mr Socrates stared after them, looking flabbergasted, his face contorted by a cold rage.

Modo put his mask back on. "Mr Socrates ..." he began.

"Don't speak of this, Modo." He waved his hand. "Lizzie, get us out of here on that airship. Who knows whether or not those natives will be back in force. Or Miss Hakkandottir, for that matter."

They hurried down to the *Prometheus* and boarded. In no time, Lizzie fired up the boiler and soon they were airborne, the roaring engine announcing their departure. As the *Prometheus* rose slowly above the ruins, Modo looked out over the edge of the car, searching for a sign of the Rain People in the forest. Nothing. He could clearly see the Sphinx and the tomb entrance they had escaped from. The temple where a replica of him, a part of him, had been waiting for over two thousand years. The God Face hadn't driven him mad, but trying to understand how it had come to exist just might.

Octavia stood beside him and put her hand on his shoulder. He wanted to lean into her but was afraid to. Instead he leaned even farther over the edge of the car.

"What do you see down there?" Octavia asked.

"My new beginning," Modo answered.

CHAPTER 54

The Message

Nulu and the warriors watched as the man with the God Face climbed into a large basket and it floated into the sky, pulled by a large grey thundering cloud. Soon he was gone, returning to the heavens.

There were so many questions. Why had Moh-Doh come? Why did he give them the God Face? No rain warrior before him had been brave enough to actually touch it. And he had brought it out of the cave for them.

"Did he explain what we are to do with it?" her grandfather asked in a whisper.

She shook her head.

"It's not easy to know the will of the gods," he said to the gathered warriors and tribespeople. "It's a gift, though. A gift."

Nulu thought about that. Moh-Doh had come. There had been a battle against the grey enemies, which he had won. Then he had given them the God Face. No longer would they have to travel into the temple. They would carry it with them.

It was a new way of being, she decided. A new way of doing things. That much, at least, she understood.

CHAPTER 55

One by One They Fall

First, Miss Hakkandottir banished the voices and images of madness from her head, one by one. Then she tromped through the rain forest and, gathering what soldiers she could find, seven in all, she began the journey on foot to Port Douglas. The soldiers' minds were weaker than usual, but by pure force of will she drove them forward. Later, she discovered Visser tangled in the roots of a gnarled mangrove tree, his eyes empty, the mechanical falcons on his arm, screeching softly. She shouted at him until he got up and joined the band of weary travellers.

They marched through the mud, the vines and roots, the murky water, and didn't stop to eat. She smashed branches aside, cut through vines with the extended nails on her metal fingers. At nightfall two of the soldiers died, each struck through the heart with a spear that flew out of the darkness. This threw the rest of the troop into a muttering panic and one ran screaming into the jungle. His scream was soon cut short.

No one slept the rest of the night.

In the morning as they struggled on, a lieutenant trailed a few steps behind the group and vanished. A short time later another soldier was struck through the heart by a spear. Miss Hakkandottir had to give it to the natives: their aim was impeccable, and they were as invisible and silent as snakes.

By mid-afternoon, she and Visser were the only ones left to trudge over the stones in the gorge. Visser was still dazed, his birds clinging to his now bloodied arm. As they waded across a shallow section of the river, a crocodile grabbed Visser by the back of his neck and yanked him down. The falcons, too dumb to fly away, joined their master in his watery, bloody death. A second later the crocodile's mate lunged at Miss Hakkandottir's throat, but she slammed her metal fist into the beast's skull and it sank, dead, to the bottom of the river.

She ran alongside the river. The natives were in the trees, but hadn't struck for some time. She hadn't had anything to eat or drink for far too long and was growing weak, so she imagined they were waiting until she collapsed. But half an hour later, when the forest finally thinned and she sighted Port Douglas a few hundred yards away, she had one last burst of energy. A spear hissed next to her leg, burying itself in the red soil. She jumped over a bush, then turned her head to glimpse the blur of something passing. By reflex, she caught the spear in her metal hand. She broke it in two and kept charging forward. Another spear cut along the side of her neck, merely scratching her. Then she was on a stone-littered road leading into the port. When she paused to look back, the tribe seemed to be gone.

She stopped at the hotel to send two telegrams, the clerk following her instructions to a T and watching her with wide, fearful eyes. She did not know if it was the blood, her unkempt hair or her metal hand that intimidated him. The first coded telegram was to the Guild Master, reporting her failure and asking for the *Kraken* to rescue her. At least he would be pleased with the news that she still had Modo's finger in the tin in her pocket.

This was the third time the Permanent Association had stopped her. There wouldn't be a fourth. She vowed she would rid the world of that organisation and, in time, of the British Empire itself.

Her second telegram was to her operative in London. When the agent at the other end deciphered her code he'd be left with three words: *Burn Victor down.*

Homeward Bound

Lizzie steered the *Prometheus* northeast towards Cooktown, following Mr Socrates' directions. After two hours they'd left the rain forest behind, crossed over a small mountain range and finally passed over a series of grassy hills, catching their first glimpse of the Pacific.

Modo was happy to see the ocean but even more so when Octavia pointed out a troop of kangaroos on a hillside. He and Octavia laughed as the odd creatures bounced across the ground. They did exist after all! Until now he'd seen only illustrations in books, and would have been disappointed to return to England without having viewed a real one.

They landed on the outskirts of Cooktown. The roar of the steam engine and the peculiar sight of the airship drew gold miners from their perches on bar stools, and townsfolk from their wooden houses, and even Chinese workers from their labour; they all stared. Mr Socrates disembarked and calmly walked through the crowd with Tharpa beside him. He found the nearest hotel and sent a telegram.

A few hours later the HMS *Basilisk*, a large iron-clad steamship and one of England's finest warships, pulled into port. Lizzie flew the *Prometheus* on board, and by nightfall the airship had been dismantled and stored in the *Basilisk*'s hold.

The travellers were assigned recently vacated officers' cabins, much smaller and more Spartan than those on board the *Rome*. Modo slept like a stone, glad to at least have a cot and the comforting sounds of the ship rather than the whirring and clicking of insects and the hoots and screeching of animals.

He was awakened early the next morning by the hollers of men scrubbing the decks. He didn't bother to change his face. Instead he dressed in unadorned military clothes provided by the marines and wandered out onto the deck wearing his African mask. He watched the sun rise on the Pacific, a beautiful sight to behold.

A lot had happened in such a short time. He wondered what the Rain People were doing at that very moment. Were they waking, too, starting their campfires and setting about their daily chores? Had they brought the God Face back to the village? For all he knew they might very well have returned it to the temple. It was theirs to care for as they saw fit.

Modo heard a cabin door open and turned to see Mr Socrates on the deck, wearing an officer's uniform. He hadn't spoken to Modo since their arrival, other than to grunt a few commands and point him towards a cabin. In his heart Modo wanted to beg for forgiveness, to further explain his motives, but he believed it would be pointless.

He'd betrayed his master. His master would punish him one way or another.

"Lizzie's leaving," Mr Socrates said. "If you wish to say goodbye to her, she's departing from the port side. After that you'll be on your own for the rest of the voyage. And you'll be taking a hiatus from your training."

Modo nodded and followed Mr Socrates, not daring to walk at his side. Lizzie, Octavia and Tharpa were already waiting on the departure deck. Someone had found a grey nurse's gown for Octavia.

Lizzie had no luggage and was wearing her one set of clothes and her long coat, though they'd been laundered and pressed.

"Once again, Lizzie, I appreciate your assistance." Mr Socrates handed her an envelope, and it disappeared inside her coat.

"Good of you to bale up," she said. "And it was my pleasure." She shook his hand.

Then she shook everyone else's, leaving Modo to the last. She didn't say a word, but met his eyes with a look that he couldn't quite measure. Admiration? Sympathy? The slightest smile flickered on her tattooed lips, then she patted his shoulder.

"Safe travels," she said to everyone, then turned and climbed down the rope ladder to a waiting boat. She was rowed into Cooktown by two marines. Not once did she look back.

They soon lifted anchor and began travelling faster than Modo had ever travelled by ship, with the steam engine and the wind in the sails of the *Basilisk* pushing them to Sydney. When they arrived, Mrs Finchley was already waiting on the docks of Cockatoo Island. Once on board she was clearly pleased to see them again, but seemed to sense that all was not well.

They set sail for England. Modo spent as much time as he could on the deck, studying the horizon. The marines and sailors left him alone; he assumed they'd been ordered to mind their own business. He preferred it that way. The prow of the ship rose into the sky and sank down into the sea, each time sending a white cloud of spray into the air.

The day after they left Sydney, Mrs Finchley joined him at the forecastle. After a few minutes of silence, she looked at him and said, "What happened in the rain forest isn't my business. I've learned not to ask questions about such matters, but I must say, you seem … changed."

"In what way?" he asked.

"I'm not sure. Perhaps you seem older."

"How can you say that when you haven't seen my face since we got back?"

"It's not your face, Modo. It's in the way you carry yourself."

He didn't argue with her. She was right. He *had* changed in some fundamental way. He couldn't say exactly how, but when he thought of the Rain People and of Nulu he felt both joy and grief. If only he could live with them. Or with people like them.

Mrs Finchley touched his arm. "I do wish Mr Socrates would allow me to continue to work with you. I miss our lessons."

"So do I," he said, knowing that wouldn't happen for a long time, if at all. Mr Socrates' orders were written in stone: no time was to be spent with Mrs Finchley or Tharpa. Was this Modo's only punishment? Or a sign that he was finished as an agent?

He rarely saw Mr Socrates on board. His master usually dined with the officers or was in meetings with the marines or Octavia and Tharpa. If Modo happened to walk past Mr Socrates on the deck, they exchanged little more than pleasantries.

To Modo's eternal frustration, he saw very little of Octavia, too, during the first two weeks of their voyage home. The officers on the ship found her enthralling, and she seemed keen to spend time with them. Modo discovered a library on board and filled the long hours with reading.

One evening while he was watching the sun set over the beaches of India and wondering about Tharpa and the vast country he'd come from, he turned at the sound of a clearing throat, and was surprised to find Octavia standing beside him.

"They're singing songs in the mess, Modo," she said. "Some of them quite bawdy. Do you care to join us?"

"I don't feel like singing. What are you doing out here, when you could be enjoying the warbling of all those navy officers."

"And the bass burbling of the marines, too, don't forget." She laughed. "You're in danger of becoming a stick-in-the-mud, Modo."

"You're in danger of avoiding me, cousin."

"What does that mean?"

"We've been on this ship for weeks and have hardly said two words to each other," he replied.

She looked as though she were about to say something smart, but paused and chose her words carefully. "You're correct, Modo. I have been avoiding you."

"Why?"

"You know why."

"Do you think this is a game, Tavia?" he said, then gave himself a moment to take a deep breath. "Fine. I know why. Just tell me what you think and get it over with."

"About what?"

"My face, of course. What's your opinion of … of it?"

Octavia looked out at the sunset for a long while. "I know what you are getting at, Modo," she finally replied. "I must say I was shocked. I didn't—well, I didn't know what to expect."

"What sort of a face is it?" He was disappointed that he'd allowed a whine to slip into his voice.

"Modo, I …"

Tears began to well up in her eyes. Had he ever seen her cry?

"Girls, even me in an orphanage, we grow up dreaming of the handsome prince. I …" She paused.

"Just say it." He spoke calmly. "It's better to have truth between us."

"Yours is not the face I've dreamed of my whole life, Modo. So, truthfully, I don't know what to say."

"It's not a prince's face. That much is obvious."

"I'm not intentionally being cruel, Modo. It's what I feel."

He nodded. "I appreciate that."

"Do you, Modo? It's so hard to know what you're truly feeling when all I see is your mask. Words are never enough."

He looked away from her, pondered the waves slapping against the side of the ship. If she thought he would remove his mask for her again, she was sorely mistaken. Without looking up he said, "Thank you for your honesty, Tavia. You should go now. You've already missed a few songs."

"If that's what you want," she said softly.

"It is," he answered.

As he watched her walk away he reminded himself that the truth was often hard. He'd been abandoned by parents who couldn't stand his deformities. That was the truth. He'd been sold by an orphanage to a travelling freak show. That was also the truth. He'd been imprisoned in Ravenscroft by Mr Socrates to mould him into a secret agent. Again, the truth. And now he was here on a ship with a young woman he would die for, and she was looking for a handsome prince.

The hardest truth of all.

Modo woke up one morning, a month into the trip, with a tingling sensation where his little finger had been. Since Miss Hakkandottir had sliced it off the area had at times felt cold or itchy, but this was the first time it tingled, as if the finger were still there. He hadn't looked at it closely for over a week, but now removed the bandage. Not only had the wound healed without any scars, but a tiny nub of flesh was sprouting out of the stub!

He went immediately to Tharpa's cabin and knocked. When Tharpa opened the door, he showed him his discovery.

"Your little finger is growing back," Tharpa said, as though it were the most common occurrence in the world.

Tharpa left to tell Mr Socrates what had happened and Modo waited on the deck. He felt certain that Mr Socrates would return with Tharpa, but instead Tharpa came back with instructions to take Modo to Dr Hollom, the ship's surgeon. Tharpa led the way.

Dr Hollom was a youngish looking man with steel grey eyes. He was already wearing his white surgical coat, clearly expecting their arrival. Several surgical blades and other devices were laid out before him. Modo gave them a nervous glance.

"Are you certain I'm to show him this?" he asked Tharpa.

"Yes." The answer came not from Tharpa but from Mr Socrates, who had entered through another door. "Hollom's worked for me before."

Modo revealed his finger and the doctor, who had soft hands without a single callus, measured the growth with calipers and poked it with a pin. Modo bit back a surprised cry.

"You feel that?" Dr Hollom asked.

"Of course I do," Modo said. He wanted to punch the man and say, "Did you feel *that*?"

Dr Hollom nodded and wrote notes and asked Modo several questions about his eating habits, how often he changed his dressing and whether he consumed alcohol. Then he turned to Mr Socrates and said, "It seems his finger is regenerating, like a lizard growing a new tail."

Lizard? Modo looked at the pink stub. *Am I part lizard?*

"This is stunning!" Mr Socrates said. "A wonderful discovery. I always thought you healed quickly, but you actually *regenerate*."

Modo nodded. "Yes, it's brilliant," he said softly.

He was pleased to see the finger returning, but he chose to wear gloves until it looked completely normal again. He didn't want others to know how freakish he really was.

After a month and a half of sailing they docked in London and hired a carriage large enough for the five of them. Modo would be happy to have a bed in Victor House. Or to go back to Safe House and sleep for several weeks. Or would Mr Socrates just shove him out on the street?

No one spoke. They were all exhausted. Octavia had fallen asleep with her head on Mrs Finchley's shoulder.

Modo took the opportunity to memorise her face. The tiny freckles, her narrow lips. She was such a beauty. He couldn't predict what would happen next; after the mission was over it might be months before he'd see her again.

He was shocked out of his reverie, and Octavia from her sleep, when Mr Socrates banged on the inside of the carriage, shouting, "Keep driving!" Tharpa gave an extra knock until the driver continued on.

"What's all the noise?" Octavia asked.

Modo shrugged, equally confused, until he saw that they were passing Victor House. It had been burned to the ground. Partial walls poked out of the rubble, all that remained of the grand home.

"Good Lord," Mrs Finchley said. "Do you suppose it was a gas leak?"

"It's not an accident," Mr Socrates said gravely. "And if they've found one of our houses, they may know the whereabouts of all of them. Perhaps even the Permanent Association itself has been compromised. That clockwork spider must have led them here."

"Then what do we do?" Octavia asked.

"We find a hole to hide in," he said, then shouted out the window. "Driver! Take us back to the docks at once!"

"A hole?" Modo asked. "Where?"

"That will be a secret best kept until we arrive," he said.

Through the window of the carriage, Modo watched the familiar London streets pass by. If they weren't safe here in the heart of the Empire, was there anywhere in the world for them to hide?

They arrived at Victoria Dock and unloaded the few carpetbags they had, then Mr Socrates hurried away to buy tickets. Modo and Octavia stood with Tharpa, watching the crowds. Mrs Finchley looked calm, but Modo caught her fidgeting with her hands.

"What does it mean for us?" Modo directed his question towards Tharpa. "Has the Association collapsed?"

Tharpa shrugged. "We do not know. Better to discover this from a distance."

When Mr Socrates returned, they followed him down the pier, stopping before a ship called the SS *Canadian*.

"That's a mail steamer, sir," Modo said.

"Yes, and it leaves in twenty-five minutes. We will be on board. We have commissioned cabins."

"Are you certain you want to take me with you?" Modo asked.

Mr Socrates gave him a hard look, weighing his answer. "You need to be retrained," he said. "And I will not abandon you here."

Modo nodded. They climbed up the gangplank and then Modo turned to watch it drawn up behind them, half expecting an enemy agent to come running after them.

But no one appeared. And, just as Mr Socrates had said, soon the ship was tugged out to the Thames and they began steaming towards what he hoped would be a place of warmth, rest and safety.

Visit **www.thehunchbackassignments.com**

Arthur Slade is the author of *The Hunchback Assignments*, which won the TD Canadian Children's Literature Award and was an Honour Book for the CLA Young Adult Book Award; it has also been shortlisted for many other awards, including the Silver Birch Award and the CLA Book of the Year for Children. *The Dark Deeps*, the second book in the Hunchback Assignments series, was the winner of the Saskatchewan Book Award for Young Adults. Slade is also the author of *Dust*, the winner of the 2001 Governor General's Award for Children's Literature. His other acclaimed novels include *Tribes*, *Megiddo's Shadow* and *Jolted*. He lives in Saskatoon with his family. Visit him online at **www.arthurslade.com**.